ABOUT THE A

George G. Gilm
a small village e
schools until the e
abandoned all e he
a professional writer, with strong leanings towards the mystery novel. Wrote short stories and books during evenings, lunch hours, at weekends, and on the time of various employers while he worked for an international newsagency, a film company, a weekly book-trade magazine and the Royal Air Force.

His first short (love) story was published when he was sixteen and the first (mystery) novel appeared ten years later. He has been a full-time writer since 1970, writing mostly Westerns which have been translated into a dozen languages and have sold in excess of 15 million copies. He is married with a dog and lives on the Dorset coast, which is as far west as he intends to move right now.

The EDGE series by George G. Gilman, published by New English Library.

EDGE 1: THE LONER
EDGE 2: TEN THOUSAND DOLLARS, AMERICAN
EDGE 3: APACHE DEATH
EDGE 4: KILLER'S BREED
EDGE 5: BLOOD ON SILVER
EDGE 6: THE BLUE, THE GREY AND THE RED
EDGE 7: CALIFORNIA KILLING
EDGE 8: SEVEN OUT OF HELL
EDGE 9: BLOODY SUMMER
EDGE 10: VENGEANCE IS BLACK
EDGE 11: SIOUX UPRISING
EDGE 12: THE BIGGEST BOUNTY
EDGE 13: A TOWN CALLED HATE
EDGE 14: THE BIG GOLD
EDGE 15: BLOOD RUN
EDGE 16: THE FINAL SHOT
EDGE 17: VENGEANCE VALLEY
EDGE 18: TEN TOMBSTONES TO TEXAS
EDGE 19: ASHES AND DUST
EDGE 20: SULLIVAN'S LAW
EDGE 21: RHAPSODY IN RED
EDGE 22: SLAUGHTER ROAD
EDGE 23: ECHOES OF WAR
EDGE 24: THE DAY DEMOCRACY DIED
EDGE 25: VIOLENCE TRAIL
EDGE 26: SAVAGE DAWN
EDGE 27: DEATH DRIVE
EDGE 28: EVE OF EVIL
EDGE 29: THE LIVING, THE DYING AND THE DEAD
EDGE 30: WAITING FOR A TRAIN
EDGE 31: THE GUILTY ONES
EDGE 32: THE FRIGHTENED GUN
EDGE 33: THE HATED
EDGE 34: A RIDE IN THE SUN
EDGE 35: DEATH DEAL
EDGE 36: TOWN ON TRIAL
EDGE 37: VENGEANCE AT VENTURA
EDGE 38: MASSACRE MISSION
EDGE 39: THE PRISONERS
EDGE 40: MONTANA MELODRAMA
EDGE 41: THE KILLING CLAIM
EDGE 42: BLOODY SUNRISE
EDGE 43: ARAPAHO REVENGE
EDGE 44: THE BLIND SIDE
EDGE 45: HOUSE ON THE RANGE
EDGE 46: THE GODFORSAKEN
EDGE 47: THE MOVING CAGE
EDGE 48: SCHOOL FOR SLAUGHTER
EDGE 49: REVENGE RIDE
EDGE 50: SHADOW OF THE GALLOWS

EDGE MEETS ADAM STEELE: TWO OF A KIND
EDGE MEETS ADAM STEELE: MATCHING PAIR
EDGE MEETS ADAM STEELE: DOUBLE ACTION

SHADOW OF THE GALLOWS

George G. Gilman

NEW ENGLISH LIBRARY

A New English Library Original Publication, 1985

First NEL Paperback Edition October 1985

NEL Books are published by
New English Library
Mill Road, Dunton Green,
Sevenoaks, Kent.
Editorial office: 47 Bedford Square, London WC1B 3DP

Typeset by Rowland Phototypesetting Ltd
Bury St Edmunds, Suffolk

Printed in Great Britain by Hunt Barnard Printing Ltd, Aylesbury, Bucks

British Library C.I.P.

Gilman, George G.
Shadow of the gallows. – (Edge: 50)
I. Title II. Series
823'.914[F] PR

ISBN 0-450-05857-3

for
J.H.
a silver lady who did so
much on the long trail into
the golden west.

One

Father Claudio Rodrigues was feeling his age as he rode the sway-backed burro down the narrow defile that was the most treacherous stretch of trail between Pueblo Rojo and El Mision de Vallecito. It was hot and it was dusty, as it invariably was on a summer afternoon amid the lower heights of the Sierra Madre in north eastern Sonora. Also invariably at this time of day, no matter what the season of the year or his surroundings, the priest began to experience a powerful thirst: of a kind that would only be made harder to endure should he take more than an occasional sip of tepid and brackish-tasting water from one of his canteens.

But he smiled with self-satisfaction as he reined in the burro at the foot of the gentle but dangerously rock-littered slope, and cast an upward glance between the splayed walls of limestone. Then he raised a hand to touch a forefinger to the brim of his sombrero in a gesture that he considered served two purposes: it bade farewell to the place where the burro could have taken a leg-breaking fall or a fresh collapse might have cascaded crushing fragments of rock on rider and mount, and it also acknowledged to the cloudless sky that Father Rodrigues still had faith that God was looking out for this wretched sinner.

And wretched sinner was surely what he was, the priest confessed silently to himself yet again, as he rapped his heels against the flanks of the burro and worked the reins to command a left turn: heading north in the afternoon shade of the elongated escarpment through which the defile cut. It was probably not noticeably cooler in the shadow of the sixty-foot-high rock wall than out in the full glare of the sun that beat down on the cracked and pitted, monotonously flat floor of the alkali plain that stretched away into the shimmering heat haze to the east and south: but it looked a great deal hotter beyond the shade line.

So, just as he had taken no reckless risks in negotiating the defile, and did not seek to intensify his need of strong liquor by gulping down water, he elected to ride close to the base of the cliff, drawing a modicum of comfort from the impression that it was likely he would be sweating and his body would be smelling a whole lot worse if he were to submit to the impulse to veer the burro out of the shadow and into the sunlight. It also had to be taken into account that the animal was innocent of sin, and to make his mount suffer during this journey of penitence would be a despicable cruelty. Of course, with such a short way left to go, he could dismount and walk to his destination without fear of total exhaustion and the certain death that such a state would mean in this desolate area of Mexico. But as the priest leaned back his head and tilted the canteen to his lips, the expression in the eyes that were thus turned again toward the pale blue sky was a mixture of the quizzical and a plea for understanding that he knew would be favourably received.

Father Claudio Rodrigues was tacitly communing with God on a man-to-man basis out here in the harsh and secular mountains. And when he was through he hung the canteen back on his saddle and displayed another fleeting smile of contentment. Feeling secure in the knowledge that both he and his God were aware that the long and arduous journey was almost over: and soon, at El Mision de Vallecito, there would be ample time for reverence within the consecrated confines of his place of pilgrimage.

The age the priest had felt as he neared journey's end

was sixty-two. Seldom did he feel, or look, so old while he went about his duties as parish priest of Pueblo Rojo: for although he was perhaps a little underweight for his six-foot-tall frame, he enjoyed good health and had lived for most of his life by the rule of thumb that dictated moderation in all things. He carried himself well, untroubled by stiffened joints, sagging shoulders or any tendency to drag his feet. His once jet-black hair was now entirely white, but this had a distinguishing rather than an aging effect in the way it contrasted so starkly with the Hispanic darkness of his facial skin, wrinkled but with lines not excessively deep. His eyes were clear and bright, his teeth were many and white, and only in the early morning before he shaved were there pepper-and-salt bristles on his cheeks and jaw to give a strong clue to his actual age. Mostly he was convinced he felt no older than fifty, and this pleased him. And he was far from disgruntled by the knowledge that the consensus of opinion among his parishioners was that their priest was no older than fifty-five.

But after such a long, slow ride from Pueblo Rojo – he had set out before sunrise and paused just once at noon to rest and feed the burro – he presumed he was not looking his best. Not that this was of the least consequence, for out here in the sun-parched wilderness there was no-one to preen for. No eyes to look critically at his unfamiliarly sweat-run and dirt-grimed face, more gaunt than usual, and in repose expressing a grimace of discomfort beneath the broad brim of the straw sombrero. Nor to see that his worse-for-wear but customarily spotlessly clean clothing – he was attired in clerical vestments except for the substitution of the sombrero for a biretta – was heavily powdered with the grey and red dust of travel.

Except for the eyes of God, of course. But He saw everything; and penetrated every vainglorious attempt at pretence. The belief the priest held in this aspect of his faith was the reason he was once again engaged on this annual pilgrimage to the derelict mission church at Vallecito. The way there – and back again to his parish – was not easy for a man who was sixty-two, no matter how sprightly he felt or how much younger he seemed to others at the best of times. And it had its dangers – other than those inherent in the harshness of the elements allied with the rugged desolation of the terrain. For it was ideal country for bandits to run to from the law; and once, a few years ago, Father Rodrigues had seen a party of Mescaleros riding into the heat-shimmer as he emerged from the defile in the escarpment that was now less high and steep to his immediate left.

Before the burro carried him much further, the cliff would cease to cast its shadow over the priest and his mount. And man and beast would thus be exposed to the full glaring heat of the sun over the final stretch of the journey. But the head of the elongated hollow for which Vallecito was named would have been reached by then, and the little church would be in sight: less than thirty minutes of relatively easy walking to the north. And walk he would, leading the wearily doleful burro by the rope bridle as he did every year. Thus abiding by one other self-imposed rule that had evolved during his first penitent's pilgrimage so many years ago. Rules that were meant to cause him a certain degree of discomfort and distress while he deprived himself of the best and the easiest that was available to him: but which drew the line far short of total mortification. The sins for which he sought atonement were within bounds, and so Father Claudio Rodrigues considered it acceptable that the extent of his suffering should also be limited.

Suddenly, just after he had reined in the burro and was preparing to dismount, the dazzling brightness of the Sonora sun was dulled. And a moment later the oven-hot Sierra Madre air was no longer heavily inert. For the next moment the priest felt a tightness in his chest and sensed himself petrified in the saddle as awesome thoughts of the wrath of God whirled in his mind. Then, instinctively as a priest, he directed his uneasy gaze toward the heavens and was able to escape the restraints of dread: but could not prevent a mild blasphemy from rasping through his exposed teeth, gritted in a self-deprecating grimace.

'Que demonious, imbecil?'

This as he saw that the Almighty was not so concerned by the compromises of a lowly Mexican parish priest that He felt it necessary to express a sign of divine displeasure. There was simply an abrupt change in the weather, that would not have taken him by such unsettling surprise had he been able to see the sky in the west. For ever since he had emerged from the defile to begin his northward ride along the base of the cliff, a bank of ominously grey cloud had started to encroach across the vast expanse of blueness that all day long had been blemished only by the dazzlingly bright sun. Now, just before the preoccupied priest had been about to advance out of the diminished area of shade thrown by the lowering cliff, the cloud raced across the face of the sun to blanket this entire region with shadow. And the wind that drove the clouds swooped down to create a minor dust storm: so that he had to hold on to his sombrero and compress his lips firmly as he cracked his eyelids almost closed to the assault of whirling debris that was hurled up on all sides of him. This as he needed to cling tightly to the burro with his free hand and both legs so that he would not be hurled to the hard-baked ground by the animal, which bucked and reared and wheeled in terrified reaction to the suddenness of the weather change.

For perhaps half a minute the man had to concentrate all his attention on the burro: firstly staying astride the frightened animal and then calming him down with softly spoken words and a gently stroking hand as he gingerly dismounted. And he did not feel safe until he stood firmly on the ground and had fastened a firm grip on the bridle. A broken leg or some other serious injury in a fall would surely have proved fatal out here. But to have the burro bolt away through the dust storm and be lost with the meagre supplies he carried: that could be just as bad.

One hand fisted on the bridle and the other raised to hold the sombrero on his white-haired head, Claudio Rodrigues took another few seconds to get his bearings: which was easy enough to do in spite of the swirling dust that reduced visibility to less than a hundred and fifty feet. For although he only came this way once a year, the landmarks never changed. It would take a million years of wind and rain and sun to make any noticeable impression on the terrain. Unless, of course, men like those who had built El Mision de Vallecito were to come here and leave other marks of their presence.

'*Avanzar*,' the priest encouraged as he tugged on the bridle, pitching his voice just loud enough to be heard above the mournful moaning sounds the wind made as it veered and eddied and strengthened and lessened at the foot of the rock face that at this point was less than twenty feet high.

And much to the man's relief the burro responded without protest: moved forward in the same docile manner as he had carried his rider from Pueblo Rojo to the place where the wind-storm had spooked him. Soon the end of the escarpment was behind them and the priest began to feel less tense himself as he sensed the final traces of uneasiness leave the animal – this change taking place as the more eerie sounds of the wind receded in back of them. And, too, it blew and hurled dust motes in a constant direction, from the south. They moved northward at a measured pace, covering ground that took a down slope into the valley in which the church stood. The adobe building was now hidden behind the wind-borne dust, but Claudio Rodrigues knew it was still standing. For he had glimpsed its familiar form, a little blurred by the heat-shimmer, during those moments he had halted his mount before the cloud pushed back the haze but the wind erupted the heavier veil of swirling dust.

Now the priest began to pray. He did so tacitly and without bowing his head or raising his tight-lipped and narrow-eyed face toward the dust-hidden sky. Talking to his God again in a less than conventionally reverent manner as he asked to be forgiven for his profanity and for his arrogant vanity that had caused him to regard himself as important enough to be worthy of a divine sign.

There was just time enough for the priest to conclude with a thanksgiving for his deliverance from possible injury before the wind began to moan again. Up ahead this time. And the man endured the taste of dust as he moved his lips to speak comforting words to the disturbed burro. Uttered them through clenched teeth exposed in a smile of contentment as he realised he was almost at journey's end. It was the mission church around and through which the wind was whining and growling, as if in inarticulate complaint at the obstacle to its northbound progress along the low-sided valley.

Perhaps because of the placating tones of the priest, or maybe because the burro recalled that nothing bad had resulted from the last time the wind had created such macabre effects, the animal quickly overcame the impulse to fresh fear. And allowed himself to be led without balking between a leaning gatepost and the end of a crumbling adobe wall towards the time-ravaged church that was now visible, and which became clearer to see with every pace that Father Claudio Rodrigues took.

It was an unimpressive building architecturally. Constructed of adobe that had weathered to countless shades of brown and grey over the fifty-odd years of its existence, it had never been a beautiful church. And the effects of neglect since it had been abandoned more than twenty years earlier meant that it had not aged gracefully. The only doorway – a stout timber door was still on its hinges in the arched frame – was at the foot of what had once been a three-storey-high belltower. But the jagged top of the tower, open to the elements and now bell-less, protruded just a few feet above the flat roof of the main body of the church, which was some forty feet wide and three times as long. There was a narrow window to either side of the tower, and the priest knew there were six similar apertures down each side wall. They had never been glazed and the shutters had long since become detached. It was in whining through and out of these windows that the hot and dust-stinging wind made the most noise.

There was no porch sheltering the doorway, and as he reached for the rusted but still serviceable latch the priest lost his sombrero: the hat in an instant wrenched off his head and flung out of reach and sight. But, he rationalised, better to lose a hat than the burro: and, not entirely trusting the animal to remain so dolefully docile, he tightened his grip on the bridle to stress it was his intention that they were both going to enter the church. Then he lifted the latch and pushed the door inwards. Managed to bite back on another profanity as the wind crashed the heavy door away from him with the same forceful ease it had whipped the hat off his head. His fingers stung from the violence of the latch being torn out of his grip, and the grimace of pain became more deep-set as he heard the door slam back against the inner wall of the roofless tower.

Then a frown of confusion displaced the grimace for a moment, and he was unconcerned by the bite of the swirling dust as he gazed in wide-eyed surprise toward the far chancel end of the church. In the next part of a second he was frozen in a grip of a terror more powerful than the dread he had felt back at the place where the dust storm erupted so abruptly. This as a man sprang up from where he had been hunched down on one knee. And spun around to face the priest on the threshold. There was a vivid threat of violence in the fluid speed of the move: so much so that the newcomer took note of the revolver in the man's hand in the manner of an unimportant afterthought.

It seemed impossible that the man would be able to keep from firing the handgun, even if he wanted to. The squeezing of the trigger must surely be an inexorable concluding act to the rise off the knee, the draw from the holster as the turn was made and the smooth stop in a half-crouch with the revolver held in a rock-steady aim from the hip. To expect the man to check his finger on the trigger would be like hoping for a rock tossed upwards to remain suspended in mid-air.

The muzzle spat black powder smoke and a streak of flame. A bullet, too, of course. But even as he saw the gun fired, the priest knew he would be alive to hear the sound of the shot an instant later. For, as the man became aware of his inability to hold back from the shot, he was able to turn his wrist the fraction of a degree, which was all that was required to miss the target over a range of some hundred feet.

The report was loud enough to sound clearly against the blustering barrage of less strident noise made by the wind. The priest had his wits about him sufficiently to realise that it was only in his imagination that the thud of the bullet impacting with the adobe wall to his right sounded thunderously more loud.

The man straightened to his full height and pushed the revolver back in the holster that hung with the ties unfastened down his right thigh. And as the final traces of the intent to kill seeped out of his expression and left in its place a look of total impassiveness, he drawled:

'You and the burro want to step inside the church and close the door behind you? Be just as noisy but not so dusty.'

The priest gulped and struggled to suck up some moisture into his arid throat. Managed to force out: '*Santo Dios, senor . . . yo . . . estar muerto de miedo . . .*'

'So come on in and thank God for your good fortune, preacherman. Better to be scared stiff than to be one.'

Two

CLAUDIO RODRIGUES needed to summon a greater degree of willpower to move than was required to speak. And he did not trust himself to be able to do both at the same time until the burro had shown himself willing to be led into the shelter of the derelict building without protest.

'I tell you this,' he said then in a tone of deep sincerity, still speaking Mexican. 'I think you just frightened me more than half to death when I see you turn that way and point the gun at – '

'Guess even that wasn't close enough to see what it's like when you get to go all the way?' the American, who understood Mexican but chose not to speak the language, cut in. This after the priest had let go his hold on the burro to devote all his attention to forcing the door closed against the gusting power of the wind.

When the latch was securely fastened, the Mexican turned and leaned gratefully back against the rough-hewn timber door. And then used the sleeve of his cassock to wipe some of the dusty sweat off his now old man's face as he answered morosely: 'Because I am a sinner who is *el veruenza* . . . the disgrace to the cloth I wear, I am surely destined for *purgatorio, señor.* And because I am certain of this, I have no wish to be shown so soon how I must suffer to expiate my sins.'

'You're probably right, preacherman. If you're living a hell of a life it has to be better not to know what comes next.'

The priest came away from the arched doorway to start down the centre of the church that had been stripped of almost all its furnishings and sacred artifacts. And the burro that had been waiting submissively nearby now moved hesitantly away, to where an unsaddled chestnut gelding stood patiently near a side wall which was closer to the chancel than the belltower end of the building. When the weary-eyed, white-haired Mexican was halfway along the former aisle, he could see a saddle with a rifle in the boot, and a bedroll, on the floor immediately in front of the only surviving pew in the church.

The American – who had a blood-, sweat- and dirt-stained bandage around his head – backed away from in front of the spot where the altar had once stood, and lowered himself cautiously onto one end of the pew that was long enough to seat a half dozen average-size worshippers. He was forty or more years old, but the priest thought he perhaps looked older in the present circumstances because he was quite obviously weary and suffering pain. The manner in which he sat down so carefully maybe indicated he was hurting in other parts of his body than just his head. He was about two inches taller than the six-foot height of Rodrigues, and was much more powerfully built – looked to weigh in the region of a well-distributed two hundred pounds. Although he was quite obviously from an American background, there was more than a mere hint of a Mexican bloodline in the shape and hue of his features that were structured on the same lean lines as his frame. The priest regarded the man's looks as menacingly ugly, but was prepared to allow that the mix of Hispanic, and a second line of heritage that had formed the angles and curves, might well seem handsome to others in different circumstances.

The skin coloration was dark: of that shade which stated plainly it had never been pale – that the elements he had been exposed to through a life spent mostly out of doors had merely darkened the pigmentation a little deeper.

Furrows across the forehead and the wrinkles that were visible beyond the reach of at least two days of bristles suggested that they had not all been etched into the taut skin by the aging process – that the suffering he was now enduring was not a new experience for this man. Dominating his features were his eyes – no more than threads of ice blue that the priest was sure were permanently narrowed to slits beneath their hooded lids. His cheek-bones were high and flanked an aquiline nose above a broad, thin-lipped mouth. Because he was in need of a shave, the line of an understated moustache, worn in the drooping Mexican style, was barely discernible. His hair was a mixture of jet black and dirty grey which was a match for the stubble on his cheeks, jaw and throat. The darker colour was still predominant and the hair was still thick. He wore it long, something in the manner of an Apache, the ends falling to his shoulders and below the nape of his neck. Perhaps the comparison with an Indian would not have come so easily to mind had it not been for the badly-soiled bandage that encircled the skull in such a way that it resembled a head-band. The area stained with blood spilled not very recently indicated the wound was on the right side just above the ear.

There was also a suggestion of the Indian about the necklet of dull-coloured beads that was visible above the loosely-draped kerchief, but in all other respects his attire was white American western – shirt, pants and spurless riding boots as black as the kerchief. There was no hat in sight, but there was a sheepskin topcoat lashed to his bedroll on the floor in front of the pew. On his unfancy gunbelt there was a bullet in every loop, and in the just-as-plain holster was a revolver which the priest, unfamiliar with firearms, did not recognise as a Frontier Colt. He could see the pistol was far from new. The repeater rifle jutting out of the boot on the saddle – a Winchester – looked to be of more recent manufacture. The priest did not notice the elongated bulge in the man's shirt at the top of his spine: and even if he had seen it he could not possibly have guessed that there was a straight razor in a pouch concealed there.

In moving away from the centre of the chancel, the American allowed the Mexican clear sight of the crudely carved wooden crucifix mounted high on the wall. Rodrigues halted in front of this and executed an earnest genuflection. Then with an expression that was remarkably serene in the wake of the violence and fear he had experienced just moments ago, he turned to the injured man and said apologetically:

'I think, *senor,* that I was guilty of *interrupcion* of your *rezar?*'

'You didn't interrupt anything worth a damn, preacherman,' came the sour-voiced reply from a mouth set in the twisted line of a scowl.

Not prepared to be deflected by the other's discouraging attitude, the priest insisted in the same earnest tones: 'You are troubled, *amigo.* If you think it will ease your mind to *confesarse*, I will hear – '

'I ain't of your religious persuasion. And if I was it would take too long to get it all said. You just go about whatever business you have in your church and don't mind me.'

The priest looked like he was about to take issue with the contention and the invitation. But then he shrugged his narrow shoulders and said conversationally: 'My name is Claudio Rodrigues, *señor.* I am the parish priest of Pueblo Rojo which is many hard miles to the south and west of El Mision de Vallecito – this church, as perhaps you know? Which is not my church. I visit here *anual . . . ir en . . . peregrinacion . . .* You understand what I mean, *senor*?'

The American had taken a tobacco poke from a pocket of his shirt and now began to roll a slender cigarette as he replied: 'You're on a pilgrimage. You come here every year.'

The priest showed a fleeting smile of satisfaction as he bobbed his head. 'Ah, I thought you had more Mexican than the average *gringo.*' He broadened the smile to emphasise that he did not intend the term to be taken in a derogatory sense. 'Because you have some Mexican in you, I think?'

'I'm called Edge these days. Learned your language from my Pa whose name was Jose Aviles when he started out.'

'You do not like to speak the language of your father?' There was implied censure in the priest's expression.

'My Ma was from Sweden. Never did pick up much of the language she spoke. When they had kids they figured it best we all used American. On account of we were all Americans by then. It avoided confusion. Pa forgot the rule more than Ma.'

'*Si,* I can understand that – to *impedir* the confusion.'

'It sounds like you're a little mixed up yourself.'

'Señor?'

Edge ran the cigarette paper over the tip of his tongue, then allowed his thin lips to remain apart and thus reveal his very white teeth in a sardonic smile as he murmured through them: 'You're the wrong religion to be a pilgrim, father.'

'Como?'

Edge struck a match on the butt of the holstered Colt and lit the cigarette that was angled from a side of his mouth. And he no longer smiled as it bobbed when he growled: 'Early American joke, feller. *Chiste malo.*'

The priest looked perplexed, then shrugged that it did not matter to him that he was to remain the non-comprehending butt of a bad joke. Then, as he moved to sit wearily down on the other end of the pew from Edge and the both of them became aware of the force of the wind diminishing, he expressed concern again. And suggested earnestly:

'*Mi amigo*, since it is apparent that you speak Mexican better than I understand your language, would it not be better if we speak the Mexican?'

'Far as I'm concerned, preacherman, we've said as much as we need to each other. Except maybe I think you should take care of your mount before you get too comfortable yourself.'

The priest was briefly perturbed by the coldly voiced criticism. Then shared a puzzled frown between the two animals and the man: who seemed now to have withdrawn into a mood of detachment. A state that might be as far removed from the here and the now as that which had captured his awareness before he returned so violently to the reality of no longer being alone in El Mision de Vallecito.

But now there was no suggestion of a man at private prayer in a house of God. Edge was reflecting upon thoughts that were emphatically ungodly, if the silent snarl fixed firmly to his face were a true sign of what preoccupied him. The glittering slits of the bluest of blue eyes gazed through the drifting tobacco smoke and seemingly saw nothing in the direct line of his sight.

The dust storm was taking longer to subside than to erupt but there was already a very appreciable lessening of wind sound. Which meant Claudio Rodrigues could repond to Edge in a voice pitched little louder than a normal conversational level.

'You are correct, *mi amigo*,' he said anxiously. And rose from the pew with a slowness and an economy of movement that had less to do with his weariness than with taking pains not to surprise Edge into another sudden and explosive physical reaction.

'Sometimes I get things right,' the half-breed answered evenly, and this caused the priest to be surprised. For although the other man continued to be apparently withdrawn into a pensive trance filled with people and events that he viewed with snarling rage, the answer had shown him to be totally aware of his present circumstances.

The priest moved more quickly now as the storm became less obtrusive by the moment, and the level of light got brighter with the settling of the dust. But the sun remained hidden behind the blanket of dirty-looking cloud and perhaps because of this the heat felt strangely more oppressive than Claudio Rodrigues could recall it from before the storm. Or maybe, he allowed to himself as he uncinched the saddle from the burro, this was a symptom of delayed shock from almost getting killed. Or was it simply because he was still afraid of the *gringo* who continued to express a vicious hatred for whatever or whoever inspired his present thoughts?

Then the priest found that he did not welcome the encroachment of peace and quiet in the wake of the storm. Which was perplexing, since silence was one of the qualities he came to the mission to seek each year. But silence out of solitude, *por supuesto!* Sharing the church with this *gringo pistolero* who was wounded and troubled by dark thoughts . . . That was a different matter. And he felt a compulsive need to keep silence at bay by talk.

'It is right that a man should tend his animal before he takes his ease. Normally I would not need to be reminded of my *obligacion* but the gunshot . . . You saw that I brought the beast into El Mision because of the *mal tiempo?*'

'Sure, preacherman,' Edge replied in the same even tone as before. And did not turn to look at what the priest was doing. Smoke continued to rise at intervals as he drew against the cigarette and expelled it just often enough to keep the tobacco burning. 'You're a regular Saint Francis of Assisi, Mexican style. But you don't have to give excuses to me. I'll be making tracks pretty soon. Meantime, like I told you: go ahead and do what you have to.'

While he said this his tone of voice did not alter. But his whole frame suddenly stiffened, and then he raised a brown-skinned hand to press the finger-tips gingerly to the bloodstained area of the bandage above his right ear, so it was obvious that a bolt of pain had hit him.

'Señor?'

'Yeah?'

The priest carried his saddle to the pew and set it down beside Edge's gear on the floor. Thought, as he resumed his seat and the half-breed looked quizzically at him, that the injured man might have come close to losing consciousness under the assault of the unexpected wave of agony that had just washed over him.

'It is in the care of men's souls that I am something of an *experto, mi amigo*. But if you will permit me, I would be willing to look at your wound to see if – '

'Much obliged, feller,' Edge cut in, and again touched the tips of his fingers to the bandage. 'But right now I'm in no frame of mind to do anybody any favours.'

'*Señor,* it is I who wishes to – '

'Always pay my way. Always repay favours.'

The priest shrugged his shoulders, lost the look of sincere concern from his features and murmured as he leaned down to open one of his saddlebags: '*Como usted quiera, hijo de p* – '

'Usually do suit myself, preacherman,' Edge said before the curse would be completed. 'And I guess I'm a sonofabitch more times than I ain't.'

Claudio Rodrigues was momentarily disturbed that he had forgotten Edge was half Mexican with a fluent understanding of the language. But his impulse to apprehension was checked when he saw the half-breed was grimacing with fresh pain instead of scowling – at the priest, or a notion in his hurting head.

'Few of us are not on occasion guilty of being the sonofabitch, I think,' the priest said thoughtfully. And spared the most fleeting of contrite glances for the crucifix as he spoke the profanity in a foreign tongue. Then he came close to showing a wan smile of satisfaction as he withdrew a bottle of wine from the bag and saw Edge do a double take at it. As he held up the bottle in an offering gesture, a break in the cloud allowed the sun to stream down through air that was now unmoving and free of dust motes. And in the brighter level of light that entered the church via the roofless and truncated belltower and the slit windows of the side walls, the wine showed up vivid red. 'I bring for the Holy Communion, *mi amigo.* In past years I have returned to Pueblo Rojo with just one swallow gone from the bottle. But in past years I have not been almost killed as I enter El Mision de Vallecito.'

'I told you, I don't need excuses from you, feller.'

'God is listening, too,' was the unruffled reply. But there was something akin to apology in the way he looked longer this time toward the crucifix before he added: 'You may satisfy your principles by exchanging a smoke for a share of the bottle, *señor?*'

'You sure are the damnest priest.'

The Mexican held the bottle in an attitude of being about to remove the stopper, but he did not do so; instead eyed the half-breed in expectation and confessed: 'I tell you already that I am surely damned. It is no secret among my Pueblo Rojo *feligresia, mi amigo.* I spend more time in the *cantina* than in my *iglesia*, is the opinion of many. I am more familiar with the many forms of poker than I am with the *Biblia*, others say. And if the *Viuda* Ravel was to tell all she knows of certain events . . . I would most certainly be unfrocked.

'I do not believe that my annual pilgrimages of penitence to this place will atone for my countless sins, *Señor* Edge, but I know the people of my parish are happy that I come to El Mision de Vallecito.' He looked at the wall-mounted crucifix again, in the manner of a child who seeks at least permission if not approval for a known misdeed in the making. Then added pointedly to the half-breed: 'Usually I do not smoke tobacco in the *iglesia.* But today . . .' He shrugged. 'It is not usual?'

He uncorked the bottle and the look of anticipation in his clear eyes was displaced by a conspiratorial grin that was augmented by the reshaping of his mouthline when he saw Edge take the poke from a shirt pocket. The expression of happiness on the travel-wearied face of the priest drew no response in kind from the more exhausted half-breed, though. And Edge's features, lean to the point of haggard, projected a mood of brooding bitterness as he carelessly tossed the poke so that it landed on the pew immediately at the side of Father Claudio Rodrigues. The gaze in the ice-blue eyes shifted for no more than a second to the smiling face. And in that time it was as if, the priest felt, there had been another sudden change in the Sierra Madre weather – like the sun, although bright as before as it streamed through the west wall windows, had abruptly been drained of all heat. The sweat beads dried on his flesh and he was sure he would have shuddered had the menacing eyes not switched the direction of their stare – toward the infinity where images of haunting memories were on vivid view.

'There you go, preacherman,' Edge drawled absently.

'*Gracias, mi amigo,*' the priest acknowledged and needed to make an effort not to stammer. He swallowed hard and struggled against an impulse to self anger for allowing himself to be provoked to such a degree of fear by this man: who was certainly dangerous, but not to him. Then he leaned far to the side to set the open bottle down within easy reach of the half-breed, and forced himself to speak without a tremor in his tone as he invited: 'Here, *Señor* Edge. I think that perhaps your need is greater than mine. Tequila would be better for what troubles you, no doubt, but . . .' He shrugged.

The half-breed glanced at the bottle to ensure he did not knock it over with a clumsy move as he fisted a hand around the neck. Returned his disenchanted attention to the middle distance as he replied: 'Time's all that'll heal what ails me, preacherman. But I'm obliged for the thought.'

'Ah,' the priest exclaimed in the manner of a man who has just solved a troublesome puzzle. 'You have lost somebody close to you? *Acompanar en el sentimiento* – '

'Forget it, preacherman,' Edge broke in curtly. 'I got more than enough pity of the home grown brand. Time to think and some quiet to make that easier.' He first gestured with the bottle to suggest a tacit toast. Then added before he tilted it to take a swallow: 'But maybe this will help some, too.'

He looked set to take a long pull, but cut short the drink. Seemed about to spit out the mouthful of wine, but then gulped it down with a face that pointedly displayed his opinion of the taste.

'You do not like, *señor?*' Claudio Rodrigues asked in perturbation, freezing in the act of rolling a cigarette.

'You're a priest and you don't normally smoke in church, feller,' Edge growled, resuming his embittered scowl into the past as he saw it unfurled on the time-pitted and discoloured adobe wall beneath the crucifix. 'I'm a most-of-the-time sonofabitch that hardly ever goes to church. Guess I wouldn't normally cuss in one, though. But I have to say that your wine is like screwing on the bank of a river, preacherman.'

'A river bank with the *mujer?*' the perplexed priest questioned. '*No le comprendo, Señor Edge?*' Then he abruptly looked enlightened. 'Unless it is another *chiste malo?*'

'You got it, preacherman,' Edge told him with a mirthless smile slightly upturning the corners of his mouth as he dropped his cigarette butt and ground it out beneath a boot heel. 'This wine's fucking near water.'

Three

THE HALF-BREED neither recalled nor cared how much time had elapsed since the start of the series of events that had led him to seek shelter from the impending dust storm in the mission church at Vallecito where he came within an ace of killing the hapless Father Claudio Rodrigues.

It had begun at the end of a day when the sun was far enough below the jagged western horizon for the final traces of the crimson of its setting to have surrendered to the black advance of night. And so he had been able to see the aura of a small fire as it started an unequal competition with the glow of the moon and stars that made starkly contrasting shadows and light on the Sierra Madre landscape some thirty miles below the New Mexico Territory-Sonara border. The arc of pale red light occasionally expanded and diminished when flames flared or smoke billowed, but it never swelled to the proportions of anything larger than a night campfire as the lone rider narrowed the gap that had been something over two miles when the falling of night first revealed the existence of the fire.

It was freshly lit, he knew. Because he was certain he would have seen the woodsmoke before the onset of evening twilight if the fire had been burning then. And once this was decided he gave no more attention to the fire's glow than to any other facet of his surroundings as he rode on down the trail, turning up the collar of his sheepskin coat so that it brushed the underside of his hat brim at the rear and sides to guard against the cold touch of the mountain night air.

He headed toward the site of the fire for two reasons: it lay directly in his intended path and he figured it was worth checking to see if whoever had lit it was amenable to sharing its warmth and its cooking potential. But if the nightcamp looked like it would have no place for a near destitute drifter who had recently completed a less than successful trip from north of the border then so be it. The Mother Range was plenty big enough for another camp far enough away for neighbourly attitudes to be irrelevant.

While he rode slow and easy with a half smoked cigarette angled from a side of his mouth, he maintained his customary watch over the mountainscape in all directions: looking for the first sign of lurking menace and prepared, behind a dispassionate exterior, to respond instantly if something more intimidating than a distant campfire should warn of the presence of other men in the quiet night.

Then, with startling suddenness, the tranquil peace of the rugged mountains was shattered by a shrill cry. And the chestnut gelding broke stride and snorted with a violent toss of his head. Edge reined in the horse and murmured softly-placating words as he gently stroked the neck of the animal. And for the stretched seconds while the scream of agony lasted he ignored all else in the shadowed night and peered toward the hidden source of the sound. Which was in the same area as the flickering dome of the firelight's glow. Then the sound was ended as abruptly as it had started. And in the silence that immediately followed, the animal under the man quivered and explosively vented breath that became a visible vapour in the cold night air. The half-breed's expelled breath was similarly visible as grey steam, thicker than the tobacco smoke that curled up from his cigarette as he murmured:

'Sounds like there's hard times all round, feller.'

Then he touched his heels to horseflesh and moved the

reins to urge the calmer, but still unsettled, gelding into forward motion again. And resumed his all-around surveillance as he rode closer to the firelit scene of a man's suffering. On his face was an expression of embittered resignation now.

The trail he rode was a well used one that at this point ran along the eastern rim of a narrow and steep-sided *barranca* that became less deep and more crowded with vegetation as it stretched southwards. To the west of the ravine that looked like it could be the course of an infrequent creek, the terrain reared up and swept down over a gradually rising grade in a series of barren rock formations that in the glittering moonlight looked spectacularly like an enormous torrent of angry water frozen in a single instant to become a glacier. While to Edge's left there was a less rugged slope, although a sharper one. It was as empty of visible life as the petrified ocean to the west, but was featured with stunted and wind-bent trees up on the crest and quite heavily cloaked with brush and some grass down near the trail along the *barranca* rim.

To the north, in back of the slow riding man, the country had been just as rugged and spartanly featured with green vegetation on the day-long trek from San Sarita where the half-breed's last trail had ended. There had been purpose to taking that trail from the north to the south of the border – the aim to overhaul a man who deserved all he got when the revenge ride reached its violent conclusion.

Now, as Edge rode through the night, southwards toward a massive expanse of terrain that looked as inhospitable and dangerous as the ground in every other direction, there was no motive to keep him moving: beyond an almost lifelong compulsion not to stay in one place for more than the time it took to complete his business there. The business in San Sarita had been to retrieve from a thief certain property belonging to the half-breed – specifically a Frontier Colt revolver, a Winchester rifle and a bankroll. That he had failed to achieve this aim – and also had been denied all but a peripheral role in the death of the man who robbed him – was the reason he now surveyed his night-shrouded surroundings with a jaundiced gaze. The disgruntlement, not far short of vicious anger, that triggered the expression on his lean and unshaven face, was totally unconnected with whatever view of man's inhumanity to man he might witness when he rode within sight of the fire that created the half halo of wavering glow.

In fact, he heard further vocal outlet to suffering before he was in a position to see what brand of cruelty was taking place. This as the rim and the floor of the *barranca* reached a common level amid a thick stand of timber through which the trail cut a curving swathe. Scattered pieces of rock and other debris on its hard-packed surface suggested it became the creek bed after the heavy rains had lashed this and more distant, higher areas of the Sierra Madre. He thought he was now less than five hundred yards from the fire, but the density of the timber that grew so lushly on the banks of the sometime water course provided an impenetrable barrier that blocked out his view of the glow from the flames. But faint whimpering sounds filtered through the trees and brush. And it was these that caused Edge to once more rein in his mount as, on this occasion, the horse responded with no more than a sudden pricking of the ears to the intrusion of the softer cries of human suffering on the peace of the night again.

The half-breed resumed his impassive expression as he ran a hand gently over the neck of the gelding. Then smoothly swung down from the saddle and moved around to the right side of the horse before he began to lead him by the bridle. Thus his right hand was free to go for the revolver in his tied-down holster if a draw was called for. Likewise, he was closer to the rifle that was slid into the forward-slung boot on this side of his saddle.

Both these firearms were still relatively unfamiliar to him, for each had belonged to other men until a short time ago. Both the previous owners were dead now. And the weapons he had taken from them would serve his purpose until he had an opportunity to obtain less ancient and ill-used replacements for those stolen from him.

The whimpering, moaning and occasional attempt at a word that Edge listened to as he moved cautiously along the curving trail suggested a meaning that went beyond the suffering of pain, plain and simple. There was helplessness and hopelessness discernible in the timbre of the voice – brands of the emotions such as a man might experience when his body has been abused beyond the point where it is sensitive to greater agony but his mind is still open to an assault of perhaps equally punishing – in its own way – remorse.

'I'm real sorry, squaw!' a man said, harshly insincere, in Mexican-accented American. 'Usually *El Malo* gives his women better service than that, uh? But he likes the woman to make the *apasionado* moans and cries, uh? But you, you are like *madera* . . . like wood with the hole of the knot in it, uh? While the new gelding who was once your proud *caballo padre* – your stallion – he whines and weeps for his loss. And thinks of how it used to be with you, uh?'

Another man said something in quieter tones, his voice just loud enough for the straining ears of Edge to detect that the language spoken was Mexican. Then came a burst of raucous laughter from perhaps three or even four throats that totally drowned out the pathetic sounds made by the man who, it was now obvious, had been castrated before those who mutilated him began to make free with his Indian woman. Then, as the derisive laughter faltered and was checked, the half-breed saw the firelight's glow again. And in a period of two or three stretched seconds he was far enough forward to see the flames and the scene they illuminated. Less than five hundred feet away.

Beyond the fringe of the timber, in the shadows of which he was effectively hidden, the ground was open again and sloped gently downward toward the start of another, broader *barranca*. And it was to one side of the ravine's mouth, at the base of a towering and near sheer, hundred-foot-high cliff that the camp had been pitched. Where three men now took time out from torture and rape to drink some coffee laced with liquor.

The group had reached the site of the camp on four horses and a burro. These animals, unsaddled and hobbled, formed a *remuda* on the *barranca* side of the fire which warmed and lit a broad area spread out from the base of the cliff. The flames also heated the contents of two coffee pots and a large skillet. Halfway around the fire from the animals the three men who were taking a coffee break squatted on their haunches or their gear and fell to easy talking: utterly detached from the castrated man and the abused woman who were across the fire from them.

Had Edge not heard what took place during the past few minutes he might have thought the captives were dead as he made his initial survey of the scene at the foot of the slope. For neither the naked woman nor the man with his pants part down made a sound nor appeared to move a muscle for the first several seconds that the half-breed watched them.

The squaw lay on her back in a spreadeagled attitude, arms stretched wide above her head and legs splayed: like she was staked out. But there were no restraints at her wrists and ankles. She was close enough to the fire for it to warm her nude body, though not so close that the flames scorched her flesh. But, the impassive-eyed Edge thought fleetingly, this positioning of the woman was doubtless arranged more for the comfort of her rapists than from any consideration for her feelings.

Because she was so close to the flickering flames, her body and face were clear to see. And Edge saw that she was neither young nor a beauty in features or form. A skinny woman with a prominent ribcage and breasts that were almost non-existent as she lay on her back, she was dark-skinned and dark-haired from her Indian bloodline, and looked to be closer to fifty than forty. But maybe suffering at the hands of her captors had put many years on her true age. From such a distance, Edge was not able to see any movement of her breathing. But then he did catch sight of a clenching and unclenching action of both her hands as a sign she was alive before he shifted his unblinking gaze to the man who was enduring far more than the squaw.

He was some fifteen feet away from where she lay and was in a seated attitude, rump on the ground and back against the base of the cliff. His arms were lashed tightly to his sides by a length of rope that had been looped around him many times, from above his elbows down to his wrists. There was an awesome discoloration of the ground to both sides of him. But the brutal wound from which the massive loss of blood had spurted and oozed was hidden to Edge's view because his only partially removed pants were bunched up.

Until the squaw began to make fists with her hands his head was tipped forward. But then he brought his chin up off his chest as a first signal that he was not dead. And Edge saw that under a mop of dirty yellow hair was the face of a fifty-year-old man, bristled and sweat-drenched. An angular, ugly face: the unattractiveness of its structure emphasised by the agony he was suffering. The style of his clothing – including the Stetson that lay on the ground some way off from where he sat – was Western American. Similarly, the garb of the three men who once more passed the bottle around, and drank the uncut liquor from the neck instead of lacing their coffee this time, stressed their Mexican nationality. From hats to boots there was a south of the border stamp to their clothing – not least in the way that two of them wore crossed, bullet-heavy bandoliers.

Just the one who had been taking the squaw as Edge drew near – and who with pride had called himself The Evil One – wore an American style gunbelt. It had a holster at each side, revolvers jutting from both. The other two did not carry visible handguns. All three were of matching heights and powerful builds and were in a thirty to forty age group. *El Malo* looked to be the oldest, or perhaps he was simply wearier than the others after his exertions above the unalluring body of the unresponsive squaw.

Edge gained these first impressions of the decadent night camp in no more than ten seconds. And as he did so he draped his free hand over the butt of his holstered revolver. Then, his movements cautiously slow and guarded against the risk of making tell-tale sounds to reveal his presence, he let go of the bridle and the Colt butt to turn and ease the Winchester from its boot. And brought the rifle to the aim from his shoulder, angled down the slope at the heart of the fire between the coffee pots and the skillet.

He did not adopt this attitude with the prime intention of trying to save the captives from further torment and torture at the hands of the sadistic Mexicans. Rather, his motive was entirely selfish. For while he had been studying the component parts of the campsite scene he picked up snatches of what the men were saying. And after *El Malo* was through with complaining about the squaw's lack of passion, and the other two had improved his humour with appreciative comments on how good the appetizing-smelling food in the skillet was going to be, mention was made of the '*gringo* bounty hunter'. But because of the burst of harsh laughter that accompanied the remark, the half-breed was only able to discern that it was spoken in a black-humoured way in connection with the wounded man's missing parts. He had never heard of *El Malo*, but such an alias suggested the man was a bandit chief – and the presence of a mistreated bounty hunter surely meant there was a price on the head of the Mexican who now rose up off his saddle and completed a threequarters turn.

He drank from the tin mug that he held to his lips with both hands while he peered into the moonlit night beyond the fire's glow on three sides of the camp, then said in his native tongue: 'On a night as cold as this, my friends, a man needs a woman of warmth and passion to keep him from the cold.' As he began to speak he was gazing through the heat shimmer and the slow rising smoke above the fire at the woman. Then he gave a pronounced shake of his head and peered down at the men at his feet to conclude: 'But Cody's squaw is useless for such a purpose. I tell you from experience. I say we kill them now and eat and go to our own women – '

'I wish you no disrespect, José,' one of the other Mexicans broke in as he unfolded up off his haunches, leaving his mug on the ground. 'But we are a long way from home. And it is my opinion the Apache is better than nothing at all.'

The top man assumed a determined stance for a few moments, but as his other companion came erect, he shrugged and allowed in a sour tone: 'All right, Miguel. If you must, you must. But get to it quickly, my friends. The food is almost ready and I'm hungry. But if I have to eat with the stink of those two in my nostrils . . . ' He shrugged the broad shoulders of his powerfully-built frame as he spread a grimace across his fleshy, heavily-bristled face.

'Hell, José, all we need is the Apache,' the Mexican who was shortest by an inch growled. 'I'll take care of that bounty hunting Ed Cody right now if you give me the word.'

Edge continued to aim the Winchester at the heart of the fire, index finger curved to the trigger and thumb resting on the uncocked hammer. But he did not ease back the hammer while the Mexican he had heard named as Luis reached behind him to draw a knife from a long sheath hung from his belt at the base of his spine.

'No!' José snarled. And whirled toward the knife-wielding man, the grimace of histrionic revulsion turning into a scowl of anger. Then he made a move as if to launch a blow at the suddenly afraid Luis. 'Dead bounty hunters feel no pain, idiot!' Next his volatile temperament underwent another abrupt change. And after Luis had been held in a frozen attitude of fear for two stretched seconds, José threw back his large head and directed a burst of harsh laughter at the moonlight-flooded sky. But curtailed this as suddenly as it had started and barked out in a tone of command: 'Get on with what you want of the squaw. *El Malo* is as strong in the stomach as he is in all other things, you humourless fools!'

Then the Indian woman ended the clenching and unclenching movements of her hands. While Luis was pushing the knife back in the sheath and Miguel was looking at him just as scornfully as the top man. And for a moment it looked as if the squaw had willed herself to die: or into some kind of trance-like state very close to death. But an instant later she made a move that was so sudden it startled Edge at a distance to almost the same extent as the trio of Mexicans just around the fire from her. She flung herself up into a sitting attitude, then powered into a turn as if to assume an all-fours crouch. But instead she sprang toward the fire. From her throat burst a shrieking sound that seemed to be an expression of all the world's hatred for that which all the world hated most.

It was this awesome sound, perhaps, more than the glimpse of the sudden lunge into action, that caused the gelded Cody to jerk his head up again and stare at the squaw. Certainly it was the shrill wail that compelled Edge, with an almost palpable force, to thumb back the Winchester's hammer. Then, for a stretched second, the rifle was aimed at the narrow back of the naked woman. This as she seemed intent upon hurling herself toward an agonising death in the heart of the fire where the repeater had always been drawing a bead. And during that brief sliver of time that seemed to be eerily warped by the seemingly insane actions of the Apache squaw – and the sound she made that suddenly altered key to express agony rather than hatred – the half-breed needed to struggle consciously against submitting to the compulsion to squeeze the rifle trigger. He beat it and confined his reaction to a rasping curse against the stock of the unfired Winchester:

'Sonofabitch, you crazy woman!'

Perhaps Ed Cody said, or tried to say, something very much like this as he found his own suffering diminished while he stared at the woman and worked his mouth open and shut. But if he did manage to find his voice, the sound of it could not compete with the shrill scream of the Apache and reach up the slope to where Edge was hidden. Likewise, he heard nothing the three Mexicans might have yelled while they were rooted to the ground by the suddenness of the move and anticipation of what appeared to be the only possible end to it.

But then she halted her seemingly unstoppable lunge to a searing death in the fire. Planted her bare feet firmly on the ground and folded forward from the waist. Reached through the tongues of flame and the billowing smoke. And was somehow able to cut off the awful screaming from her throat as she came partly upright and turned her whole frame.

'Shit, you stupid – ' Cody could be heard to snarl.

Maybe he finished it off, but the explosive burst of Mexican obscenities voiced by the three men on the other side of the fire from him swamped his words. This as they stumbled backwards, seeking to get out of the way as the squaw viciously hurled the scalding contents of the two coffee pots toward them.

Perhaps it was just a trick of the dancing firelight that caused an illusion: but in the moments after the coffee had been flung out of the pots and the man named Miguel took both lots full in the face, it seemed that the Apache woman's gaunt face was spread with a broad grin of pure pleasure. More likely, though, it was an expression of silent suffering as she struggled to control a vocal outlet to the agony she felt as she continued to tightly grip the blisteringly hot handles of the pots.

She held fast to them for just part of a second longer,

as Miguel threw his hands up to his scalded face and bellowed his pain. And Luis made to draw his knife again. But José beat him: had both his revolvers clear of the holsters before the other man had fisted a hand to the knife. Luis was snarling a whole string of obscenities, his stubbled face set in a snarl of hatred that was a near match for the sound the squaw had vented. While José was now silent and displayed an expression that was as impassive as any of which the half-breed in the trees was capable.

Luis was not a knife thrower. He had the blade clear of the sheath but needed to get in close. He had taken only one step toward the woman before she hurled the empty pots at him. Some flesh from her fingers and palms was torn off the bones and she was not able to prevent a scream from escaping her throat now. Luis halted his advance and ducked. He was struck without force by one of the pots. The wailing Miguel dropped hard to his knees beside the man with the knife, still clinging with both hands to his burning face. Beyond and a pace in back of Miguel, José fired both his revolvers. And in the immediate wake of the double report that could be heard echoing on a diminishing note down the *barranca*, the woman was silent, Luis curtailed his cursing and Ed Cody allowed his chin to drop to his chest, as if to commence a tacit prayer. Just Miguel added to the unobtrusive crackling sounds from the fire, whimpering his anguish.

'You sound like a bawling infant!' José accused. And his harsh-spoken accusation acted like a gag on Miguel, choking him into miserable silence before the Apache woman was sprawled out on the ground. Spreadeagled, like before. Where she moved convulsively for a number of seconds until her nervous system died. Then just the trickling of the blood that seeped from the two holes beneath her unpronounced left breast kept her entire emaciated frame from being utterly still for a little longer.

Edge, as dispassionate as the Mexican with the smoking guns in his hands, tracked the aim of the Winchester from the fire: to draw a bead on José. And he was within a part of a second of taking a risk on whether *El Malo* was wanted alive or not. But, before he could apply more than the start of first pressure to the trigger, a cacophonous fusillade of gunfire shattered the tense stillness.

He turned his head away from where his cheek had been pressed to the stock of the rifle and spat a globule of saliva out of the side of his mouth. Murmured cynically against the barrage of shots: 'So okay, you fellers have the bounty. It never really was much to my taste.'

Four

MIGUEL WENT down first, spurting blood from many wounds. He slammed sideways out of the kneeling attitude, his hands flying away from his scalded face in a doomed, vain attempt to break his fall: dead before he was slumped on the ground. Luis had time to begin a move toward the heaps of gear where he and his companions had taken their ease to drink coffee. It was obvious there was a gun there, but his effort to reach it was as ill starred as the defensive move Miguel had tried. For he had already taken several bullets in his body as he began to swing around in response to the volley of shots. Then, by concerted skilled shooting or by sheer chance, his legs were blasted out from beneath him at the same time as his head seemed to explode under the impact of many bullets smashing into his face and neck.

Both men were down and dead within the space of five seconds. And in this time José, who was the only member of the trio to have a weapon to hand, spun around and thumbed back the hammers of both his revolvers: turning the cylinders to displace with live shells the empty cases of the two bullets that had tunnelled into the flesh of the Apache squaw.

Near silence had returned to the campsite. There was just the crackling of the flames and the scratching at the ground of shod hooves as the *remuda* of mounts calmed in the wake of the barrage. Then the hardly audible ping as the toe of José's boot accidentally came up against one of the empty coffee pots. Perhaps it was just in imagination that a distant echo of the firing of a dozen or so rifles could be heard faintly from far beyond the reach of the fire glow. But no sound more obtrusive than this now came out from within the shadowed confines of the *barranca* where the gunfire had blazed just a few moments ago.

El Malo froze at the completion of his turn that found him facing into the ravine, his twin revolvers levelled from the hips. And perhaps in the first second as he halted the turn he might have died. For it would have required just a glimpse of a living target moving in the shadows and the triggers of the cocked guns would surely have been instinctively squeezed. And in the brittle tension that was clamped down over this small area of the Sierra Madre, those two shots would certainly have drawn a mass response. And the surviving Mexican would have been cut to pieces amid a greater torrent of blood than had sprayed away from the dying forms of Miguel and Luis. But then the moment was gone. And it was a voice, rather than another fusillade of gunshots, that shattered the new silence. The voice of Ed Cody as the man reached far into his vastly diminished reserve of stamina to shriek:

'Kill him! Kill the friggin' sonofabitch! Do it now! So I can see it happen. Like I saw them other two friggin' bastards get it!'

José was startled at first when the bounty hunter who was no longer a man began to bellow his demands. And he stiffened in a visible display of the alarm he felt. But he did not turn toward his former prisoner: and before Cody was through with his yelling, the Mexican had dropped his revolvers to the ground. And slowly he started to push his arms skywards, fingers splayed and palms toward the *barranca* to emphasise the emptiness of his hands.

'*El Malo* is not stupid!' he called; and if he needed to exert any conscious effort to keep his voice from quavering with fear, it could not be heard. 'He knows when it is better to fight and when it is best to surrender to a superior number of the enemy!'

'Superior in every way, Sanchez!' a more highly pitched and more cultured voice responded from the dark mouth of the ravine. 'But that is nothing much of which I and my men can be proud, I think. Since you are nothing more than a sackful of animal excrement that walks and talks like a man.'

'I'm in no situation to argue with you, Captain,' José Sanchez admitted, and now there was either fear or anger being held on a tight rein in back of his stance and his voice. A tall and slim Federale officer led a group of more than a dozen other uniformed men out of the *barranca* and into the fringe glow of the firelight.

'Move away from your weapons, excrement,' the top man of the troop commanded. And pushed his own revolver back into the flapped holster on his hip.

But all his men carried rifles that they aimed menacingly toward Sanchez, who moved to comply with the order with a swaggering arrogance that the circumstances patently invested with bravado. He came to a halt after three strides had carried him well clear of his discarded revolvers and the slumped corpses of Miguel and Luis.

The bearing of the Federale officer was a perfect match for his tone of voice: further stressed that he was a man of good breeding who had been privileged to both enjoy and suffer the best and worst that comes with rank not necessarily of the military kind. His gait was upright and measured, and there was on his classically handsome face as he advanced toward Sanchez an expression of a supercilious contempt that implied that the civilian was literally what the captain constantly called him.

'What are you going to do?' Sanchez asked nervously, on the point of backing off from the uniformed man who was of an age with him. The officer had taken the ivory-butted revolver out of the holster again, and now came to an elegant halt four feet away from Sanchez. Thus the frightened bandit felt able to hold his ground. But probably he was too afraid to move anyway as he watched the Federale cock the gun. 'You can't shoot me like a dog!'

'You are lower than a dog, Sanchez. You are what comes from a dog when the animal squats and raises its tail.'

The rifle-toting men under the captain's command shuffled to a halt in an uneven semi-circle to either side of the officer who aimed the revolver at the chest of the shaking Sanchez. There was a brief silence, perhaps the most tense yet, that again only the crackling of the flames kept from being absolute. Which held until Sanchez was at last able to force sounds out from between his frantically-working lips. This as he lowered his arms and clasped his hands at his chest in an attitude of prayer.

'Please, Captain. I am unarmed and helpless and . . .'

Now Ed Cody revealed he was still conscious after his draining outburst, and that he had a knowledge of the language being spoken. But he used his native tongue as he snarled without raising his chin up off his chest: 'So was I when you cut off my *cojones*, shithead.'

'Not just the head, *señor*,' the captain corrected. And speaking American he sounded even more cultured than when he used his own language. 'From head to toe he is excrement.'

Sanchez pleaded: 'You can't kill me! Not now I have surrendered to you!'

The bounty hunter managed to bring his head up, and there was a grin of pleasurable anticipation on his gaunt face as he relished the prospect of watching his torturer shot down. He snarled in triumph: 'You wanna bet on that, shithead?'

'*Señor*, I allow no gambling within my area of jurisdiction,' the Federale officer said with vehemence. Then angled his revolver away from the chest of the trembling Sanchez. Squeezed the trigger to send a bullet smashing through his victim's kneecap. Waited for the scream of shock to diminish into groaning pain after Sanchez had collapsed on to his side, his hands now clasped to his bloodied leg before he concluded with an arrogant smile: 'Since, as I have demonstrated, I am not myself a man to take chances.'

'Seems to me, feller,' Edge rasped, his voice a barely audible whisper while the words squeezed out through teeth clenched in a scowl, 'that for somebody who doesn't gamble, you're one hell of a mean crapshooter.'

Five

As soon as José Sanchez was made a secure prisoner by the Federales, the half-breed's interest in events at the campsite beside the mouth of the *barranca* was ended. But since his intended route lay south and the easiest way in that direction was on the trail through the ravine, he continued to watch what was happening in the area of the dying fire while he waited for the soldiers to do what the officer demanded of them.

He continued his less than eager surveillance from the same position at the side of the trail in the fringe of the timber. His Winchester was back in the boot but he remained close enough to the gelding so that he could quickly slide the rifle free of where it rested if this proved necessary. And with such a bunch of trigger-happy men under the command of the coldly vicious captain, anything might happen. Which was the main reason why Edge elected to wait out their departure rather than take the risk of riding openly down the slope. Trouble usually located him easily enough. He never needed to invite it.

It was not a lengthy delay, since the terse, peremptory manner in which the officer had ordered the raid on the camp – and brought it to such a sudden and violent end – had set the pattern for what followed. Two men were despatched to bring the horses that had been left back in the depths of the *barranca*. Doubtless they had been temporarily abandoned when Ed Cody's shriek of agony had warned the riders there was trouble on the trail ahead. Then four men were ordered to saddle up the horses and the burro in the camp *remuda.* The corpses of Miguel and Luis were searched and anything of any value found was confiscated. The wound of José Sanchez was treated to the extent that his right pants leg was cut open and the bullet hole bandaged with a strip of fabric ripped from an undergarment earlier worn by the Apache squaw.

Men not engaged in carrying out the captain's orders occupied their time with smoking or helping themselves to whatever was in the skillet. And as they took their ease they exchanged ribald remarks about the naked corpse of the woman: mostly concerned with how the youngest of their number had better go with her, since her unprotesting body presented the best chance he had yet been given to lose his virginity.

After he had given the commands to his men, the captain remained apart from the activity. He squatted on his haunches beside the almost exhausted bounty hunter, interrogating the helpless man in a quiet but vicious manner. His brutality seen most times in the way he reached out to jerk Cody's head up whenever it dropped weakly forward. Then once, when the American felt provoked to argue with him, the Mexican countered with a blow to his face. And the impact of the back of the gloved hand brought a sharp cry of pain from the gelded Cody.

This caused Sanchez to briefly check his own groaning response to suffering and to snarl: 'That is good, Captain. That *gringo*, he tries to capture *El Malo* singlehanded. He is a fool who deserves – '

The men sent into the *barranca* had brought the horses close enough to the camp for the sound of their trampling hooves to be heard. The captain spoke without shouting, but his cultured tone carried the menacing words clearly up the slope to where Edge waited patiently and watched disinterestedly.

'Sergeant Mendoza. If the excrement utters one more word, you will shoot him in the other knee.'

'Yes sir,' the non-com who had bound up the bandit's wound answered. And in the way he smiled and drew the revolver from his holster there was an unmistakable eagerness to carry out the order.

Sanchez assumed his former position – curled up on his side with both hands clasped beneath his bullet-shattered kneecap. And remained so, with the sergeant aiming the gun down at him, while the string of horses was brought into the diminished area of glow spread by the flickering fire. Then, after one last hostile exchange of questions and answers between the captain and the bounty hunter, the officer rose to his feet and issued the final orders to signal a departure.

These were as swiftly obeyed as all the others. Just the groans and sometimes screams of José Sanchez as he was bundled astride a horse and had his wrists tied to the saddlehorn detracted from the quiet efficiency with which everything was accomplished. The captain was the last man to mount, after running a cold gaze over the campsite area and the double file of men already in the saddle. His manner indicated that he did not think there was the slightest chance his orders had not been complied with to the letter. Rather, he was double checking to see if there was anything he had overlooked. And a curt nod before he swung astride his horse was the signal that all was well.

Then he glanced at the bounty hunter, whose bonds he had ordered cut, and touched a finger to the peak of his cap as he said in American: 'Goodbye and good luck, sir.' Reverted to his native tongue to command a forward walk.

Edge watched these final activities about the campsite from a different vantage point – had led his gelding off the trail and deep into the timber at the side as soon as it became apparent the Federales were not going to back-track into the *barranca.* Instead, were northward bound and so would move up the slope toward him as soon as they were ordered to start. And by the time the column moved, the half-breed was astride his horse: poised to lunge the animal into an instant gallop if the coolly unruffled attitude of the Federale captain should prove to be a mask for something more sinister. But all was well, even though Edge was convinced the officer was like him in at least one respect: would have a nose . . . a sixth sense for being watched. But maybe too much had happened already tonight and all the man's senses were dulled by the triumph he now experienced as he led his prisoner and the troop away from the carnage-ravaged scene at the foot of the slope.

Edge gave a just perceptible nod that this was probably right as he glimpsed in the pale moonlight a smile that flitted for no more than a second across the angular-featured face of the captain. For it was a smile of almost childishly gleeful enjoyment at how events had turned out. A secret smile that might well have broken out into a foolish giggle had not Sergeant Mendoza and José Sanchez been riding immediately behind him, with the double file of uniformed men in back of them.

In the same shaft of moonlight the face of each passing rider was briefly in view and Edge saw a variety of expressions displayed. The prisoner with the smashed kneecap was enduring pain that he made no attempt to conceal. The sergeant was grimly watchful of Sanchez; despite the fact that the bandit had his wrists lashed to the saddle the non-com rode with a hand draped over the butt of the revolver in his holster. Some of the men were grinning as broadly as the captain, but uncaring about who saw them. Perhaps continued to enjoy the obscene jokes about the young virgin and the dead squaw. Others showed grim expressions: were scornful, filled with remorse or stone-faced. Maybe each of the men reflecting his attitude to what had just happened, or perhaps their thoughts came from further back in the past. Or they could even be contemplating a depressing future.

The last two riders in the column had lead lines on the horses of Miguel, Luis and Cody and the squaw's burro. And after these animals had trotted out of Edge's field of vision he returned his attention to the camp where the former riders of the confiscated mounts were sprawled. But he continued to keep track of the departing troop, his ears straining to pick up any tell-tale change in the rhythm of the slow-moving hooves that would signal an interruption of the north-bound trek. And not until there had been utter silence from behind him in the timber for more than two minutes did he touch his heels to the flanks of his horse and ease him forward, out onto the open slope. Again kept an apparently indifferent watch on the terrain to all sides as he rode slowly down to the camp. Where for a long time just the occasional flame and the smoke of the fire could be seen to move: this seeming to accentuate the perfect stillness of Miguel, Luis and the Apache squaw. And Ed Cody, too, from a distance looked to be as dead as they were as he slumped on the ground with his back against the rock wall, his legs splayed, his freed arms limp at his sides and his chin sunk on his chest.

And the bounty hunter was as silent as the corpses until Edge rode close enough to see the shallow rise and fall of his breathing. He seemed unconscious then. Until, of a sudden, he dragged his head up and turned it so that he could peer toward the newcomer. As he did this he needed to brace his hands on the ground to keep from toppling on to his side.

'Hey, you had second thoughts, uh?' he asked in a weak, croaking voice. His lips trembled and his eyes glistened, hope shining through the tears of earlier despair.

'It's you best think again, feller,' the half-breed said after he had reined in his gelding close enough for the glow of the fire, which was flickering toward extinction, to supplement the moonlight that fell on him. 'On account of I'm not who you think I am.'

'Hey, you're American, uh?' Cody replied with a degree

of excitement giving a little strength to his voice. And he raised a hand to knuckle the blurring tears from his eyes: eager to get a clear view of the man who swung smoothly out of the saddle. 'You just come out here on the San Sarita trail . . . ? There's a whole bunch of Federales under a real mean . . . Shit, I must've passed out!'

He moved his gaze from Edge, to the trail up the slope behind the half-breed, and then the fire. And remained confused as he recognised the fire had not died down enough from the last time he saw it to validate his unconscious conclusion.

The gelding was disconcerted by the presence of death, even though the stink of it had not yet permeated the night air that was aromatic with woodsmoke and chilli. Edge hobbled the horse before he answered:

'I was up in the timber for awhile. Thinking about taking on the job you and your squaw fouled up. Damn Federales beat me to it. Waited out them leaving and then came on down here. Guess you ain't too hungry?'

If Cody was feeling any physical pain he hid it well. Maybe the horrific wound from which so much blood had spouted had become numb with the passing of time and the way he had been able to remain unmoving for so long. Or maybe he had simply grown accustomed to it. But emotional suffering was plainly visible on his haggard, never handsome, and now ugly face.

'How long, mister?' he demanded to know, ignoring the virtually rhetorical query that was posed as the half-breed squatted on his haunches beside the fire and peered into the skillet. 'Were you up there when that sadist Sanchez hacked off my balls?'

Edge used his kerchief to wrap around his hand so that he did not burn it with the handle of the ladle that the last Federale to eat had left in the pot. Supplied: 'I was better than a mile to the north when that happened, I guess. Heard your yell. Before that, just knew there was this fire up ahead.'

He scraped up some of the contents of the skillet with the ladle and eyed the food without enthusiasm as he sniffed it. Then he took a tentative taste of what turned out to be chilli beans with maybe a few small chunks of meat mixed in. It would do, and he began to eat more quickly.

'You ain't worked in this part of Sonora before, have you?' Cody asked and he sounded and looked like the pain of his castration was getting to him again.

'No.' The half-breed did not take the time to empty his mouth when he responded to the suffering man.

'What's your name?'

'Edge.'

'I ain't never heard of you.'

'That's all right. I ain't trying to get famous.'

'Then you're bounty huntin' in the right piece of country, mister. On account of that Sanchez shit is the biggest bird between San Sarita and Punto de Honra. And a lotta miles east and west. But he ain't nothin' special. Just figures he is. Two hundred bucks was his price last I heard?' His expression rather than any variation in his croaking tone of voice added the query.

'Dead or alive?'

'Either way. No difference, I was told. But that Federale sure wanted him still livin'.'

Edge scraped the skillet clean of food and said: 'Guess no difference is what it makes now. Since the Federales got him for free.' He made to eat from the ladle, then paused to direct a questioning glance at Cody to ask: 'You sure you don't want to eat? This is the last of it.'

'Eatin's the last thing I want to do, mister,' the gelded man growled and there was scorn in back of the anguish of his voice and expression now.

Edge shook his head and countered: 'No. Dying's going to be the last thing you do, Cody. But I always figured a condemned man having a final meal was a waste of good food.' He began to eat again.

'I ain't condemned!' the man at the foot of the cliff blurted. 'I ain't the first guy to have this done to him! Screwin' ain't everythin'!'

'I figure that hard-nosed Federale captain didn't make you any promises, feller?'

'Uh?'

'About sending a doctor out from San Sarita? Or maybe a wagon to give you a ride into town?'

'Damn right, he didn't, the shithead! All I asked him was to leave me my horse and gear. Like you said about the food . . . He said it'd be wasted on me. I wouldn't be able to sit a saddle for long. And in not too long I'd be dead. When I said I'd manage somehow, the shithead back-handed me across the face.'

Anger was an emotion too strong for him to sustain. His voice became weaker and he was visibly having trouble keeping his head from falling forward. The glitter in his eyes was again caused by tears and in back of the salt moisture was a plea.

'I'd have left you the horse and gear, feller,' the half-breed said, and dropped the licked-clean ladle back in the empty skillet. Then he eyed the two overturned and drained dry coffee pots with a baleful gaze as he straightened up from off his haunches and delved into a shirt pocket for the makings.

'But there ain't nothin' you're gonna do for me?' Cody accused bitterly.

'No. On account of there's nothing I can.'

'You're just gonna leave me here? With the dead? Just like that bastard Federale captain? Come sun-up the buzzards'll be here. And if I ain't dead by then I'll be too friggin' weak to beat them off me. Or maybe the coyotes'll be around soon as the fire goes out.'

Cody's voice rose in pitch but he did not have the strength to talk louder as he visualised being living food for the scavengers of the Sierra Madre: seeing vivid images of the horror played out on the insides of his squeezed shut eyelids. Then he snapped open his eyes to the sound of a match being struck. And in its first flare he saw the butt of the holstered Colt upon which Edge had scraped the match into flame.

He swallowed hard and then blurted: 'Hey, you're right, mister! I'm set to cash in my chips for sure. But I don't have to die slow. That Colt you got . . . let me have the loan of it? I'll just use the one bullet. That ain't askin' so much, seems to me?'

Edge lit the cigarette and tossed the matchstick into the glowing embers where it flared as the fiercest point of the once bright fire for a second or so. Then he turned and moved carefully around the naked corpse of the squaw so that he was close to the mutilated man.

'While there's life there's hope, Cody.'

'Uh?'

'One bullet would be maybe all it'd take to kill me. Then you'd have my horse and my gear and you could maybe drape yourself over the saddle and ride a few yards. Even a mile. Hurting like hell. Until you slid off. Hurt even more. But maybe you'd be able to haul yourself aboard again. Seems to me, though, you'd have faint hope, feller. And you'd soon run out of life.'

Cody had to crane his head to the side to peer up at the tall half-breed who towered above him at such close quarters. At first his expression was a pathetically unsuccessful attempt to show that Edge's assertions were totally wrong. But soon his glistening eyes, the line of his slack mouth and the small sounds that escaped from his bobbing throat all contributed to an involuntarily genuine display of total despair. Ed Cody had played the last card in a hand that had been a loser from the start. Now he could only invite an end to the whole game. The strength required to sustain the attitude of looking up at Edge was abruptly drained and his chin fell, rather than was lowered, to his chest. He seemed to try to clench his hands into fists – as the squaw had done so many times before she made the move that led to her death – but he lacked what it took to more than form claws of his fingers.

'Ain't too much to ask . . .' he began to force out, his voice childlike as he fought against the threat of weeping. 'A man like you . . . You'd do it for an animal without no chance. Anyone would, I'd say. And I reckon that most of my lousy life I been actin' more like an animal than a human bein'. Worst kinda animal. Huntin' down men for a few measly bucks. And treatin' my women not much better than that bunch of greasers treated the squaw. Maybe I didn't deserve no better than what they done to me. And I don't reckon I deserve to die easy now.'

Edge had reached into the hair at the nape of his neck as soon as Cody was no longer looking up at him. And after he had drawn the straight razor out of the pouch he took the time to firm his grip around the handle. Held it low down and behind him as the bounty hunter, weakening by the moment and soon to die, dribbled words down over his chest.

'Real dumb of me . . . haulin' that Apache hag along on a huntin' trip. Drunk, that's for sure . . . Seemed like a good idea . . . Was humpin' her and she wasn't so much better with me than with that shithead . . . Sonofabitch, how dumb can a guy get . . . Screwin' a dried-up old crone when he oughta have been lookin' out for . . . I was thinkin' of this whore back in Tucson . . . Just gonna get my rocks off . . . And he rammed his rifle barrel up my bare ass . . .'

Ed Cody's voice was hardly audible by now, but probably he was not aware of this. Edge dropped down on his haunches again and the bounty hunter knew this happened – rolled his head to the side and forced his eyes to the limit of their sockets to try to look into the half-breed's face.

'You gonna put a bullet in me?' he rasped.

'Too quiet out here, Cody. Gunshot would carry a long way. I don't want that bunch of Federales coming back here until I've left.'

The man who was sitting on a massive patch of congealed blood made a final attempt to screw his head around far enough so that he could scowl at the half-breed. He failed, and acknowledged failure with a strangely gentle sigh. Then: 'So get the hell away from here, mister,' he murmured and the lack of rancour in his voice sounded as odd as the sigh had been. 'Far away, if you'll take my advice. Go back north and over the border. Ain't nothin' worthwhile to hold a man in this stinkin', lousy, rotten, friggin' no-good country.'

Edge reached out with his left hand, cupped it over Cody's eyes and brow and eased the man's head up until the crown was pressed against the cliff. The slack mouth opened and closed in spasms, but only inarticulate growls escaped from the vulnerably exposed throat. Then the razor was brought forward and up. And with a smooth action that was completed in part of a second the keenly-honed blade was slashed across the scrawny neck.

The slender length of shiny steel plunged in deeply enough to sever the vital jugular vein and windpipe. And blood spouted from both the massive gash and the suddenly-gaping mouth as Edge snatched away his two hands before they were stained in the torrents of crimson. He was unsure of whether it was anguished condemnation or grief-stricken appreciation that he saw in the tear-bright eyes of Ed Cody in the final half second of the bounty hunter's life. And then the man was dead, head hanging down again: now his stubbled chin resting on a shirt front sodden with dark, arterial blood. Edge wiped both sides of the blade on an unstained sleeve of Cody's shirt before he returned the razor to the pouch and unfolded up to his full height. Took the cigarette out of the corner of his mouth for long enough to say to the corpse at his feet:

'If you figured to tell me thanks, it's okay. Kind of state you were in, it was no sweat to help you out.'

Six

At noon the next day Edge was the only customer in the cantina that was only one of two places of business in the tiny community of Punto de Honra. The other was a general store which was right next door to the cantina across a narrow alley. Both places were run by a Texan named Morton Reed who looked and smelled like he had not taken a bath since he won the cantina in a poker game. Which he thought was twelve or thirteen years earlier. Just as he could not be precise about the length of time he had also owned the store: possession of which he had acquired by marrying the widow of the man who first opened it. Too damn long was all that concerned Morton Reed who was a compulsive talker.

The half-breed was not interested in the commercial history of Punto de Honra and neither did he care at all about how the Texan's marriage of convenience had turned out to be such a bad deal. But the tequila was good, if not the best, and was going down easy. And the smell of food that wafted into the room from the kitchen out back gave appetising promise of a fine meal to come. And Reed was the kind of talker who enjoyed most the kind of conversation in which he held the floor – demanded little more than the physical presence of a listening ear with just an occasional nod or affirmative sound of agreement. So it was an undemanding exercise to sit in the small, squalid cantina of a small, squalid village; out of the direct glare of the midday sun, and think of nothing or anything at all – with a bottle of better than average liquor now, the prospect of a well cooked meal in the offing, and with not the least sign of any trouble from any quarter.

'Hey, I ain't gettin' on your nerves or anythin' like that, am I, Mr Edge?' Reed asked anxiously after a short, frowning pause during which he had apparently been reassessing something he had just said about his wife.

Edge looked up from the corner table where he sat on the chair that placed his back to the angle of the two walls. And his narrowed eyes checked the sunlit, empty doorway before he glanced at Reed and answered: 'I'll let you know.'

The man behind the bar was sixty or more. Texas tall but no longer wide – there was a suggestion about his thin frame that once he had been built like the side of a house – he had a hollow-cheeked, sunken-eyed, slack-mouthed face that had lit with a bright smile when he discovered his only customer was an American. Now, for the first time in a quarter bottle of tequila, he looked a little less than happy.

'Just that we don't get so many Americans passin' through this neck of the woods. Guess I've gone near native myself, but it sure beats a lot else to have a fellow-countryman to crack the jaw with every now and then.' He looked down at himself and glanced toward the straw sombrero that rested on the end of the short length of bar counter. Without the leather waist apron and with the broad brim of the hat throwing shadow over his dark-stained, heavily stubbled face, Morton Reed would look as one with the handful of peons Edge had seen as he rode into the village.

'Guess not,' the half-breed said and began to roll a cigarette.

'Come to that, we don't get many people of any kind passin' through,' the man behind the bar added, and now seemed almost morose in comparison with his earlier delight. 'Weeks . . . sometimes months can go by and we don't see no-one except them that live here. Then I get the closest there is to a rush of trade. Here and at the store. Like this week, for instance. Monday, someone same as you came into town. Well, not like you. Just that he was American, too. Ridin' with an Apache squaw. He wasn't a good guy to talk with. Just asked a whole lot of questions I wasn't about to give him answers to. Spent pretty well at the store, though. Then, yesterday, a bunch of Federales came by. The officer – Captain Miranda – he was a real hard-nosed sonofabitch who looked over this place like he didn't figure it was classy enough for him to take a leak in, you know what I mean?'

Edge lit his cigarette and nodded. Thought about topping up his half empty shot glass but decided against it. 'I saw them on the trail, feller.'

Reed pulled a face. 'You pass the time of day with that Miranda pig?'

'Passed nothing but by. The food about cooked yet?'

Reed sniffed deeply and nodded. 'I reckon so. How many *enchiladas* you want, Mr Edge?'

'Two.'

'Comin' right up. In the unlikely event I get any more customers while I'm out back, you tell them to wait, okay?'

He had to come out from behind the bar that was along a side wall of the room to go through the bead-curtained square arch that gave onto the kitchen in the centre of the rear wall. He looked older when he walked, but perhaps this was only because he had a pronounced limp. He whistled a familiar tune as he busied himself with making Edge's lunch, and the sounds he made were the only ones to infiltrate the small, overheated but shaded room where the lone patron sat at a corner table. And the half-breed found himself involuntarily realising how it could be that a drifter wearied by a life on the move might feel a strong inclination to call a halt in a place like Punto de Honra. If the circumstances of a game of poker were right. He had stopped by the store before he stepped into the cantina: and now he decided he could not visualise any set of circumstances that would manoeuvre him into marrying the woman who sold him some basic supplies.

'So you came into town from the north, Mr Edge?' Reed interrupted the half-breed's meandering line of thought as he carried from the kitchen a plate laden with two large *enchiladas* thickly covered with red chilli sauce. 'If you saw the Federales, I mean?'

The aroma of chilli was not quite pungent enough to mask the stink of Reed's unwashed flesh. And Edge waited until the man had returned behind the bar before he picked up the fork and tested the food. His slow nod of appreciation was accepted by the Texan as a reply to his query.

'You come down by way of San Sarita, Mr Edge?'

'Right. Feller, your food is as good as your liquor.'

Reed waved a filthy hand in the air. 'You can see I don't have to supply anythin' in quantity. Gives me all the opportunity I need to go for quality. Hey, there's been some trouble at the San Sarita Federale post, that right?'

'You heard right.'

Reed was not perturbed by the uncommunicative attitude of the half-breed who was eating with the manner of one who wants the pleasure to last as long as possible. 'Some of the guys in the troop, they were okay. After Miranda and his sergeant were through with me and started in to ask questions around the rest of the town. Told me they were from Sonora headquarters down in Hermosillo. Headed for the post at San Sarita. And not none of them lookin' forward to it, neither. They'd heard the post commander got himself killed in a cantina brawl. Miranda's gonna replace him.'

'The scuttlebutt about the feller getting killed was right,' Edge confirmed.

'Antonio Gomez?'

'That's him.'

'He was through here every once in awhile. On patrol or on his way to and from headquarters down in Hermosillo.'

'Not any more.'

'Didn't run such a tight post. More interested in featherin' his own nest than in maintainin' law and order? Brawl got started on account of some prisoner Gomez figured to make a fortune out of and – '

'All sounds about right, feller.'

Reed had been starting to talk with great enthusiasm again. But now he did a double take at Edge and saw that he had been right. The hardness he thought he had detected in the soft-spoken words was backed up by a dangerous glitter in the ice-blue slits of his customer's eyes.

'Real sorry, Mr Edge.' He dry-washed his dirty hands and then wiped the palms down the sides of his already greasy pants. 'I was just askin'. I didn't have no idea I was puttin' my snout in your business.'

'No sweat, feller. How much I owe for the liquor and food?'

'Buck and a half okay? US or pesos, I don't mind.'

'If it's okay with you, I'm happy.'

Edge had not half eaten the meal when this exchange brought an end to Morton Reed's fishing for details about the trouble at San Sarita. The Texan also found himself unable to resume his earlier dissertation on his life and times since arriving in Punto de Honra. For whenever he thought of a suitable remark to get himself started, a glance at Edge caused him to remain silent. For the lone patron of the cantina was eating without any display of relish now. On the lean, darkly-stained, deeply-scored and thickly-stubbled face was an expression that – perhaps without intent – warned against interruption. An expression somewhere between a frown and a scowl that told of preoccupation with bitter memories called to mind by the recent talk: or perhaps with a bleak future heralded by the events at San Sarita of which he did not wish to talk. Then he was through eating and rattled the fork on the empty plate.

'I'm obliged,' he said and delved a hand into a pants pocket. Produced some coins and counted out a dollar and fifty cents which he heaped on the table. Then he retrieved the part-smoked cigarette and re-lit it. Picked up the still half full shot glass but did not yet drink from it as he leaned back in the chair. And presented the image of a satisfied man – after the last vestige of the earlier expression had slipped from his face.

Morton Reed could not abide the silence for more than a few seconds. Said as he came toward the corner table: 'That Miranda guy won't run a sloppy post, that's for sure. Some of the men with him were tellin' me, Mr Edge. He never had too much chance to throw his weight about at state headquarters. Captains common as flies in the necessary down there. But, like Gomez was, he'll be king of the castle up at San Sarita.' He transferred the coins to his pocket and picked up the plate. Edge gestured that he should also take away the bottle and he did so reluctantly. Acknowledging this as a sure sign that he would soon lose the company of his fellow-countryman.

'I don't guess it'll make much difference to the likes of me. Or any other law abidin' citizens. Unless Miranda has better luck than Gomez at catchin' up with José Sanchez and his bunch.' He leaned through the bead curtain to deposit the dirty plate in the kitchen. Then went on as he carried the bottle back behind the bar: 'You heard about Sanchez, Mr Edge?'

The half-breed, no longer looking so at ease on the chair, seemed detached again: but his attitude was of alertness as he paused in the process of taking the cigarette from his mouth and raising the glass to drink. Then Reed heard the sound that had captured the attention of his customer. The distant clop of shod hooves that signalled the approach of a small group of riders.

'The feller who calls himself the Evil One,' Edge replied at length, and sucked half the remains of his drink.

'That's right. *El Malo*. And he can live up to that name

when he's crossed, the way I hear it. You ain't . . . ?'

'What, feller?' Edge queried as he appeared to be totally at ease again: indifferent to anything that was happening beyond the confines of the cantina.

Morton Reed was suddenly the very opposite of what the half-breed seemed to be. He was sweatingly nervous, and after rubbing his greasy hands down his pants he felt the need to pour himself a drink. And he gazed at the sun-bright doorway as he said in anxious low tones: 'Just that the guy who was through here Monday . . . the American . . . He was a bounty hunter. Name of Cody. He was askin' a whole lot of questions about José Sanchez, Mr Edge. Same kind that Miranda was askin'. Me, I couldn't tell neither of them nothin'. But even if I could've, I wouldn't. That guy Sanchez . . . Even if the stories they tell about him was just a quarter true . . . Well, I sure wouldn't want it to get back to him that I even mentioned his name in passin' to a bounty hunter or a Federale.'

The eyes in their sunken sockets remained in a transfixed stare at the doorway as the clop of hooves rose in volume and the sound slowed in cadence. Three, or perhaps four, men checking their mounts from a trot to a walk as they rode into the tiny community. Then the Texan peered at Edge, the expression in his eyes expanding the query in his tone to something akin to a demand.

'Sometimes I bounty hunt,' the half-breed supplied, but needed to augment this before the other man's anxiety began to diminish. 'Most of the time I don't.'

The riders had reined in their horses and were dismounting out front of the general store. Edge finished his drink and stood up as he heard the animals being hitched to the same rail where his gelding was tied. Now, in underscored contrast to his attitude before the riders were heard outside, Morton Reed was eager for his customer to leave. And relief at getting what he wanted gave him such a lift that he did not need to drink the liquor he had poured himself.

'You made mention in passing – ' Edge began.

'Yeah, but that was only – ' the Texan broke in, suddenly anxious again.

Edge counter-interrupted: 'Of the necessary, feller. You got one here?'

'Sure, out back.' He jerked a thumb to indicate the way was through the beaded arch.

'I'm obliged.'

'You're welcome, Mr Edge. You're ever through this way again, you be sure to stop by my place. And I'd surely appreciate it if you'd tell other folks that Mort Reed does the best he can for his customers . . .'

The half-breed did not hear the cantina owner complete his request for recommendations, for he had already gone through the archway. The kitchen was smaller than the room he had just left. Just as poorly furnished and decorated. But it smelled better because the atmosphere was still permeated by the aroma of highly-spiced cooking that totally masked any taint of Reed's stink that the Texan may have trailed behind him out here. The yard beyond the rear door smelled of rotting garbage. The air within the hole in the ground privy was no heavier with the familiar stench than that in others Edge had used – many in places with far greater pretentions than the squalid little cantina in Punto de Honra.

The half-breed emerged through the bead-curtained archway less than a minute after he left. The first change he noted was that there was a small plate on the table where he had sat. On the plate was a quarter segment of lemon and a pile of salt. Beside the plate was a brimful shot glass.

'*Señor, bienvenido Punto de Honra!* You will take the drink with me, okay? Drink the tequila with me the only way there is to drink it, okay? With the salt and the lemon?'

He was standing at the bar. A fine looking man in his early twenties. His handsomeness was shallow and his build was slim, but with the passing of time maturity would give character to his clean-shaven face, and if he took care of himself his frame would fill out in the right proportions. His tone expressed genuine pleasure but there was something wrong with his smile. The mouth was right in the way it was open to display a perfect set of teeth, but although there was a bright sparkle in the dark eyes they looked like they were prepared in an instant to switch to malevolence. Or, Edge thought for a moment, perhaps it was Morton Reed's patently obvious discomfort with the situation that made it so easy to distrust the young Mexican's attitude.

'Obliged, but I pay my own way,' the half-breed said.

'This is Esteban Sosa, Mr Edge,' the Texan squeezed out from a frantically working throat and through teeth exposed in a forced smile. 'His mother lives here in Punto de Honra. There's always a celebration when he visits. He insisted on buyin' you . . . I told him you were about ready to leave . . . I figured you might have gone around the side without . . .'

'Hey, you look like you have some Mexican in you?' Sosa said in his native tongue.

Edge had been looking down at what he was doing as he fastened the toe ties of his holster around his thigh. Now he surveyed the too-brightly smiling youngster again. Saw that almost everything about his mostly black garb was of Spanish influence. Just the Remington revolver in his tied-down holster was of American origin.

'Half, feller,' he said in American. 'Sometimes that half has me drink tequila your way.' He jerked a thumb toward the table where he had sat. 'Not today.'

A little of the sparkle dimmed in Sosa's dark eyes before he turned to look away from Edge and across the bar counter at Morton Reed. For a moment the never securely fixed, sick-looking smile on the haggard face of the Texan was in serious danger of slipping off. But a tacit threat secretly communicated by the much younger man forced the cantina owner to become even more falsely bright as he watched, mechanically, the ritualistic way in which the Mexican poured salt on the back of a hand, touched his tongue to the heap, took a full measure of tequila at a single swallow and then sucked noisily on a segment of lemon.

'Hey, I went north of the border one time, *Señor* Edge,' Sosa said.

Two youngsters of similar age to the one at the bar stepped on to the threshold: swinging in from either side of the doorway. At first glance the number of their years seemed to be all they had in common with Esteban Sosa. Their mode of dress was more ragged Western American than elegant Spanish, and they were far less self-assured. Looked to be just as anxious as the Texan in the tension-heavy atmosphere that their entrance made more weighty.

It was their sudden appearance to block his exit through the front door of the place that caused Edge to check his move away from the bead-curtained arch. Rather than Sosa's comment that was spoken in thickly accented but clearly understandable American.

'They say travel broadens the mind, feller,' he countered, and shifted his suddenly dangerously glinting gaze from the nervous pair on the threshold back to the bar. Where, by pre-arrangement or another silent and secret message, the increasingly perturbed Reed was ordered to bring two more glasses up on to the counter top.

'*Si.* I did not like the United States of America, so I returned soon from there. But I learned that, of course, many good things come out of the United States of America.'

'Esteban, you didn't oughta – ' Reed began, abandoning his unsuccessful efforts to pretend he was enjoying what was taking place.

'Just pour, *gringo!*' Sosa snapped, bristlingly vicious for the moment it took to make the demand. Then he was smiling with an almost impenetrable veneer of amiability as he turned just his head to look toward Edge and say: '*Si, señor*. The many good things that come out of the United States of America are the trails into Mexico.'

It was a well rehearsed joke he had used often, but he burst out with riotous mirth as though he had just realised how funny it was.

'Mr Edge, I sure wish you'd – ' the Texan tried again to make a point. But he was driven back into trembling silence by a mere glance from Sosa this time. And sweat beads stood out on his high forehead and coursed down his crinkled neck while he gripped the neck of the bottle so tightly it seemed the glass was in danger of shattering.

'Hey, Manuel, Raoul,' Sosa said eagerly as he glanced over his shoulder in a charade of pretending he had just realised they were there. 'The horses, they are okay? You come have a drink *Señor* Reed has already poured for you. There is another *Americano* in the cantina today. *Señor* Edge is his name. He is buying, okay?'

Manuel and Raoul moved in off the threshold. The uneasiness that was suggested by their expressions was more clearly visible in the cautious way they advanced across the cantina. They looked like they wanted to say something to Sosa, but after a glance at each other neither was encouraged to risk advising there should be a change of plan. One of them gasped and the other made a clumsy move toward drawing his revolver from its holster when Edge swung around to go toward his old table. The apprehension they suddenly experienced at a higher level was also felt by Sosa to a lesser extent and Reed to a degree that brought a moan from his pumping throat as he needed to hook his free hand over the bartop to keep himself from stumbling.

Then the dramatic moment was gone, as the half-breed picked up the glass of tequila and turned to bring it toward the bar counter. The expression on his face was utterly impassive, but there was an uncaring nonchalance about his ambling gait. Manuel and Raoul now grinned as broadly as Esteban Sosa as they joined their obvious leader at the bar. And Morton Reed seemed abruptly to be weak with relief instead of terror when Edge bellied up to the bar on the other side of the most stylishly garbed of the three youngsters.

'Okay,' Sosa announced and there was triumph triggering unbridled glee now. 'In the United States of America I also learn the custom of taking the turn to buy drinks. We now all drink and *Señor* Edge will pay after I have paid for – '

He had nodded to Reed who for part of a second directed a glance at the half-breed that seemed to be a combination of a little contempt and a great deal of pity. This before his free hand released its steadying grip on the top of the bar counter and reached below. Where a chinking sound signalled what he was doing before he brought into sight five shot glasses, held in a bunch by his fingers and thumb pressing them tightly together. The sounds of the glasses being lifted from under the counter and set down on top of it was not loud enough to mask the shuffling of feet as a close-knit group of men crowded up to the cantina's front doorway. Then Edge glimpsed Morton Reed reaching down for more glasses as he glanced at the threshold and saw the men there were all peons: all past middle years, wearied by lifetimes of unrewarding labour and sullenly resigned to being a part of something they had no stomach for.

'I am most popular in this village, *Señor* Edge,' the beaming Sosa went on after he had broken off to look at the throng in the doorway. 'I have many friends who like nothing better than to drink with me. Come in, my friends. *Adelante, amigos!*'

Morton Reed gave a short sigh and a curt shake of his head as he set down the second clutch of glasses and started to pour tequila into one of them. Manuel and Raoul giggled their relief that the period of tension was ended and made to toss back their drinks without ceremony. Those at the head of the group of men in the doorway made to advance tentatively into the cantina.

'You are cowardly dogs and are as uncouth as – ' Sosa began to snarl at his partners. And interrupted his ritual with the salt. Paused in his intention to swing around and execute a victory toast to the half-breed. Took the time to glower at the men on his left, who were suddenly frightened again. He spoke the native language, and it was his enraged words that brought the influx of reluctant peons to a nervous halt as they perhaps thought the young man's ire was directed at them.

'Oh, my God!' the Texan blurted shrilly and flung himself backwards. Dropped the bottle he had been pouring. And collided with the shelves in back of the bar with a force of impact that brought several more crashing down to the floor.

Sosa snapped his head around. And wasted just a part of a second on glowering at Reed before he realised the man behind the bar was reacting to something Edge had done.

'You talk so much . . .' the half-breed accused coldly. And slammed down his untouched drink on the bar with his right hand. As his left seemed to throw a punch at the startled Sosa's face. But the clenched fist that began the short jab from the shoulder did not deliver a blow. And in the final instant before contact was made, the handsome young Mexican saw what it was that had triggered Reed's fear: glimpsed the blade of the razor that Edge had slid smoothly from the neck pouch. '. . . you don't take the time to listen, feller.'

One of Sosa's hands was wrapped around his glass and there was a heap of salt on the back of the other. He continued to express anger rather than fear as he started to pivot his body: had the presence of mind to hurl the salt at Edge as he let the glass smash to the floor as part of the move to draw his Remington. Edge squeezed his eyes shut for a moment against the shower of salt. But by that time the razor had already served its purpose. Had made two deep, slashing cuts into the right cheek of Esteban Sosa. In the form of a cross. Each stroke about three inches long. Blood was beading up out of the slits when Edge snapped his eyes closed. It was running freely down the Mexican's cheek, obliterating the shape of the wounds, when the half-breed re-opened his eyes: and pushed the muzzle of his cocked Navy Colt into Sosa's belly.

'I said I pay my way. Nobody else's.'

The young man's dark eyes expressed terror. His throat was working frantically like he was having to fight a threat of nausea. His lips were trembling. He had seen the razor Edge now lowered to hold loosely down at his side. And he could feel the sticky warmth of blood on his face and knew it was a gun barrel that was sticking into him just above his ornate belt buckle. But he managed to find the words to rasp in Mexican:

'He will kill me if anyone . . .'

He had brought up the hand that had gone for the Remington and never started to slide the revolver out of the holster. And he now laid it gingerly on his doubly slashed cheek. Seemed only then to become aware of how much blood he was losing.

Edge filled the silence that was left after horror and perhaps a first bolt of pain caused the Mexican to break off his plea. He warned in the same language: 'I'll kill anyone who draws a gun against me! That's the only time I'll tell you!'

Manuel and Raoul were the only bystanders, all shocked into silence, who were visibly armed. They had pushed away from the bar and hurled down their empty glasses too late to do more than stare at the end result of the half-breed's sudden attack. Now they exchanged anguished looks and thrust their hands high into the air. Within a few moments, all the peons in the area of the doorway had imitated the two men behind Sosa. Perhaps because they were all much older, or maybe because they had been unwilling participants in the young men's trick, they recovered more quickly from the shock of the speed and violence of the half-breed's move.

'Perhaps, Esteban,' one of the old-timer peons said in a melancholy tone, 'the painful lesson you have been taught will – '

'It was just a joke, Edge!' Sosa broke in, speaking American. 'A stupid joke that we sometimes play – *Madre de Dios!*'

His tone had been of recrimination when he began to explain. Horror was in process of changing to misery in his eyes. But then he pulled his hand away from his face, saw the blood on the palm and fingers and felt compelled to lower his gaze and look at just how much blood had drenched his shoulder and chest. His lament in Mexican was gasping, and his eyes rolled up in their sockets as his mind blacked out and his muscles ceased to function. He collapsed into a sprawl between Edge and his two partners and the sharp crack of his head against the floor caused fine droplets of blood to spray away from the mutilated cheek.

Everyone could now see the ancient Colt in Edge's hand, with the hammer back and his forefinger curled to the trigger. But then it was the movement of his other hand that held the massed attention as he was seen to fold the blade back into the handle of the razor: before he returned it to the pouch that was concealed under his shirt and the long hair at the nape of his neck.

'You people want to get back to what you were doing before you got mixed up with these three jokers?' the half-breed said, motioning with his free hand toward the doorway. Before he went down into a crouch, took the Remington out of Sosa's holster and came upright again.

He had spoken American. One of the peons who understood the language began a rapid translation. And he was not even half-way through it before the exodus started: all of them keeping their arms raised until they were out in the glaring sunlight of early afternoon. While this was happening, Edge gestured with his own gun and placed Sosa's revolver on the bartop. And, with apprehension, Manuel and Raoul lowered their right hands, eased their guns out of the holsters and deposited them alongside the array of glasses there.

'Edge, you oughta – ' Morton Reed started, his stance less rigid now, but his voice sounding breathless.

'I hear this feller's mother lives in Punto de Honra,' Edge said to Manuel and Raoul in Mexican after the young men had both hands raised again. 'You should take him to her, I think. Unless there's a doctor in – '

'There ain't no doctor here!' the thick-set Manuel cut in. He spoke American and as he did so he got some kind of a hold on the self-confidence he had last felt before the Texan signalled violent trouble.

'We will take him to his mother,' Raoul said in the same language, his tone meek and his manner obsequious as he stooped and lowered his arms.

'Get his ankles!' Manuel snapped, thrusting the taller, but more slightly built, man out of the way as he hunkered down. Then he picked up Sosa's dislodged hat and gently turned the head of the unconscious man to grimace at the cross cut in his cheek – the shape of the wound clear to see now that the flow of blood had subsided to a meagre ooze.

'I figure you've heard of *El Malo, gringo?*' Manuel rasped, the grimace becoming a scowl as he shifted his gaze to look up at Edge.

The half-breed had placed his own revolver on the bartop and was starting to make a cigarette.

'He has,' Morton Reed answered and his voice still sounded like his chest was as tight as a drum. 'I was tryin' to tell him that – '

'Esteban's mother is the sister of José Sanchez, *gringo*,' Manuel said menacingly. 'Esteban is his favourite *sobrino* . . . nephew?'

'Nephew is right,' Raoul confirmed as the two of them rose, the limp form of their oblivious partner sagged between them.

'So be warned, *gringo*. By doing as you have done to Esteban Sosa, you have signed your own death warrant!'

'*Manuel, vamos!*' the still afraid Raoul urged.

'That ain't no idle threat either, Edge,' Reed warned ominously as Sosa was carried out of the cantina.

'If I have to sign anything, feller, I can write my name,' the half-breed countered evenly, and paused to moisten the paper so he could complete the cigarette. Added in an ironic tone as he glanced toward the doorway through which the Mexicans had gone: 'Though it does seem I made my mark. On the face of it.'

Seven

WHEN EDGE rode away from Morton Reed's cantina in Punto de Honra he was itchingly conscious of being watched from the sun-shadowed interior of every building. He sensed hostility from some quarters but in the main it seemed to be nothing more powerful than frustrated resentment that was directed tacitly out at him through unshuttered windows and open doorways.

The community, which was sited on a shelf of rocky land midway up the eastern side of a massive valley, was comprised of just a broad plaza and a short and narrow street that soon became the trail south. So it did not take long, even holding the gelding at an easy walk, to get clear of the huddle of weather-stained and crumbling adobe buildings. And then the itch was concentrated between his shoulder blades, but gradually diminished as he followed the wagon-wide trail down the valley slope that often placed craggy outcrops of rock between himself and the village.

Within ten minutes he felt confident he was out of effective gunshot range – unless there was in Punto de Honra an expert marksman with access to a better than average sharp-shooter's rifle. He took the cigarette from his mouth and directed a globule of saliva to the side: this to demonstrate to his irrational inner self what he thought of such an unlikely chance. But then, as he first mopped at the beads of sweat on his forehead and the runnels that moistened his neck, next struck a match on the butt of the revolver in his holster, he acknowledged with a grunt and a brief scowl there had been good reason for the heavy sweat and the forgotten cigarette. Something called fear.

He was a stranger and – worse in Mexico – a *gringo* stranger, who had badly hurt the son of a village woman. To compound the iniquity, Esteban Sosa was a favourite kin of a much-feared bandit. Who might choose to consider the entire population of Punto de Honra were guilty of a crime: because a lone *gringo* had been allowed to ride away whole and free after committing such an outrage. The rights and wrongs of how the prelude to the violence had been staged were immaterial.

The gimp-legged Texan had said as much in far more words while he set about cleaning up the mess of broken glass and spilled blood and tequila in the cantina which again had just the one customer. He undertook the chore with haste and inefficiency as he talked too earnestly and too fast – sometimes was close to incoherent as he struggled to keep at least a fingertip hold on his unstable composure.

'You gotta understand, if that high-handed whipper-snapper wasn't connected the way he is, I'd have been up on the bar cheerin' for what you done to him, Mr Edge. And so would most of the folks that live around here. He's always been too big for his britches, that snotnose sonofabitch. Ever since he was old enough to figure out he could throw his weight around and get away with it.'

The smell of spilled liquor had for a time negated the stink of Morton Reed. But as he worked with the dustpan and brush and submitted to the compelling urge to babble out his thoughts, fresh sweat triggered again the familiar pungency from his unwashed flesh and clothing. Edge could not fail to be aware of this, but did not allow the fetid taint in his nostrils to distract him from what was his prime concern just then. This was the forming of an opinion about which of the three confiscated revolvers was the best.

'Naturally, of course, if the little shit wasn't kin to Sanchez, I don't suppose he'd have got away with so much in the past,' the Texan hurried on, shaking his head. 'I guess you figured out that wasn't the first time he's pulled that stunt? Stands a passin'-through stranger a drink, then gets him to ante up for all them guys that he's fixed to crowd in. Only he don't stand the first round at all. That's on me, Mr Edge. And if you'd stood the round, I wouldn't have had your money for long. Him and his two buddies would've relieved me of it. Their kind . . . the same kind as José Sanchez . . . they figure all Americans are fair game for stealin' from and trickin' out of their money.'

The Remington looked to be the best of the three handguns, but that was only because Esteban Sosa had spent a lot of time and effort keeping it clean and polished to match his neat outfit. The action was stiff from not being oiled in weeks or maybe months. Raoul's revolver was a once finely made, now battered but well cared for Smith and Wesson with an ivory grip and some fancy engraving on the cylinder. Edge like the feel of the weapon best of all three but it was chambered for .44 calibre ammunition. Like the old Colt Navy Model conversion from percussion he was intending to change. So he selected Manuel's Frontier Colt which fired the same .45 calibre bullets as the Winchester which was outside in the boot on the saddle cinched to his gelding.

The Texan's stiff leg caused him pain when he had to crouch and rise during the cleaning chore in back of and out front of the bar counter. And he was forced to interrupt his earnest chatter sometimes, so that he could concentrate on confining his reaction to a grimace while his lame leg protested his demands for unfamiliar positions.

'I got to say, though, that I reckon you went a little far, the way you cut him the way you did, Mr Edge. Wasn't one of them guys with him – his buddies nor the village guys, either – that had too much stomach for what he was doin'. Especially, I'm thinkin', after all of them except

Sosa himself took a second glance at you and saw you weren't the kind to mess with. And it's my opinion that if you'd gone easier on him, they'd all of them been secretly thankin' you right now, Mr Edge. Yeah, even his buddies and, I bet, his Ma as well. Been real pleased to know that the high and mighty snotnose got took down a peg or two. Just a pistol pulled to make him back off. Or maybe a smack on the jaw . . . hard enough to lay him out, even.'

There were still several small shards of broken glass glistening in sunlight against an area of floor patterned with a brushmarked stain of blood diluted by tequila, but Morton Reed came painfully upright and set down the cleaning materials on the bartop in a manner that signalled he was through for now. And he watched with a doleful gaze as the half-breed switched one Colt for another. Then started in surprise when Edge spoke for the first time in several minutes.

'His gun's got a foresight missing and I don't think much to the wooden grip plates, feller. He's getting the best of the bargain in my opinion, but I have good reason for preferring the Frontier.'

'You could've took all the guns and left it at that. No need to be so rough on that Sosa sonofabitch. Wasn't nobody lookin' to cause hurt – or get hurt.'

'Opinions are something everybody has a right to. Another of mine is that the penalty should fit the crime.'

The Texan looked bemused as Edge swung away from the bar.

'He crossed me, feller. So I crossed him.'

'You got a smart way with the words, I'll say that for you, Mr Edge,' Reed called in the wake of the half-breed heading for the doorway. Then he snatched up a part-filled shot glass that had survived the recent upheaval, and tossed back its contents in a single swallow. Raised his voice so that it was sure to carry out over the threshold to where Edge was unhitching his horse from the rail in front of the general store. 'But I don't hear no one chucklin'! On account of that mean streak that's just bound to make decent folks think the worst of you!'

Now, far enough down into the valley for Punto de Honra to be lost to view whenever he checked the terrain behind him – the existence of the tiny community up on the promontory-like wedge of rock was betrayed only by a pall of smoke from a number of cooking fires – Edge allowed his mind to remain open. Receptive to whatever notions might drift into the forefront of his consciousness after his brief reflections upon events in the Texan's cantina. And he was dispassionate as the expression on his face when he discovered he was not to be assailed by conscience-triggered doubts.

And he felt no sense of satisfaction as he rode down into the depths of the valley through the high heat of the Sierra Madre afternoon: beyond a mild contentment as he relished the taste and effect of the tobacco smoke whenever he drew against the cigarette. Beneath such a transient and insubstantial feeling of well-being there was an emotional void into which nothing good nor decent nor tolerant would fit. The kind of vacuum that could be filled only by bitterness and cold fury and hatred. Which was not a new experience for the man called Edge.

On this occasion the strange emptiness had been created in the aftermath of the violent events in that other cantina: at San Sarita. How long it would take for him to become as normal men are again remained to be seen. The time-scale was never the same. And if other unsuspecting victims of his total lack of compassion were to suffer to the same extent or even worse than Esteban Sosa, so be it. That was the way it had been so many times before. First the Confederacy was to blame. Then a bunch of Union troopers. Next a band of renegade Sioux. Now a man named Delmar Pyle . . . If there was need to apportion blame. Which Edge, in this state of mind, did not consider necessary. If people bothered him, they got paid back in kind. And there was an end to it: simple. Just why the punishment he meted out was sometimes so brutally severe was his business – and nobody messed in his business without inviting trouble of the worst kind!

After this brief period of introspection, his mind became as empty as the mountains appeared to be on every side. And for a long time after he had finished the cigarette he remained at a level of composure derived entirely from being alone in this wilderness without need or inclination to occupy his mind with the past or the future. But this was a state of perfection for the man called Edge that could not endure for long. And as the sun began to dip its leading arc behind a distant ridge in the south west, the first pangs of self-doubt penetrated his peace of mind. As the air became perceptibly cooler and the level of daylight faded, a question insistently demanded and immediately gained access to the forefront of his consciousness:

What are you doing here?

Then another:

Where the hell are you headed?

Again:

What are you searching for?

Finally, before the gunshot:

Whatever the hell it is, why should you think you can find it in Mexico?

He had shaken his head in a negative response to each unbidden query. And each time the movement had gotten more emphatically angry. Then the extent of his self-anger was transmitted to the trail-weary gelding when he accompanied the final shake of his head with a snarled obscenity. The horse started to shy, as if as an expression of resentment at being unjustly mistreated. The rider had not expected the abrupt interruption to the steady pace, and instinctively leaned forward to keep from sliding out of the saddle.

This combination of sudden moves by the animal and the man either saved the life of the half-breed or jerked his head into the path of the bullet that might otherwise have missed him. The first curse was spoken when he saw the spurt of black powder smoke among a scattering of boulders off up the valley slope to his right. Maybe three hundred yards away. Although he only caught the most fleeting glimpse of the smoke, he knew instantly and for certain what it was. He started to rasp a second curse through clenched teeth exposed in a snarl. But then, before it was half vented and before the sound of the rifle's report carried down the slope to him, the bullet struck him. Delivered a searing bolt of pain that reached to every cell of his brain as it opened up a gory furrow across the side of his head.

He felt a compulsion to scream a response to the agony, but also felt a boundless rage that had struck him dumb. Then he was blinded. And, as he became aware of the sensation of falling, he found himself unable to experience anything else. When, it seemed for only a stretched second or so, he had the answers to all those probing questions that had been needling him so irritatingly before.

He was no different to any other man in terms of what all those questions added up to: he was searching for happiness. And now, at last, he had found it. A state of ecstatic euphoria that was filled with a luxuriously warm darkness in which he had the sensuous feeling of falling without fear through a silky soft void as infinite and as mysterious as the universe.

Then the downward plummet came to an abrupt end that was not immediately uncomfortable. And the darkness retreated when his eyelids flickered open: but the light was not disconcertingly bright.

A voice gasped breathlessly: 'Oh, thank God, thank God. I'm so happy you have come back. Now I know you will not die. I am sure of it. You have recovered from your unconsciousness and I know that soon you will have back your health and your strength. Oh, how I love you. I love you so much, my most wonderful . . .'

The light became even less bright as the face of a young

girl seemed to swim above him, seemingly disembodied. She was Mexican and her features were beautiful: the face round and smooth, blemish-free and youthfully innocent. She was smiling with perfectly matched, very white teeth and enormously large, sparkling eyes.

Edge blinked several times, like he was checking to see if she was a figment of the dream of pure joy into which he had plunged a few moments ago. But she did not float away into oblivion, and he saw that the beautiful face was not disembodied. He continued to experience something akin to joy as he swept his gaze over her torso. But his thoughts were far from pure when he looked back at her glowing face while his mind held an image of the mounds of her breasts smoothly contoured by close-fitting fabric.

'Hey, you wonderful man, how does it feel to be loved as much as I love you?' she murmured and bent down toward him. To press her soft cheek to his stubbled one as she hugged him at the shoulders with cupped hands that were cool, and gently rested the twin peaks of her warm breasts on his chest.

He tried to move, but found it was impossible. Like he was paralysed from head to toe. But there was a stirring of motion in the pit of his stomach. Before he was able to tell if there was any physical response, though, he became uncomfortably aware of a dull ache that started to throb in every muscle of his body.

'You hear what I ask of you?' the girl asked, suddenly anxious, as she raised herself up from him.

She looked even younger – maybe no more than sixteen, or even less – when her dark eyes were filled with apprehension. And Edge tried to form his features into a semblance of a wry grin, was not sure he succeeded, when he rasped:

'Sure, kid. And I have to tell you, you've just made a happy man feel very old.'

Eight

A SHUDDERING laugh gripped the girl and a large tear of happiness splashed down off one of her cheeks to sting the half-breed's right eye before she folded down on him again. She kissed him over and over again, and as her body continued to shake with the delight of heartfelt relief the movement of her breasts over his chest produced an unmistakable physical reaction in his crotch. Which was so demanding that the pleasure it produced almost totally negated the pain.

'That's real funny . . . Mom was always telling me how you made funny cracks all the time . . . Even when things weren't funny at all . . . How you'd make them not so bad by saying something . . . Oh, thank God! It's like a miracle! Us finding each other after all these years. Gee, dad, it has to be fate that you got shot and they brought you here where I – '

'Sonofabitch! What did you say, girl?' The half-breed's voice was a vicious snarl. This as whatever was starting to happen between his legs suddenly ended. And all the points of pain throughout his body fused into a single powerful bolt of agony that hurtled along his jangling nervous system, to explode with excrutiating effect within the confines of his skull. But the sure and certain knowledge that he had heard clearly what the girl had called him acted to keep him from crying out in response to the physical agony. And the groan that forced an exit through his teeth clenched in a grimace was a small sound that only scratched the surface of his anguish.

'What?' she blurted: and she almost sprang away from him this time. And he knew just how powerful was the ugly scowl on his face when he saw the look of fear close to terror that she expressed. 'I called you – ' she began tremulously. Then her dark eyes were flooded with understanding and she threw both hands to her face. 'Yes, of course! Oh, my God! How could you know? You were out of your head from being shot . . . rambling in your sleep! Oh, what a stupid little fool I am! What you said while you were unconscious . . . dad . . . Edge! It was true, I know it! And since it is true, it means that I, Conchita Lopez . . . I am really your daughter!'

The pain in his head was too compulsively insistent to be ignored after the initial shock of her revelation had diminished. But because of the vital importance of every word she spoke, the half-breed forced himself to concentrate with a miniscule part of his awareness on her voice while he struggled with what remained of his willpower to refuse the demands of the pounding ache. Demands that he cry out, that he contort his features into a harder grimace, that he throw up, pass out or ignore Conchita Lopez to indulge his every fibre in suffering.

It could not continue for long. Certainly not while he also fought to keep his heavy eyelids from snapping closed so that he could see as well as hear this beautiful young daughter he had never known existed. And so he compromised to that extent: allowed his eyes to close now that he knew what she looked like – could envision her in sharp definition even against that tiny area of his mind that he was not prepared to surrender to agony. This as she was saying:

' . . . in Arizona Territory. A town called Peaceville. Gail worked for a Mexican with a funny name. In a restaurant . . .'

It was a mistake to close his eyes. Her voice was receding

and sounded at a more shrill register, like she was moving away from him and was having to shout in desperation to make herself heard. He made a single weak and weary attempt to get his eyelids unstuck, but the pain in his head was diminishing at the same rate as her voice was fading. And the luxury of not having to contend with that pounding under his skull was a reward too tantalisingly desirable to turn down.

Anyway, he had heard and seen enough for now.

It had been in the summer of eighteen hundred and sixty five. When the vengeance hunt for the killers of his brother had drawn him from the ravaged farmstead in Iowa to a town close to the Arizona Territory border with Mexico. He had started out on the long and hard trail as Josiah C. Hedges, lately a captain in the victorious Union army. And he reached the violent end of the journey as the man called Edge, wanted for murder.

But that killing for which the law wanted him had happened in the state of Kansas. In Peaceville, Territory of Arizona, they made him sheriff. The pay was low but there was a free roof and bed beneath it out back of the law office, no charge for three square meals a day in the restaurant owned by a Mexican with the unlikely nickname of Honey, and a tall, full-figured, darkly-blue-eyed, red-headed, long-haired woman named Gail.

Gail did not come as a fringe benefit with the job as sheriff of Peaceville. She waited tables at Honey's restaurant and it was by her own free will that she gave her large-breasted, narrow-waisted, powerfully-hipped body to the man named Edge as often as he felt the need for it during his four weeks as the town's peace officer.

Gail . . . ? He had not even known her full name. But what had it mattered? He didn't have but a single name himself now. How old had she been? A little younger than he was? Maybe a little older. Around thirty, anyway. He could recall the dark blueness of her expressive eyes. The way the corners of those eyes crinkled when she laughed, while her mouth always went a little lop-sided. He had a vivid memory of the russet shade of her long and hardly ever tidy but always sheened hair. But he could not call to mind a clear composite of all the features that formed a face short of beautiful but far better than homely.

And that smooth-skinned, firm-fleshed body he had lowered himself onto and into so often . . . ? There had been a few before. And some since. Not so many as there had been opportunities. But enough so that all but one would have been less than clearly remembered even had that exception been the last woman he took, and she just a minute ago: rather than the wife he had loved so deeply for such a tragically short time. So, now, the image of the body of the woman named Gail was as frustratingly difficult to recall clearly as her face. Yet at the time he was making use of her freely-given submissiveness, she was perhaps providing him with something he had never before or since needed so desperately: while not once did she complain of his selfish taking from her while he salved the hurt of what had brought him to her body . . .

All the pain was still confined to the inside of his skull. But it was less intense now. Then, when he cautiously eased open his eyes it did not hurt very much more. But he was aware of a smarting sensation on the outside of his head. The right side. His arm felt stiff, but only from inactivity, as he raised it: needed to pull it out from under the weight of some kind of cover so that he could explore the pained area above his right ear. His fingertips touched rough-textured fabric. But it was not so coarse as he traced the dressing around where it was banded across his forehead. Back where the bandage covered the wound, he discovered the roughness was also flaky. He decided this was because a great deal of blood had soaked through and congealed.

He also decided, as he brought down his arm to rest it across his chest above the covering that draped him, that he had not dreamed any of the jumble of memories that suddenly came torrenting into his pain-wearied and sleep-numbed mind.

He had started to get mad at himself for his aimlessness as he rode through a valley of the Sierra Madre range in Sonora. Somebody had blasted him out of his saddle with a gunshot. He had been unconscious for long enough so that he could be brought to some kind of man-made shelter before he came out of it. Came out of it suffering a greater degree of pain than now. To see, by light of day, a beautiful young girl named Conchita Lopez. Whose uninhibited display of love for him had sexually aroused him. Until she revealed she was his daughter by Gail.

Now it was night, for he recognised that the flickering red- and yellow-stained light on the ceiling directly above him was thrown off by a well established fire. Outside of whatever kind of building in which he had been left alone – the light of the dancing flames and a little of their heat entering the place through an open doorway. He could not hear the crackle or spit or hiss of the fire. So it was some way off. Within the room where he lay on a narrow bed under covers that no longer felt so heavy, only the sounds of his breathing kept the silence from being absolute. And he now trusted his re-awakened awareness sufficiently to be certain that he was alone in the room. But someone watched him from outside. Until the door crashed closed.

His stomach rumbled emptily and his throat both felt and sounded parched when he swallowed hard. His naked arm was suddenly cold outside of the covers, and when he pushed it back beneath them he had to clench his teeth tightly to keep them from chattering when the goose-bumped flesh brushed his naked side.

He vividly recalled the hardness of the girl's nipples at the centres of her firmly soft breasts when she pressed herself down on him in the heat of the day. Then cried out softly through his still clenched teeth and squeezed his eyes closed, conscience stricken by having carnal thoughts about his own daughter.

An image of Conchita's mother came suddenly into his mind. And for a part of a second he almost saw her as clearly as if she had been a part of his life yesterday: before she backed off into a shadowed recess of his mind. Just short of disappearing into a blurred silhouette against the dull ache that was now worse with his eyes closed than when they were open. So he cracked the lids again and peered up at the pattern of real light and shadows on the ceiling. And knew he had not been asleep and dreaming when he recalled memories triggered by Conchita's startling revelations. It had all been so precise and so concise as he recollected the sequence of events that had involved the redheaded Gail. Which, he felt sure, had to mean he had been voluntarily considering what had happened back in the town of Peaceville after he avenged the brutal killing of Jamie. Had applied his mind to this exercise as he crossed the threshold from natural sleep into a waking state where physical pain and emotional anguish were no longer the dominant sensations to the exclusion of all else.

Now, with his wits about him as he gazed up at the constantly changing shapes of light and dark above him, he was able to dispassionately reflect upon everything he knew about his present circumstances: and relate each factor to all the others. And right then, as a direct result of the relative dates, Conchita Lopez should have been no older than thirteen or maybe fourteen.

Yet he had seen her as at least two or three years older than that. And, at risk of arousing himself again, he acknowledged that her body had felt like that of a developing young woman rather than an adolescent girl. But he could not trust his own judgment in a matter such as this. He seldom came into contact with the younger generation, so could have no reliable opinion on how some children might mature faster than others in the same age group. Also, he had to take into account how Conchita Lopez had flung herself across his naked torso, babbling words of love while he was still disorientated. That must surely be influencing and probably clouding his attempt to discredit the girl's claim . . . ?

Or was he trying to prove her a fraud . . . ?

Perhaps it was the very opposite. Maybe he wanted irrefutable evidence that the beautiful young girl was his child by Gail?

Or any of the other women who he had taken sexually and so by the basic law of nature could have conceived from his seed?

Not Beth, of course. She was cruelly dead before an embryo would have had time to take the shape of a human infant in her womb.

'Goddamnit, you crazy bastard!' Edge snarled as the moving pattern above him was abruptly blurred and his cracked-open eyes started to sting with salt moisture – that in the coldness of the room, removed from the flickering fire, could not be beads of sweat.

A booted foot stamped on hard-packed ground, a latch rattled and the door of the room was flung open. It crashed violently against the inside wall and a brighter glow of firelight rushed in over the threshold. But the cold of the night rather than the warmth of the flames streamed in behind the light.

Edge rolled his head to the side when he discovered he could not raise it up off the pillow. And blinked away the tears of grief for a long-dead wife. So that he could see in sharply defined silhouette the man who stepped into the doorway and aimed a rifle at the bed. An almost dwarfishly squat man with an oversize straw sombrero on his head and a *serape* draping his shoulders with the corners almost reaching down to the ground.

'So, *hombre*, you are awake again?' the little man said in heavily accented American. He sounded like he was recovering from being startled. Then he allowed the barrel of the rifle to dip so that it was negligently aimed at a spot on the dirt floor of the room. And went on, as Edge realised he must have spoken the curse with harsh loudness: 'I should warn you, *hombre . . . El Malo* would be *estar furioso o colerico* – real, real mad as hell – if he heard you call his favourite *amante* a crazy *bastardo*.'

He spoke the caution in a sardonic tone, and as he turned his head to glance toward the sound of approaching footfalls his decayed teeth could be seen exposed in a grin. This as Edge felt an ice-cold ball of anger start to form in the pit of his stomach after he conjured up a fleeting image of Conchita Lopez in the spreadeagled attitude of the Apache squaw when he first saw her: and José Sanchez rising up from her showing an expression similar to that of the man on the threshold of this room.

'Francisco, quitar!' a second man snapped irritably. And Edge checked the urge to rage as Francisco stepped back from the doorway. So that the man who issued the command could take his place. Along with the young girl who said she was the half-breed's daughter, and who the man with the rifle claimed was the favourite mistress of a bandit chief.

Edge thought the ill-humoured voice had sounded familiar, and so he was not entirely surprised when he recognised the short, thickset Manuel who he had last seen helping Raoul to carry the unconscious Esteban Sosa out of the cantina in Punto de Honra. What did jolt him was the way the girl's wrists were lashed together in front of her and how she was forced to lean a little to her right by the pressure of the revolver muzzle Manuel held against the left side of her neck. As an indication of how the pain in his head was still affecting his ability to think clearly with a correct sense of the priorities, he found himself momentarily engaged in wondering if the revolver was the Frontier Colt Edge had captured off him in Morton Reed's place.

'Francisco speaks of how it was in the past, *Americano*,' Manuel said coldly.

The girl gasped and shuddered as she heard at such close quarters the metallic sounds of the handgun being cocked.

'*Tener cuidado, muchacho!*' somebody in the group beyond the open doorway warned earnestly.

'*Callate!*' Manuel snarled to the older man who had warned him to take care. Then lowered his voice but kept his tone hard as Sierra Madre granite when he said to Edge in American: 'When The Evil One was a free man, this girl – your bastard, it is true to say – was the one he chose most often to comfort him and to keep him warm in his bedroll at night, *Americano*. But what is any woman that she cannot be replaced by any one of a hundred others? Unless she be a dearly loved close *relativo?* But when she is not . . . When she is no more than a *ramera* – '

'Daddy, it's not true! I'm not a whore!' Her voice was shrill with fear. 'I was made a prisoner! But if José heard what he's saying about me, he'd – '

She was forced to break off with a squeal of pain as Manuel brought his free hand across to fasten a clawed grip on her upper arm: to hold her still so that he could force her head into a more unnatural position by pressing the gun muzzle harder into her neck.

Edge vented an inarticulate cry that was compounded of anger at Manuel and response to the bolt of agony that felt like another shot to his head as he jerked his back up off the bed. Then he had to fight for breath and struggle against what seemed the only options facing him – to collapse back down out of the sitting attitude or to lose consciousness and fall into whatever position was dictated by gravity. But then he was able to reach deep down into the well of his stamina and find it was not totally exhausted. But the simple act of breathing continued to tax him so much that he did not dare to expend energy with the string of curses he had in mind to snarl at the man threatening his daughter.

He could see the couple, but not so clearly, while he strained to keep from passing out. He could imagine the fear and pain on Conchita's lovely face, as he heard Manuel continue:

'What is any woman to a man who is enclosed in the condemned cell, *Americano?* Waiting for the hangman? Which is the situation of José Sanchez this very night. She is nothing . . . Unless she is the means to free him and save him from the gallows. Then the situation is very different, *Americano.* Would you not say so?'

'I'd say . . .' Edge forced out through gritted teeth as he levered himself up the bed with his arms until he was able to rest his back against the bedhead, '. . . that whatever you want me to do, I've got to go along with it.'

Manuel released Conchita's arm and drew back the gun far enough so that she could straighten her head on her shoulders. And the same brand of relief that sounded in her sigh was heard in a low murmuring of talk from the group beyond the doorway.

'It is good you realise that,' Manuel said in a gloating tone.

'Seems to me I don't have any choice, feller,' Edge answered, mildly satisfied with how quickly he recovered from the debilitating effect of this latest move. 'Relatively speaking.'

Somebody laughed and yelled in delight: 'Hey, a father and daughter are related. He made a joke.'

'A lousy one,' Edge murmured as he recognised the voice of Raoul – the third youngster from the Punto de Honra cantina. 'But I got the excuse I feel lousy.'

Manuel directed a globule of saliva at the floor midway between the threshold and the bed. Warned harshly: 'I tell you, *Americano.* You better be in good shape by daybreak. For then we will leave here for the Federale post at San Sarita.'

He holstered the revolver now, then took hold of Conchita's bound wrists to jerk her viciously out of the doorway as he turned to stride away. The girl half stumbled and vented a sharp cry of alarm and pain as she was wrenched out of Edge's field of vision. And the half-breed needed to exert energy-draining conscious effort to check a roar of impotent rage while at the same time he forced himself to remain immobile on the bed. It helped him to beat the impulse to feeble action fired by futile anger when he snapped his eyes closed and willed his ears to be deaf to all sound. And he seemed to be blind and deaf and mute for minutes while his imagination tormented him with a thousand obscene and violent tableaux in which his daughter was the screaming victim. Her voice pleading for him to save her while her dark eyes accused him for allowing her to suffer.

'*Hombre,* they will do nothing bad to Conchita if you do what is asked of you,' Francisco assured earnestly.

He sounded like he was speaking in a whisper, until Edge cracked open his eyes. When he saw the dwarfish little man in the act of lighting a candle, and only now became aware that it had been an imagined roaring inside his head that had deafened him. For a moment longer the sweat that beaded his face and naked torso remained warm and sticky. Then he felt the assault of the cold night air streaming in through the open doorway and he shuddered as he slid down into the bed again, and clutched the covers to his throat with his arms beneath them. This as Francisco concluded in a voice that was dull-toned but with no note of intrigue:

'She truly is José's favourite and when he is freed, any *hombre* who has harmed her *sin motivo* – without the just cause . . . That *hombre* would have to answer to *El Malo.*'

The candle was held by old hardened wax to the centre of an upended crate that served as a table against the wall on the other side of the room from the bed. A smaller crate next to it was a matching stool and with the candle lit, Francisco lowered himself gratefully onto this. When he took off the too-large sombrero Edge could see that a cruel nature had not been content to provide him with a stunted frame. For his decayed teeth were just one contributing feature to a face of misshapen ugliness. One cheekbone was higher than the other, as were the brows above eyes that bulged from out of deep-set sockets. His mouth was crooked to the extent of deformity. All this against a backdrop of loose and heavily wrinkled skin and in a frame of thin, straggly hair that was perhaps silver behind the greasy dirt. From simply looking at him, Francisco might have been aged at any number of years between thirty and seventy. The way he moved suggested he was closer to the lower end of this scale.

'*Feo, hombre, si?*' he said with a slight shrug after he had settled himself comfortably with the rifle resting across his thighs, as a warning rather than a threat. 'Ugly as sin, yes? Maybe you look at me and not feel so bad about your *situacion?* Soon, the *herida* to your head, it will be healed. And if all goes as we hope, you and your *hija* will be free and in time all this will be forgotten, *si?* Francisco Cortes, he will always be ugly as sin, no matter what takes place.'

Edge had been gazing up at the timber ceiling of the adobe walled room since he finished his brief scrutiny of his guard. He continued to do so as he told the man: 'It ain't working, feller.'

'*Que?*'

'Your bedside manner. I figure that waking up ugly is better than waking up dead.'

Cortes spat at the floor and rasped: '*Vete al cuerno!* It is nothing to me how you are. But for the sake of Conchita – your *hija* – and for your own life, *hombre* . . . you better be in good shape to leave this place at sun-up tomorrow.'

'Be a better chance of that if my belly wasn't empty and my throat didn't feel like I was breathing dust, feller.'

'You will get *desayuno* with the rest of us, *hombre*,' Cortes said sourly after he had pushed his face toward the candle to re-light the stub of a cheroot he'd found in a shirt pocket. 'Before we pull out.'

Still peering up at the ceiling, that was now spread with an egg-shaped patch of yellow light from the candle flame, Edge murmured through pursed lips: 'If I'd done that one night back in Peaceville all those years ago, I guess I wouldn't be in this mess now.'

'*Que?*' the ugly little man across the room posed, but sounded disinterested in hearing a response.

Edge said sardonically: 'Pulled out.'

Nine

EDGE DID not sleep. Although he gave himself the opportunity: unprepared to fight whatever demands for rest his punished body and tortured mind might make. But, apparently, the period of unconsciousness that came immediately in the wake of the gunshot in the valley, and then the time he had spent in exhausted sleep after the shock of learning he was the father of a beautiful young girl, had combined to provide him with as much dark oblivion from harsh reality as his physical being and emotional reflexes required.

For a long time – perhaps even an hour or more – he lay as if asleep. Almost comatose, with just the soft sounds and slight movements of his shallow breathing to signal that he was still alive. During this time, when he would have drifted into sleep had it been involuntarily necessary, he allowed his mind to roam at will over the events that had preceded the spurt of smoke from a rifle muzzle; which was the final conscious image to impress itself upon his mind before he was thrust into a seeming dream that had turned into a waking nightmare.

From out of this period of calmly detached reflection upon memories of what he knew had taken place, he drew certain facts and connected them with theories about his present situation, and projected what the future might hold. And when the pain had diminished to a point where hunger and thirst were of greater discomfort, and he no longer felt clammily cold beneath the bed covers, he rolled his head on the pillow to ask of his ugly little guard:

'What did I say that makes Manuel think I can stop the Federales stringing up Sanchez, feller?'

Francisco Cortes was sitting in the same place, with the Spencer carbine still resting across his lap, held there in the loose grip of both hands. But he was no longer peering with his bulging eyes across the candlelit room at where Edge lay in the bed. Now his chin was down on his chest so that his misshapen features were concealed. In the soft light of the steadily burning flame of the candle – not a breath of a draught entered the room through the open doorway – the bald crown of the little man's head had a dull sheen against the dirty silver of the encircling hair roots.

For stretched seconds that were so taut with tension that the half-breed held his breath without realising he was doing so, he wondered if he had merely formed the query in his mind: and had not yet spoken it aloud. But then he knew this was crazy, and he was not. He had posed the question and the dwarf-like Cortes was too deeply asleep to be disturbed by the sound of a voice. He was even snoring; softly and regularly. And except for the subdued sounds of the burning fire that was now throwing far less light across the threshold, the breathing of men at rest was all that disturbed the otherwise utter silence of the Mexican night. Doubtless some were snoring more loudly than Cortes, but they were all enjoying their untroubled rest close to the dying fire several yards beyond the doorway.

It was about fifteen feet from the bed against one wall to where Cortes was hunched in sleep on the crate against the far wall. A little less from the bed to the open doorway that was the only way out: there was not even a window in any wall or a smoke hole in the roof. Edge took note of these aspects of his surroundings after he had come up into a sitting attitude on the bed. He achieved this with slow caution and the ill effects were negligible. The narrow bed had a timber base with a straw-filled mattress on top, so there was nothing to creak beneath his shifting weight. But he had not moved his legs for a considerable length of time, and a small bone in each of them cracked out of their set positions as he eased his feet to the floor.

The fact that the sleeping guard remained undisturbed was proof that the half-breed's imagination was playing a trick on him: and that the sounds of his protesting bones were a lot less loud than the gunshots that had seemed to ring in his own ears. Now, only as he eased himself upright at the side of the bed, did he become unpleasantly aware again of how cold was the night. And, as he draped the blanket around his shoulders, he brushed his naked torso with his hands and knew he had been pumping sweat while he achieved the simple task of getting out of the bed. He shuddered once and gritted his teeth, because he was worried they might rattle together at the wrong time. Although his feet felt colder than any other part of him, the fact that they were bare made it easier to move silently on the hard-packed floor.

Just for a moment did he eye the heap of what looked like his clothes in the corner at the foot of the bed. But he still had on his pants and decided that for awhile the brand of peace of mind that this gave him would have to be enough. He did not think there was one chance in a thousand the Mexicans had been careless enough to even leave the razor in the pouch on the necklet among his clothing. And it was surely the Frontier Colt that had changed hands in the Punto de Honra cantina which Manuel had thrust against Conchita's neck?

Now came the moment to test his ability to walk without weaving or stumbling or tripping over his own feet: always assuming he was able to take that first step and not feel what was left of his strength draining out of him as his body became drenched with sweat again. But he had to take the risk . . . Had wasted too much time just standing there in one place while his mind ran riot down a line of wishful thinking that got him nowhere . . . The inevitable could not be postponed further.

He moved tentatively forward, and it was not a snap decision arrived at amid flashes of self-doubt that angled him away from the bed toward the doorway. Before he had started to fold up off the bed he had it firmly fixed in his then totally composed mind that he should first discover what – and who – waited outside the confines of the four adobe walls that enclosed him.

After three or four short steps he found out the stiffness and aches in his body were less of a handicap than the fuzziness and pounding in his head. With more exercise than he could take in this small room, the disconcerting physical effects of the long period of unconsciousness would soon be overcome, he was certain. But he felt lightheaded, unable to sustain a logical line of thought for more than a second at a time, and whenever he shifted his gaze between the open doorway and the sleeping form of Francisco Cortes it seemed to take much longer than a second for his vision to clear.

Then he reached a point where he could interrupt his advance and, with the hand that was not clutching the sides of the blanket together at his throat, he was able to reach forward and accept the support of the wall to the side of the doorway. The rough-textured adobe felt like ice beneath his palm and splayed fingers, and he knew he was sweating again. And as this realisation was established, he became convinced that he could let go of the blanket and it would stay in place, glued to his torso. The fire out in the night seemed to glow bright yellow in the doorway. Next the timber frame became blurred, as if its straight lengths were seen through the shimmering effect of the fire's great heat. Then the twisted doorframe tilted to the left and the floor canted in the opposite direction. There was a rushing sound in his ears and he tasted bile on the back of his tongue. The yellow heat of the fire was so great it seemed to sear his eyelashes and the brilliance of its glow threatened to burn blindness into his eyes.

He squeezed his eyelids closed and the threat of nausea subsided. Only the acid track of the bile down his throat as he swallowed it left him with any sensation of burning. This as he let go of the blanket to thrust both hands against the wall. And now his entire frame felt it was composed of ice while the wall under his splayed hands was back to being adobe. In the darkness and the cold there was an absolute silence that he saw visually as a spider's web touched by frost. It was that fragile; but should it be destroyed it would shatter with a sound louder than any since the Creation.

But then the hallucination was ended. Much more abruptly than it had begun. He recognised a soft, long hiss as the sound of his own pent-up breath rasping out through his clenched teeth. Then he detected the regular rise and fall of another man's respiration, and knew Francisco Cortes slept on a few feet away. Next he picked up the more distant and less evenly spaced sounds of a fire that was almost out, and of several sleepers who were as oblivious to him as was the little man with the Spencer in his lap.

Now Edge cracked open his eyes and tensed himself to meet whatever new shock to his system the real world or his wild imagination might spring upon him.

Reality was upside down, that was all. But he knew at once why this was: he was leaning forward with both hands braced against the wall, his body canted sharply and his head hanging down between his outstretched arms. In bringing up his head, shuffling his feet forward and then easing his hands down to his sides there was just a fleeting sensation of dizziness while the right-side-up world issued a short-lived threat that it was going to fade out of focus. When this danger was withdrawn, and he was troubled only by the cold of the night air and the pounding but bearable pain under his skull, he took the longest stride yet in what had seemed such a gruelling trek from the bed.

And came to a sudden halt for part of a second when he caught his first glimpse of part of the outside world. Then drew in a deep breath through flaring nostrils as he stepped fully into the doorway.

'You *gringos* have the expression I have heard, Edge,' one of the four women aiming rifles at the half-breed said, her voice a monotone until she spoke his name – and invested it with the harshness of the worst obscenity she knew. 'I think it is correct to say, best you get back inside before you catch your death.'

All of them were older than Conchita, but none by more than a half dozen years. None was as beautiful as his daughter, but this opinion had less to do with parental prejudice than with the menace, backed by hatred, that seemed to emanate from every fibre of their beings. And was checked just a hair's breadth back from their fingers on the rifle triggers. Such a degree of dark emotion made them look to Edge more ugly than Francisco Cortes.

'Nice you ladies are so concerned about my health,' he countered, and his voice sounded off-key to his own ears. And he knew the sour note could not be blamed on the after-effects of being shot. Instead, he was plain scared that if one of the women found it suddenly impossible to suppress the urge to fire at him, there would be a chain reaction. And he knew he would not survive a barrage of gunshots from such a dedicated firing squad.

'*Francisco, despiertate!*' the spokeswoman of the quartet snapped harshly.

The dwarfish sentry came awake with a start and for part of a second his bulging eyes actually seemed on the point of squeezing out of their sunken sockets as he stared at the empty bed. He was also about to give vent to a bellow of rage. But then he swept his gaze around to meet the resigned look that Edge was directing at him over his broad, bare shoulder. And recovered his composure with amazing speed in the time it took him to swing the Spencer and aim it at the half-breed. It was brashness rather than anger that sounded in his voice when he counter-attacked, in American:

'I was not sleeping! I pretend, that is all! To put to the test the *vigilancia* of the guards who watch because Francisco Cortes is not trusted! *Guardia . . . ? Madre di Dios . . . ! Mujerio!* A bunch of women! It is the *insulto!*'

While Cortes was attempting his brazen bluff, Edge slowly retreated from the doorway and paused only to pick up the blanket from the floor as he returned to the bed. The prominent eyes and the muzzle of the carbine tracked him every inch of the way: and while the Spencer was a potent threat, there showed in the candle-lit ugliness of the little man a plea for support.

One woman vented an unladylike sound of contemptuous disbelief. Another accused him in their native tongue of being a lying sonofabitch. And a third began to claim in the same language that the worst women were superior to men of his kind. But before she could spell out what kind she considered Cortes to be, the fourth one commanded:

'*Silencio!*' Then switched to American and a less harsh tone of voice to warn: 'There will be no more empty talk. If anyone attempts to leave the *chabola* again before dawn, my rifle will have the one and only word to say of it!'

She rose as she spoke, came to the threshold of the shack and unequally shared a glower of ice-cold anger between the Mexican on the crate and the half-breed who was now seated on the bed, the blanket draped about his shoulders again. Edge received the greater portion of her tacit malevolence, and she did not even shift her gaze away from his face to see what she was doing as she reached in to grip the door and slam it firmly closed. The candle flame flickered in the draught this created. Then burned steadily again, for Cortes was turned away from the improvised table when he vented his long-held breath in a rushing sigh of relief.

'That, *hombre,* is Ysidora Garcia. She is the special *mujer* of Esteban Sosa – the *pistolero* who you cut with the razor in the *cantina* at Punto de Honra. I think she thinks she is more special than he does . . .' Cortes shrugged his hunched shoulders. '*No importa.* I think Ysidora Garcia did not shoot you because such a way to die is *rapido, hombre.* I hear her tell the others, when you were first brought here, that she would like to see you *crucificado.* She is *duro como la piedra*, that one . . . as hard as the nails, yes? If she had her own way, that *mujer* would surely crucify you as she has said she would like.'

There was something akin to grudging respect in his tone as he completed the warning. Then, as he saw Edge arrange himself comfortably on the bed under the blanket again, he felt he had to emphasise:

'You *comprender, hombre?* She is a mean *mujer* . . . woman. If she had the opportunity, she would truly enjoy to crucify you . . . in the manner of *Jesucristo!* You *comprender crucificado*?'

'Sure, feller,' Edge assured the man across the room. 'Given the chance, Esteban Sosa's ladyfriend would like to really nail me.'

Cortes sent a stream of saliva past the barrel of the Spencer to the floor. 'The joke, he makes,' he murmured. 'When he should be worried sick. Or are you *loco, hombre?*'

'One headache at a time is all I need right now,' the half-breed replied evenly, and touched his fingertips to the blood-crusted area of the bandage as he peered up at the patch of candle glow on the ceiling. Then he lightened his tone as he turned his head on the pillow to meet the scowling gaze of the Mexican. 'And anyway, *amigo*, there are some things you can't cross until you get to them.'

Ten

The Mexican with the stunted frame and the cruelly grotesque face was suddenly loquacious. Not because he was in the mood to be talkative: at first. He simply realised that talk served as an effective defence against the encroachment of dangerous drowsiness again.

Edge made no attempt to encourage or dissuade the flow of words that eventually confirmed or denied many of the theories the half-breed had arrived at while he was inviting sleep, before he made his ill-conceived attempt to escape. And, having seen, albeit briefly and over a severely restricted field of vision, what lay immediately outside the adobe shack, his mind's eye was able to paint in backdrops to some of the events of which Francisco Cortes spoke.

As the dwarfish man warmed to his subject, which fundamentally expressed his deeply felt resentment toward almost the entire bunch of men and women who ran with José Sanchez, he spoke increasingly in his own language. And he thus spoke more fluently. But his disgruntlement with the injustices life heaped upon him because of his gargoylish appearance kept intruding to interrupt his train of thought.

But Edge looked upon it as a measure of his own degree of recovery from the gunshot wound in his head that he was able to unscramble the salient points from the man's gabbling and place the events in a logical sequence.

* * *

El Malo's bunch of bandits had been forced to scatter far and wide when the Federales from the post at San Sarita, then commanded by Captain Antonio Gomez, had located their hide-out in a deep *barranca*, where a narrow creek that ran with sweet water for most of the year joined an often dry tributary of the Rio Moctezuma south-east of San Sarita. That was several weeks ago, and during the time since then José Sanchez and the two men he trusted most had been searching for a fresh bolt hole to where the whole band could withdraw and wait out those periods when the Federales were most actively searching for them.

And this was the place that Sanchez, riding with Luis and Miguel, had found. In another *barranca* that cut into the lower slope of a rocky hillside. Where once the *conquistadors* had used Indian slave labour to sink a gold mine. Some stories told of much ore-bearing rock being torn out of the depths, but others said not a speck of gold had been found. But gold grubbers were optimists by nature and so a succession of Mexican and American prospectors had worked the old mine in high hopes destined to be dashed. Enough of them, over many years, to keep this one-room adobe shack in some kind of repair.

This new hide-out for *El Malo* and his group had a water hole rathe than a creek, and the water in it was a little brackish: but it was drinkable. And although the small shack in which Edge was a prisoner was the only building there was plenty of shelter for men, women and animals in the network of tunnels which ran through the hillside from both walls of the *barranca*.

Because of these tunnels, and the geographical position of the *barranca,* José Sanchez had plans to turn his new hide-out into a fortress. The tunnels were to be extended and enlarged to provide living accommodation worthy of what was going to be the best and most feared bandit group in the whole of Mexico. And such a fortress was ideally placed to play an important role in the bandit chief's grand design: for from the cover of rock outcrops and clumps of prickly pear and mesquite at the *barranca* mouth it was possible to look surreptitiously down on a lengthy stretch of the main trail between the Sonora state capital of Hermosillo far to the south west and the Mexican border with New Mexico Territory to the north.

One day, Sanchez was certain, he would no longer be regarded as a bandit: for he was going to ride along that trail at the head of a great peasant army. To declare war on the *gringos*. A war that every man under his command would fight to the death, irrespective of whether the Mexican Government ordered the army into the fray. And the war would not be over until every Mexican fighter was dead, or the Government of the United States of America returned to Mexico all the territory that changed sovereign hands after the signing on 2 February 1848 of the Treaty of Guadalupe Hidalgo.

It was apparent from the tone of his voice that Francisco Cortes held in cynical contempt the grandiose scheme. He always had thought that *El Malo*'s depthless hatred for America and all things American was a sign that the man was in danger of losing his reason. This sudden surge of patriotic fervour might mean José Sanchez had at last gone off his head.

And it was ironic, was it not, that so soon after making his intentions known to his followers he had been taken prisoner by the Federales in an ambush during which Luis and Miguel were killed? Never once before, while *El Malo* and his men terrorised the countryside as plain and simple bandits, had any member of the group fallen into the clutches of the Federales. But then the head of José Sanchez had been filled with the stuff and nonsense of impossible dreams. And because of this his two best men were food for the coyotes and the buzzards and he was in the shadow of the gallows.

Of course, he should never have gone hunting for that *gringo* bounty hunter named Ed Cody. Or when he found him he ought just to have killed him quick, and the squaw who was with him, too. But that would never have been enough for José Sanchez. Because Cody was both a bounty hunter and a *gringo*, he had to suffer in full measure from the malevolence the bandit chief felt for his kind. Cut off his balls and made him watch while the three of them had their way with the Apache squaw, it looked like. Then slit his throat and shot the woman. All that, and fire smoke as well: it was madness and the three of them had paid the price for their stupidity when the newly-appointed commandant of the San Sarita Federale post ordered his men to the attack.

And as if this were not enough, the very next day the son of *El Malo*'s sister stupidly invited trouble involving another *gringo*. At the time, Esteban and Raoul and Manuel knew nothing of the Federale ambush. They knew only that this new hide-out had been decided upon, and were making for it to rejoin the re-grouping band. If they had known of the serious trouble José Sanchez was in they would not have stopped off at Punto de Honra to visit with Esteban's mother. Would certainly not have wasted time with the stupid prank concerned with drinks at the *cantina*.

It was while the razor wounds on the young man's face were being attended to, after Edge had ridden out of the village, that word came with a messenger from the north that Sanchez was a prisoner in the Federale post at San Sarita. Manuel and Raoul and the messenger who brought the news – a man named Ramon Cabello – left Esteban in the care of his mother and rode for this *barranca*. They spotted Edge on the trail ahead and Cabello who was the most expert marksman in the whole group made a wide, secret sweep to pass the man who had hurt Esteban Sosa so badly. And the shot was fired that had resulted in the half-breed being where he was now.

In the telling of this part of the story, the voice of the ugly little man revealed the low esteem in which he held the Sosa boy. And from a couple of sidetracks he wandered down after lighting a fresh cheroot it emerged that Esteban was disliked by everyone in the group with the exception of his uncle and Ysidora Garcia. There was also, in the manner of Francisco Cortes's telling of this episode, implied surprise that a man like Edge should have allowed himself to be bush-whacked in broad daylight by a trio of men that he – Cortes – regarded with no more respect than Esteban Sosa.

And it would have been easy then for the half-breed to begin fuelling with memories the stirring of self-anger at the way he had let his guard drop while he rode through the valley bottom south of Punto de Honra. Or, perhaps, his mind might well have played involuntary host again to those imponderables that had filled it and caused him to be less vigilant than was usual yesterday afternoon.

That it was only the day before he was shot was disclosed by Cortes after the little man had lit a fresh candle as the flame of the old one was about to gutter out in its own melted wax. He produced the candle from inside the crate that served as a table and took care to keep one hand always fisted around the frame of the Spencer as he performed the chore.

When it was seen just how much blood had seeped from Edge's head wound, the three men had been about to leave him for dead. But when Manuel came close to retrieve his stolen handgun he saw that the half-breed was still breathing without effort. And he figured that Esteban would welcome the chance to take his revenge personally against the *gringo* who had humiliated and disfigured him. So Edge was slumped over his horse and brought to the new hide-out. Where, when it was learned what had been done to Sosa, Ysidora Garcia had gone crazy with blood lust. But she had been forcibly restrained from attacking the unconscious prisoner with a knife: and it was fortunate for everybody concerned that this was so.

For Edge had become delirious after he had been carried into the shack and his wound was cleaned and bandaged.

Cortes was responsible for this. He got all the dirtiest and most unpleasant chores to do . . .

Only at this stage in the account, as Cortes became sullen with discontent at his lot and started another catalogue of wrongs committed against him, did Edge come close to interjecting an urgent demand for the ugly little man to get back in the main stream of his story. Felt the need to give Cortes such a nudge because he could see a thread of grey light at the foot of the door. But then the cheroot was mashed out on the crate become a table with an angry gesture. And Cortes spat at the floor and cursed himself for wallowing in self-pity.

'It should have been a moving and wonderful event,' he went on, his Mexican tinged with objective regret. 'A beautiful young girl finding the father she had never known. Who she did not even know was still living.'

There was the sound of activity and voices – both of men and women – outside. But the softly-speaking man across the room showed no sign that he was aware that the new day was breaking.

'You were doing a great deal of talking, even while I was administering to your wound. Most of what you said then was incomprehensible. Some was nonsense. Memories from long ago in your past. That came and went almost with the speed of lightning flashes. But then you slept peacefully and the women took turns to watch over you. But not Ysidora Garcia, of course. She could not be trusted. Then you began to speak again. This time what you said was less frantic: and the events of which you spoke remained longer in your mind to be remembered.

'You spoke of San Sarita. Of coming there with a woman. In search of something that had been stolen from you. You did not recover your property. There was trouble in the cantina. The Star Cantina which many of us know from having frequented the establishment where Manuel Martinez gets rich selling bad liquor for high prices. In the trouble, that pig Captain Antonio Gomez was shot to death. Which explains to us why the new captain is sent from Hermosillo to be the commander at San Sarita. You spoke of other Federales. Not officers. You knew these men. You were allowed to ride freely out of San Sarita, that was plain to us. So you are on good terms with the men at the post. With the people who live in San Sarita, too.

'It would appear, Manuel says, that you may be of assistance to us when we make the attack to secure the release of José Sanchez. If you are recovered in time. But how to make you help us if you are well? Then the miracle happens. You begin to speak again in your sleep. Of a time much longer ago. And of a woman. In truth, you speak of many women, Mr Edge. But Conchita Lopez is among those who are listening . . . she realises that one of these women is her mother.'

The level of noise from outside the shack gradually rose as more people awoke to face the new day. Orders were sullenly given and grudgingly acknowledged. The clattering sounds of carelessly-handled utensils signalled that breakfast was being prepared, and soon the aromas of coffee and frying meat began to infiltrate the shack: carried inside on a current of warming air through the gap at the base of the door. The strip of light that showed there was still grey, but of a less dirty shade.

'She was an American, like most of the women you spoke of,' Francisco Cortes went on and there was a querulous note in his tone now, as he spoke more loudly. Obviously aware that the silence of the night was no longer threatening his resolution to remain awake, but determined to get his tale told: and resentful of the interruptions. 'She was named Gail and she worked in the restaurant of a Mexican in a town of the Territory of Arizona. You were unsure of what the town is called. Sometimes you call it one name, then another.'

'It was called Warlock while I was looking for it, feller,' Edge said, and the man across the room vented a terse gasp of surprise that his audience of one was awake and paying attention. 'The war had been over a few months. Town council took a vote and it was agreed to change the name to Peaceville.'

'*Si, si,* those were the two names you say, *hombre,*' Cortes blurted, reverting to the American language. Then he swung the Spencer to the aim as the half-breed came up off his back and turned to set his feet on the floor. 'You were the sheriff there for a short time, *si?*'

Edge discovered he felt a little dizzy but that sensation was gone within a few seconds. His head wound was sore where the bullet had ploughed a furrow through the sparse flesh of his scalp, but there was just a nagging ache on the inside of his skull. This was no worse sitting up than when he had been lying down. He decided he was a whole lot better able to handle himself now than he had been when he made his abortive escape attempt in the cold dead of night. He even experienced something close to a genuine warmth of good humour in back of the smile he showed when he answered:

'A very short time, feller. Guess upholding the law needs more willpower than I had.'

The redness of the crackling fire or maybe of the newly risen sun tinged the light at the foot of the door now. And the gently wafting stream of air that came through the gap was warm on Edge's bare feet. The smells of hot food and drink of breakfast in the making had already masked those of candle grease, stale tobacco smoke and old sweat: and the half-breed was once more uncomfortably aware of the dryness in his throat and the emptiness of his belly.

'It was only then, *hombre*, that Conchita asked to be told your name,' Cortes hurried on. 'And when Manuel or Raoul or somebody else says that you are named Edge . . . Then she knows for certain you are her father. Perhaps then it was moving and wonderful, as such a thing should be. But within a few *momentos*, Manuel, he knows this gives him what he *necesariamente.* He has the hold on you to make you do whatever he wants when we get to San Sarita. As the loyal follower of *El Malo,* I understand why we must do this, *hombre.*' He shrugged and sighed, then slowly shook his head as he augmented: 'It is perhaps because I am so *feo* – such a *grotesco* apology for a man – that is the reason I am such a *romantico?*'

'Maybe, feller,' Edge murmured absently. 'Guess I ain't no oil painting and I sure as hell ain't the romantic type: but I think I'm falling in love with what's cooking out there.'

The latch rattled as he emphasised his comment with a deep sniff at the appetisingly aromatic air. Then the door was sent swinging inwards across a slow arc, opened by one of the two rifle barrels that were levelled over the threshold. The tall and slender-framed Raoul displayed a nervous frown on his youthful face, and he showed no sign that he felt surer of himself after the thickset Manuel had abandoned his menacing scowl for a confident grin.

'So, the *Americano pistolero* is fit and strong as he sounds through the closed door,' Manuel growled sardonically through his grinning teeth. 'Not so weary as expected after his *desasosegado* night? When first he must try to walk to beat the *insomnio?* Then is prevented from getting to sleep by the talk of his guard who is no longer in need of sleep.' His tone had started to become harder as he shifted his gaze from Edge to Cortes. And the scowl was back in place, to match the chilling note in his voice as he accused: 'Because he had slept enough while our prisoner attempted to escape!'

Manuel's rifle had tracked the shifting direction of his hard-eyed stare. And the dwarfish man was so certain he was going to be shot, he hurled his own weapon to the floor and thrust his short arms high in the air as he pressed his back hard against the wall. Then he squealed, eyes bulging and spittle spraying:

'Por favor, jefe –'

'Shut your slobbering mouth, you crazy runt!' Manuel

cut in on him. And jerked his Winchester back to cant it to his shoulder. 'I'm not your leader! *El Malo* is! Even if the stinking pigs of Federales have got him locked up right now! We'll perhaps need every man we have to get him free! Even half a man, like you! If José Sanchez wants to punish you for going to sleep on guard duty, that'll be up to him when he's free! So pick up your weapon and see if you can keep your ugly eyes open a few minutes more, *cretino!* You, *Americano!* Since you are feeling so well, you can get on your clothes without aid, I think?'

'You're a right-thinking feller far as that's concerned,' Edge growled. And was able to remain seated on the side of the bed as he reached for and got a hand to the heap of his clothing on the floor beyond the end.

'We leave in thirty minutes!' Manuel snapped. 'Anybody who hasn't had time to eat by then goes without the bacon and beans!'

He spared another withering stare for Cortes, then swung away from the doorway. The taller man at his side matched his move, still looking like he had the troubles of the world on his slim shoulders and knew for certain he could not carry them very much longer.

Cortes rasped: *'Hijo de puta!'*

Edge pulled on one of his boots and murmured: 'Yeah, feller, sonofabitch is right. But maybe we'll both see things differently after breakfast.'

'*Hombre,* I will never see that one as anything but what he is!' He sent another globule of saliva at the dirt floor.

'That's because you're in such a lousy mood,' Edge countered as he succeeded in pushing a foot into the other boot – and was pleased enough with how he achieved this to express another grin as he added: 'But pretty soon you'll be the same as me.'

'*Que?*' Cortes growled.

'Both be full of beans.'

Eleven

MANUEL'S TIME limit of thirty minutes until they pulled out from the *barranca* was strictly applied. He had a fob watch with an alarm bell – taken from a dead man after a train hold-up in Texas, Francisco Cortes told Edge – and he had set it to ring at the appointed time. And when the chimes sounded their plaintively off-key tones it remained only for the temporary leader of José Sanchez's bandit group to kick dirt into the fire's embers: this as he swept a hypercritical gaze over the wagon and team and the dozen men astride horses or burros.

The riders and their mounts and the former United States Army ambulance with two sway-backed pintos in the traces did not present a tableau that invited admiration. And the expression on Manuel's face did not promise he was prepared to make allowances for the circumstances that had contributed to the wretchedness of this less than impressive force he intended to lead on a rescue mission to free the condemned *El Malo*. For his dark eyes, in combination with the twist of his lips around his exposed teeth, tacitly directed at all who looked toward him a stream of epithets that he probably could not have brought to mind in the time it took him to scan the column. A single scan, from the wagon at the rear to where Raoul held onto the reins of Manuel's mount at the front, then back again. Until the alarm bell mechanism of the watch wound down.

If Edge had been so disposed, he might well have been able to think of just as many profanities as he ate his breakfast, and surveyed his surroundings and those who peopled this *barranca*: where once, perhaps, a fortune in gold had been dug.

If the bolt-hole had actually been what it seemed at first impression, José Sanchez had made a bad choice for his new hide-out. For it appeared to be a blind canyon, roughly triangular in shape: the narrow end at the mouth. From the mouth, the bottom land sloped down quite steeply, broadening between rugged rock faces that gradually became more sheer. At the blind end the cliff was some sixty feet high, and it would take an expert climber to scale it. Cover within this deep cleft in the hillside – six hundred feet long and a hundred and fifty feet broad at the widest point – was confined to scattered boulders, hollows and clumps of brush, and the small adobe shack that was sited a third of the way down into the *barranca*, at the base of the steepening north slope.

But a more careful study of this piece of terrain that would once have been a natural trap for a bunch of outlaws revealed the man-made tunnel entrances. Three of them at more or less regular intervals in the base of the rock face down at the far end. One into the north side of the *barranca* and two into the south. And maybe others were concealed by boulders or brush. All had been hewn from solid rock at their start, and thus they were of irregular shape – which may have led Edge to believe they were nothing more than small caves, had he not been told of the mine workings.

Of course, the tunnels provided more secure cover than other features of the hide-out. But by the same token they were also a more secure trap – unless some or all of them were inter-connected and eventually led to a way out of the *barranca* elsewhere on the hillside. If this were the case, then Sanchez had made an excellent choice. Or was there no such secret way out of this blind canyon? Yet?

Had the Mexican bandit chief simply seen the potential for digging an escape tunnel as a part of his scheme for extending and enlarging the old mine workings to provide underground quarters for his men and their animals?

While he sat on a slab of rock beside the dying fire, guarded by the still sullen Cortes as they both ate bacon and beans and washed down the greasy food with almost tastelessly weak coffee, the half-breed did not scan the sunlit scene out of idle curiosity. Instead, he sought an avenue of escape. But he quickly discounted the mine workings: unprepared to take the risk that all of the tunnels followed independent routes to dead ends. Which left just the mouth of the *barranca* or its sides where they sloped less steeply, close to the mouth. But two rifle-toting men stood guard at the top of the wagon-wide, well-trodden path, where it seemed to come to a dead end of its own among a clump of thickly growing vegetation. And the flanking slopes were dangerously open: sparsely featured with cover from below.

So his method of escape would have to include a hostage: and it was at this early stage – less than a minute after he moved out of the shack and began the seemingly indifferent reconnaissance of his surroundings – that he realised there was no immediate chance of getting free of his captives. For in this short time it had become apparent that Manuel did not hold only Francisco Cortes in low esteem. His attitude toward every other member of the group was equally disparaging. So it was clear he would not hesitate to sacrifice any or even all of them in a hostage stand-off situation. And, likewise, it became clear to the half-breed almost as quickly that the men and women he so harshly humiliated whenever he spoke to them would take pleasure in blasting Manuel out of the way if any attempt were made to use him as a shield.

Any pleasure they drew from such an event would be, from the look of them, the only reason to smile in a very long time. All were as raggedly dressed in similar Mexican style to Cortes, except that a few wore felt rather than straw sombreros, and one of the women had on a once-elegant dress rather than work pants and shirts. Now that the women had completed their duties as night guards, they had surrendered the rifles to the men who had first claim to them. And this ensured every man had either a rifle or handgun or both.

Just Edge and Cortes were allowed to remain at the fireside and eat a leisurely breakfast. Everyone else had to bolt their food and go back immediately to completing the preparations to depart: constantly and abusively harried by Manuel.

Conchita was among those who loaded the wagon, while others hitched the team or got the saddle animals ready for riding – including his own chestnut gelding, Edge noted. Her hands were no longer tied together but, he thought, she was probably more of a prisoner now than when she had been bound and exhibited to him with the gun at her throat. For Ysidora Garcia was never more than a few feet from her: and the older woman looked at the young girl with much the same brand of hatred as that she flashed with her dark eyes toward Edge from time to time.

The half-breed found it difficult not to watch every move that Conchita made. Had to force himself to glance at the bowl from which he ate, the cup from which he drank, the sunlit and shaded areas of the *barranca,* the almost dead fire, or those men or women who were engaged in chores away from the ambulance and the tunnel entrance out of which the supplies were being transferred. Consciously did not want to watch her, because the longer he did, the more he was convinced that she was his daughter. And the strengthening of this conviction acted to cause him deepening, unaccustomed anguish because of his total inability to help himself, let alone his daughter.

She was truly beautiful. For which he claimed no credit: except by the accident of his own birth to a mother who was beautiful. And, of course, Conchita's mother had possessed more than her fair share of feminine charms. He could see both these women in his daughter: discernible in the curve of a cheekbone, the line of the jaw and the slight uptilt at the tip of the nose. And in her mannerisms, too. The way she tossed her head, always to the left, to swing strands of misplaced hair away from her eyes. In how she thrust her right hip to the side to ease the burden each time she was told to lift a heavy weight. Even in the sneering set of her mouth when she expressed tacit resentment whenever Manuel or Ysidora shouted an order at her.

He could not identify from which woman the girl had inherited such easily recognisable features or characteristics. But he was certain he had seen them many years ago, before Conchita was born. But never in such harsh and squalid surroundings. Nor in circumstances that left him with such a forlorn sense of impotency: weak from the wound, with not even the concealed razor for a weapon. A prisoner considered as no more than a lucky break by this woebegone bunch of leaderless bandits – who intended to try to get Sanchez out of the Federale prison with or without him.

It was, he supposed, inevitable that he should find it so difficult to control his wandering gaze: much as it tortured him by emphasising his unaccustomed helplessness each time he caught sight of the slender form. She was his daughter. The child becoming a woman he never knew existed until a few anguished hours ago. He needed to adjust himself emotionally to this previously unconsidered relationship and the responsibility it entailed. Disbelief at first. Then incredulity. Next something close to awe. Now, during those moments when he was able to suppress the compulsion to sink into a slough of self denigrating ineffectuality, he felt a warm glow of pride in Conchita. That he had fathered such a fine-looking offspring. And not only was she beautiful – she also had a strength of character. This seen in the manner she responded to being as much a captive as he was. A girl with less spirit would be cowed by the harsh treatment she was receiving from those who yesterday had been her equals.

He felt he could claim, with justification, that she had inherited at least some of her grit from him. And he was thinking along these lines, relishing a deeper and warmer feeling of pride in his gutsy and beautiful young daughter, when Manuel began yelling for everybody to hurry and finish up what they were doing. Which drew from Cortes a rasping, sour-toned comment about the youngster getting to be as loud mouthed and high handed as José Sanchez. And this mention of the name of the imprisoned leader of the bandits acted to put an icily angry end to the half-breed's train of thought: as there was conjured up to the forefront of his mind that image he had glimpsed before – of his daughter, naked, writhing with passion beneath the lusting body of . . .

Obeying a snarled order from Manuel, the dwarfish Cortes rose to his feet and gestured with the Spencer that Edge should also get up. Then they went toward the wagon, as all the men with the exception of Manuel swung astride their mounts, and the women climbed into the rear of the timber-sided and roofed rig. Conchita was the first of the five women to get aboard, after she was shoved violently into a stumbling half run by Ysidora Garcia. Just for a moment the mistreated girl looked as if she were about to whirl around and lunge into a screaming attack on the woman. But for the first time in several minutes her big, dark-brown eyes met the narrowed, ice blueness of Edge's gaze. And it was almost as if she could peer into his mind and see the image of herself that was torturing him. For within a part of a second every trace of fury and latent violence had gone from her features. And in what fleeting time was left before she went from sight in the rear of a wagon she expressed a desperate plea for understanding. Along with what he saw as an even more fervent entreaty that he not judge her until she had a chance to explain.

He was not sure if he offered her any brand of silent comfort in response. For he was disconcertingly caught up in a turmoil of emotions of a kind he had not experienced for many years. Then Conchita was hidden in the wagon and he found his gaze drawn to the scowling face of Ysidora. And it was almost a relief to feel his features form into their usual impassiveness as he automatically reacted with ice-cold composure to her hatred for him – an emotion with which he was very familiar.

The alarm bell of the watch that Manuel held aloft began to chime, and the other three women squawked at Ysidora to hurry. Cortes rasped a plea rather than a command that Edge should climb up on to the wagon seat and slide across to the passenger side. Then the ugly little man tossed the carbine toward a scar-faced bandit who caught it neatly and slid it into the boot. And as Cortes hauled himself clumsily up onto the wagon and unwound the reins from around the brake lever, Edge saw that nobody was aiming a gun at him. But Manuel's malevolent eyes were not the only ones that warned him against impulsive action while the chimes were sounding and the fire was being doused. For several of the mounted men were turned in their saddles to grimace in the direction of the wagon, tacitly blaming the half-breed for whatever was needling them. And there was implicit in their baleful expressions a threat to kill him with great relish if only he would give them the excuse.

'*Hombre*, I would ask you please to not do anything *temerario* . . . anything rash, while we two are seated so close together, uh?' Cortes muttered nervously as Manuel was striding to where Raoul held his horse at the head of the column.

'They ain't all as good shots as Ramon Cabello, uh feller?' Edge said and experienced a flicker of cold anger at the pit of his stomach when he saw one grimace transform into a shallow smile.

'I am famous for my marksmanship,' the man who had

shot the half-breed said in Mexican. Unaware that he was at the top of the list of men Edge intended to kill. He was about thirty, tall and slender and handsome: with a neat moustache that by its jet blackness perhaps caused his even teeth to seem whiter than they were.

Then Manuel snarled an order for the column to move out and all the riders turned to face the front as they heeled their mounts into a slow walk that was the pace set by Manuel.

'You have nothing to worry about, Francisco Cortes,' Ysidora Garcia hissed in her native tongue, as the ugly little man snapped the reins and the wagon started to roll. 'If this *gringo* bastard makes one move that I think is suspicious, he will have another hole in his head.'

Both driver and passenger turned to look at the slot, some ten inches by three, that was cut in the front bulkhead of the wagon. And saw the eyes of the woman, burning with anger, peering through the aperture.

'Senorita – '

'I make no claim to being an expert shot,' she broke in on Cortes. 'But I have every confidence I will be able to hit my target from such a distance.'

She pulled her head back so she could push the barrel of a revolver through the slot, angling the gun so that the muzzle drew a bead on the half-breed's face no more than eighteen inches away. Although the roof of the enclosed section of the wagon projected forward over the seat, it did not yet provide much shade at this early hour of the day. The sun was still low in the sky beyond the *barranca* mouth and its light shafted through the slot to show that the gun was uncocked. But the woman's thumb was resting on the hammer.

'Lady, I don't like to have guns aimed at me,' Edge said evenly, and shifted his glinting-eyed gaze to the misshapen face of Cortes to add: 'Did I ever warn you about that, feller?'

'I warn you, *hombre!* Do not provoke her.'

'He is right, daddy!' Conchita said anxiously, and it was apparent she was riding as close to the front of the ambulance as the woman with the gun. 'This one has the bad temper. And following what you did to Esteban Sosa it will not require very much to make her lose it.'

Edge was grateful that the girl's use of the diminutive gave him pause for startled thought. For in the vocal silence that followed, he reflected fleetingly on how empty his usual threat about guns would have sounded in the present circumstances.

'Daddy?' his nervous daughter pressed for a response after several stretched seconds, while the wagon and harness creaked and the shod hooves clattered. And dust swirled up from the arid ground.

'No sweat . . .' He almost addressed her as 'lady', but checked this and completed: ' . . . girl.'

'You have no other children, *hombre?*' Cortes asked in a tone of genuine interest.

'None that I know about.'

'*Si*, I thought this was so. You are, I think, a little *desconcer* . . . It embarrasses you to be called *papa* as Conchita does? And you know not how to call her – '

'You may just call me Conchita,' the girl broke in. 'And you tell me how you wish I should call you?'

'I can give you many names to call him by!' Ysidora snarled, then vented a mirthless laugh that sounded as ugly as Francisco Cortes looked, before she added: 'But I do not think there is time enough to say them all before we arrive at San Sarita.'

'Ysidora,' one of the other women said wearily from further back in the ambulance.

'Yes?'

'It was a long night while we stayed awake on guard. There are many kilometres to San Sarita. It is time for us to sleep.'

'So sleep if you must!'

'If you will stay silent, perhaps we can.'

There were sounds of agreement with this, that were curtailed when Ysidora vented an unladylike grunt. A few moments later, the dwarfish driver of the wagon complained sourly:

'I, too, am awake all night . . . *estar de centinela.*'

He glanced over his shoulder, saw the revolver barrel had been withdrawn and that the woman had pressed forward to better see out through the aperture again. She rasped in a sneering tone:

'You could not be trusted, you apology for a man. And you proved this to be correct.'

'I did not sleep!' he protested. 'I pretended that I was to see if – '

'We don't care a damn!' one of the women snapped.

'I still think I should be allowed to rest instead of – ' He looked again at the woman peering through the slit and what he saw in her unblinking eyes did not encourage him to press on with the whining plea for sympathy. And then a sidelong glance at the hard-set profile of Edge beneath the sweat and dirt stained bandage warned him there would be no kind of understanding from that source.

Thus the wagon reached the top of the grade without further exchanges, and this was the way it remained as Cortes steered the ill cared for horses in the traces around the sharp curve through the brush and timber that effectively camouflaged the *barranca* mouth. Here, the two bandits who had been on sentry duty swung astride saddled horses that had been brought up into the stand of timber on lead lines. One of these horses was the chestnut gelding, and as Edge began to roll a cigarette the slivers of blue that were his eyes glinted more than usual in malevolent reaction to the sight of the rotund form with a black-bearded face that sat his saddle, cinched to the back of his mount.

'Hey, where you get *de tabaco, hombre?*' Cortes growled sullenly.

The half-breed did not shift his again impassive gaze

away from the broad back of the short man riding his horse as he replied evenly: 'All I have left are my clothes and what you people didn't find in the pockets, feller.'

'It seems you were half asleep when you put your patient to bed, Dr Francisco Cortes,' Ysidora hissed with reproachful sarcasm.

The dwarfish man was abruptly nervous as Edge struck a match on the side of the seat and lit the cigarette. 'I am not sure Manuel Vargas would *aprobar* –'

'Manuel Vargas can go stick his head up a chipmunk's ass, feller,' Edge cut in uninsistently as the terrain beyond the timber-hidden mouth of the *barranca* came into sight.

Cortes uttered a strangled sound that might have been either an exclamation of shock or a stifled laugh.

Ysidora said vehemently in American: 'I agree, the sonofa – '

'If he sees you, it will be –' Cortes interrupted, then was himself cut short in midsentence by the woman who reverted to Mexican to make the menacing threat:

'It may be the last cigarette of a doomed man, uh?'

All the riders had reined in their mounts, and now Cortes responded to a mere glare from Vargas and brought the wagon to an abrupt halt with a harsh working of the reins and a blurted: '*So!*'

While orders were issued and the mounted men manoeuvred their animals into the formation demanded, the half-breed showed a seemingly casual interest in this piece of Sierra Madre country which he had never seen before.

They were on the western side of a broad valley that was perhaps ten miles across from the tops of the high ground that flanked it at the widest point. This widest point was some way to the south, for they were close to the northern head of the valley, where it petered out through a combination of the bottom land rising and a convergence of the shallowing slopes. To the broad south the valley also deepened as the ground became more rugged and more sparsely featured with copal and mesquite, prickly-pear and salt-cedar, chino grama grass and greasewood. In the area immediately beyond the concealed *barranca*, though, there was more than enough greenery against the yellows and reds and greys of the sandy soil and the rock for the timber stand at the entrance to merge naturally into the background. And there were at least a dozen brush thickets close by where mine tunnels could emerge unseen from the hillside. Countless others at a greater distance. Or if brush or timber did not hide such adits, there were a number of rock outcrops or free-standing boulders which would suffice just as well. Or, if not on this side of the rise, of course, there may well have been an escape route from the old mine workings beyond the ridge of the valley's western flank.

But what he saw and what he surmised from it could turn out to be of purely academic interest, he acknowledged as Francisco Cortes complied with a snarled order from Vargas and set the rig rolling again. Downhill now and using the brake to keep the dilapidated and heavily laden wagon from forcing the sway-backed team into unwanted speed. Some riders were fanned out to the right and some to the left, and held their mounts to an easy walk as their only measure to keep from leaving clear sign on the dust that powdered the hard-baked ground. But Vargas and Raoul followed immediately behind the creaking ambulance: leaning down to the side to trail blankets that they swept this way and that and occasionally shook to create gusty draughts.

'They do this to keep us from leaving tracks that would show the old mine is no longer abandoned,' Cortes said after he had seen Edge glance back along the side of the rig. 'And with each of our men riding his own way down to the road, an easy-to-see trail is not made: as once it was.'

'You're one smart bunch,' Edge replied absently in the native language the ugly little man had used.

'This Edge, he is a man most difficult to impress, I

think,' Ysidora growled through the slit and her tone held more irony than his. 'It is not possible to teach him anything he does not know already.'

'My mother said he was the cleverest man she ever knew,' Conchita said. And Edge tried not to be affected by the childish pride that he heard in her tone.

Ysidora resumed the tone of a sneering rasp to counter: 'Then he is clever enough to know that fool, Manuel Vargas, can never allow either of you to live. After this long-lost father of yours has done what is required of him! For now both of you have seen the place where *El Malo* intends – '

The wagon and the widely scattered outriders had now reached the clearly defined trail that laid an arrow-straight line along the valley. And another halt was needed so that the column could reform. The hate-filled woman was so embroiled in the low-voiced venting of her feelings that she failed to be aware of what was happening, until Vargas halted his horse to the left of the rig and hammered on the side panel with the end of his fist. Which drew a frightened squeal from Ysidora and gasps of alarm from the other women.

'Bitch!' the temporary leader of the bandits snapped, his voice coolly controlled while his youthful, now gaunt rather than lean face revealed the effort it required to keep his rage from exploding into mindless violence. 'You are with us to do as you are told. You have been told to ensure the American's bastard daughter has no chance to help him escape.'

'Manuel, I – '

'Silence!' he snarled across her words, which had been forced from a fear-constricted throat. He paused and there was, indeed, a brittle silence that filled the entire valley – as if the Sierra Madre range and every living thing in it was cowed by the power of the man's command. For these stretched seconds, Vargas worked at getting something more secure than a finger-hold on composure. Then his scowling face gradually spread with something vaguely like a grin as he warned in a voice made more menacing by its flatness: 'That is good, Ysidora. You will continue to keep your mouth closed. In fact, if I want you to open anything but your arms and your legs until Esteban returns to us, I will tell you. You understand this, woman? Otherwise . . .?' He shrugged and heeled his horse a few feet forward, the better to see Edge across the front of the uneasy little man who was peering fixedly northward over the backs of the two horses: pointedly avoiding a clash of eyes with the coldly angry horseman. And now Vargas switched to American to say to the calmly smoking half-breed: 'You have some Mexican blood in your veins, *Americano.* So I think you maybe know the store my people set by honour. And I tell you now: I give you my word of honour, I will not harm you or Conchita Lopez. If you do what is required of you. Is that okay? You believe me, *Americano?*'

'I believe . . .' Edge began. But broke off when Vargas, with a broadening smile of satisfaction, urged his mount into motion, yelling for the column to set off again. And then the half-breed concluded: '. . . that you're a feller who likes to keep his options open.'

He removed the cigarette from his mouth for the moment it took to direct a stream of saliva over the side of the seat as Cortes started the wagon with a judder. Some of the women in the back growled their profane criticism of his driving, but Ysidora remained mute as she nurtured a new resentment for a new subject.

Cortes asked: 'What does that mean, *hombre?* Options open? What are – '

Now Ysidora broke her silence to rasp through the slit as she peered toward the head of the column where Vargas had resumed his position alongside Raoul. 'You are as ignorant as that pig is stupid if he thinks he can outsmart the *gringo.* Manuel Vargas promised only that he will not do the killing. Perhaps you can count, apology for a man? If you cannot, I can tell you how many more there are who can do the killing of the *gringo* and his bastard daughter!'

'He told you to be quiet!' one of the sullenly weary women complained. 'If you do not do that and allow us to sleep, I'll tell Vargas what you – '

'All right, all right!' Ysidora snapped, and murmured a barely audible obscenity as a final utterance before she subsided into a brooding silence.

And Francisco Cortes remained equally mute as he dwelt on a train of thought that the expression on his cruelly ugly face showed was less than pleasant.

Which allowed Edge a period lacking in any kind of distractions from outside his own troubled mind to maintain a bleak-eyed survey on the country they covered. And from the crest of the rise at the head of the valley he saw the terrain spread north and west in the form of a rugged plateau, enclosed on these horizons by an arc of jagged-topped mountains in the far distance. Already the rising heat of the new day was beginning to blur with nebulous grey haze the uneven line between dark land and bright sky. To the east the ground dropped sharply into the depths of what he soon saw was the southern end of another valley that at first gradually and then dramatically became broader and shallower. A number of miles to the north, and above the far side of this valley, a pall of dark smoke smudged the sky.

Edge guessed that this comprised smoke from the cooking fires in the *fogones* of Punto de Honra's adobe houses. Then, after the column had dropped down into the valley bottom by way of the trail that zig-zagged to take the steepness out of the descent, the guess was proved correct. For from this new viewpoint he was able to recognise rock formations and clumps of vegetation, skylines and fans of scree: features that registered as even more familiar the further north the column moved. All of them seen during a similar surveillance he had made along the length of this valley as he rode the trail in the opposite direction. Before

Ramon Cabello had triggered the rifle shot that should have killed him.

Cabello and Vargas and Raoul had meant for him to die, anyway. But his ruling fates had decreed the time was not yet right. A bullet through the head was too quick and easy. He had some more suffering to do. To pay for all those mistakes he had made. Like making a fine woman pregnant and then abandoning her, for instance? Like allowing himself to be suckered out of almost all he owned by the no-account Delmar Pyle? Like dwelling on his loss for so long and to such an extent that he failed to realise he was being watched by hostile eyes until he saw the spurt of muzzle smoke of the gunshot that came within a fraction of an inch of blasting a bullet into his brain.

He grimaced, and a grunt of irritation with himself escaped his gritted teeth as he found he was once more mulling over areas of the past that had simply gotten him into his present spot. When he should be concerned only with how to get out of the mess if he ever got the chance in the future.

'You say something, *hombre?*'

'Uh?' Edge asked of Cortes, and glanced at the ugly little man who was in process of lighting a cheroot. After an adult lifetime of smoking, the half-breed was usually able to keep a cigarette burning smoothly no matter how detached he was from the here and now. But on this occasion the cigarette had gone out. And now he took the lighted match from the man at his side and touched the flame to the tobacco ash. Shook it out and flicked it off the side of the wagon as he murmured: 'I'm obliged.'

'You're welcome,' Cortes growled morosely.

And Edge's mind was fleetingly host to an unbidden notion concerned with how welcome would be the two men who were hiding among some boulders some three hundred yards along the trail and twenty or so off to the right. Welcome to him? Or to his captors? His captors aboard the lumbering ambulance or strung out in a less than tidy column of two ahead of the rig. None of whom had signalled by word or gesture that they were aware of the couple concealed in the rocks: rocks that were large enough and numerous enough to effectively hide the men and their horses, also. Or was there anything sinister in the fact of the men secreting themselves? Perhaps they had seen menace in the approach of the column along the trail from the south and were merely hiding until it had passed?

Edge grimaced again, but it was a barely perceptible narrowing of his eyes to slivers of ice blue and a movement of his lips that caused the cigarette to dip lower away from the corner of his mouth. And he made no sound of self-censure that his mind was so receptive to inconsequential and capricious thoughts that did nothing outside of filling the time. For it was either that or a mind that was blank, since he had decided at the outset that he was in no position to make a first move in whatever was to develop out of this new situation.

He had spotted the two riders as dots in the distant north while the column was making its tortuous way down into the valley. Then intervening ground on the uneven bottom land had hidden them for all but a moment – when the wagon had crested a low rise and Edge glimpsed the rump and tail of a horse just before the animal moved out of sight among the scattered boulders. Right there and then he had reached the decision to keep what he had seen to himself: and now did not allow intrusive side issues to mar his concentration as he scanned the sun-bright terrain for a sign that he could be wrong in his assumption that both men were concealed in the same area. Hell, just because he had seen only two did not have to mean there were only two men in position to spring an ambush.

He could see not a trace of other men who might be watching the column of riders and the wagon as it moved slowly northward ahead of a low and elongated cloud of disturbed dust. But he could sense hostility emanating from the area he knew to be a hiding place. Whether directed at him or the group as a whole he could not decide.

'Daddy, don't you want to know anything about how I came to be – '

'Shut up! If I am not allowed to talk, then neither are you!'

Conchita had spoken her near accentless American in a whisper. Ysidora snarled her embittered reprimand in Mexican. And both Edge and Francisco Cortes felt drawn to glance at the face partially visible at the slit between them. When, for part of a second, the half-breed wondered if he was wrong about the men among the rocks watching the column with menacing malevolence. Maybe, he was tempted to acknowledge, his sense for such things had been impaired by the degree of burning enmity the scorned woman was directing out over the column toward Manuel Vargas at the head.

Then a rifle report cracked out. And the powerful, deep-seated emotion was abruptly gone from the dark eyes of Ysidora Garcia. While, just for a split second, she showed nothing more than mild surprise: this in response to the bullet that tunnelled into her skull through a hole above the bridge of her nose. A hole that was black at first. Then red. She was hurled backwards by the impact. So just a scant few droplets of blood sprayed out through the aperture to splash on to the seat. Which by then was vacant. For Edge had thrown himself off it to the right, and Cortes went to the left.

Horses and burros were suddenly reined in, and the broken-down animals in the traces needed no more encouragement than this to come to an abrupt stop. Men yelled in a mixture of shock and fear and anger, counterpointing the shrill screams of horror that sounded from the enclosed rear of the wagon.

Edge hit the ground painfully hard, certain of only one fact – there had been just the single gunshot. From this, allied with the knowledge of how close the bullet had come to hitting him, he made an educated guess that he had been the intended target.

'Esteban, don't be crazy!' a man yelled. And Edge thought he recognised the voice of Vargas, but could not be sure. His head was starting to burn with pain again from where he had banged it hard on the wounded side at the end of the dive for safety.

Then a chorus of voices was raised, and the sense of what was being said by anyone was lost to the half-breed by the sheer volume. Horses, too, whinnied and snorted: and their nervous movements stirred up dust that stung his cracked-open eyes. He started to rise, eager to get his head above the billowing dust: and was on all fours when he felt something small and hard and round pressed into the middle of his back. He froze and screwed his head around so he could look up at the arc of five women who peered down at him. One held a rifle on him and another had what looked like a painfully firm grip on Conchita's left elbow. The white dress of the one with the rifle was stained with wet blood and it was difficult to judge whether it was horror or malice that glinted in her rapidly blinking eyes.

Against a lessening of the barrage of noise, Edge said in even-toned Mexican: 'I'm going to get up on to my feet, lady. I'd ask you to keep it in mind that, up or down, I've got the same snowball's chance in hell of – '

'Stay as you are!' the woman ordered, and her voice lacked authority from having to be forced up from a throat almost closed by whatever emotion lit the cold fires in her eyes.

'You feel that strongly about it, pull the trigger, lady,' Edge told her. And looked down at the dirt between his splayed hands as he pushed himself up into a kneeling attitude.

The shouting had subsided to the level of two voices engaged in a heated exchange. This took place at the far end of the column from where Edge now needed to take a double-handed grip on a front wheel of the wagon to haul himself fully erect. His head hurt worse and he needed to squeeze his eyes tightly closed to rid his mind of the notion that the world was visibly tilting one way and then the other as it slowly rotated. He was aware of the rifle muzzle still being pressed against a midway point of his spine. Maybe the woman had tried to blast a bullet into him. But he had seen the hammer was not back.

Conchita blurted anxiously: 'Daddy?'

Francisco Cortes started to urge: 'Margarita, it will be best if you – '

A man, closer to Edge than the far side of the wagon, snarled with far greater force: 'Get away from him, all you women! He is well covered!'

Now Edge opened his eyes, as the muzzle of the Winchester was withdrawn from his back. And he saw the man astride his gelding was aiming his own rifle at him. But the half-breed looked at this man only briefly, before his attention was drawn toward three other horsemen who were moving their mounts slowly back along the straggled column. The trio were Vargas, somebody he did not know, and Esteban Sosa. Sosa, dressed as elegantly as at Punto de Honra, had his head swathed in far more bandages than the half-breed. They were wound under his chin and over the crown of his head, so that they covered both his slashed and his uninjured cheeks. The whiteness of the bandages contrasted starkly with the darkness of his Stetson brim and skin tone. Because such a restricted area of his shallowly handsome face could be seen, the expression of savage malevolence it wore seemed more powerful than it perhaps was as all three riders reined in their horses alongside the man who covered Edge. His voice was granite hard as he said, his eyes fixedly staring down at Edge:

'When Vincente Vallejo comes to my mother's house to tell me of Manuel's plan, I am not convinced it has any merit, *gringo*.' He made a hand gesture toward the skinny little man with an oversize drooping moustache who the half-breed had not recognised. Then he touched the bandage where it covered his wound as he went on in the same ice-cold monotone: 'But Manuel has warned that my eagerness to kill you so you are paid back for what you did to me has clouded my judgment. This view I will now accept. Until I am able to think clearly. I am now in command, until the time when we free *El Malo!*'

As he made this claim to the top spot, he shifted his gaze away from the face of the half-breed to glower at the women, Cortes, and then over his shoulder at the disarranged double file of men. Several of the men nodded or muttered briefly to acknowledge that this was as it should be.

Margarita, who was broad of hip and large of breast and had the least attractive features of all the women, spoke out loudly and silenced the men. 'There is something you should know, Esteban. This blood on my skirts is that of Ysidora Garcia. The bullet that missed the American killed your woman.'

Sosa's malevolent scowl did not waver by even the batting of an eyelid in response to the revelation. 'She is still inside?'

'Yes.'

'Get her out. There is no point in us travelling with anything that is useless.' He looked pointedly at Edge as he said this and began to wheel his horse.

'You wish her to be buried out here in the wilderness?' Margarita asked.

'I wish to be rid of her useless carcase,' Sosa answered. 'If you wish to make a grave for her, you must catch up with us when you have done this. Rest of you women, get back into the wagon. Francisco, Edge, get aboard. We are leaving for Punto de Honra immediately.'

Vargas and Vallejo turned their mounts to trail him toward the head of the column and the slap of hooves on the hard-packed ground masked to all except those close to her the reaction of Margarita:

'Empedernido hijo de puta!'

The black-bearded man astride Edge's horse gestured with the half-breed's Winchester for him to comply with Sosa's command. And he did so, having to squeeze his eyes closed again as the world threatened to tip off its even keel once more. Cortes resumed his position on the driver's side of the seat and pointed out:

'*Hombre,* the *venda* has slipped up from the wound. It is bleeding again. Maybe there is dirt in it. There is no time to tend it here.'

'Obliged,' Edge acknowledged, and reached up with both hands to tug the bandage cautiously back in place on the right side of his head.

He did this with his eyes still closed and only opened them to the sun-bright world that looked stable again when he felt the wagon start to roll.

'Francisco, we have not removed the body yet!' a woman yelled anxiously.

'Best you do it quickly, before Esteban knows his order was not carried out.'

'You mean just throw Ysidora out from the back of the wagon?' Margarita snapped.

'Unless you wish to do as he suggested and – '

'Mother of God!'

'Let us get it over and done with!'

There were sounds of the women straining as they struggled with the limp weight of the corpse. Then, because everyone aboard the wagon was listening for it, the sound of the dead woman slapping against the trail was probably louder in imagination than reality. Next, for stretched seconds there was just the clop of hooves, rattle of wheel-rims and creaks of wagon timbers and harness. Before Cortes apparently found the vocal silence unbearable and ended it.

'I knew he would not care that the woman was killed,

hombre,' he said sourly. 'Always she thought more of him than he of her. She was the latest of many such women. He attracted them as easily as that.' The ugly near-dwarf clicked his thumb and finger, then sighed and shook his head. 'But that was before you cut him and make the bad *chirlo*. He is not so handsome now. I think perhaps he will not be able to attract the women so easily now?'

'You never can tell, feller,' the half-breed answered and leaned to the side to look back across the settling dust behind the wagon to where the inert form of Ysidora Garcia showed as no more than a dark heap on the trail. 'Maybe later, but so far getting cut up didn't seem to cramp his style too much. He's still quite a ladykiller.'

Twelve

DURING THE hour or so it took for the column to get to Punto de Honra up on the east side of the valley, the pain in Edge's head lessened to the extent that he experienced more discomfort from the lumps and bruises of the dive off the wagon.

But he did become disconcertingly aware of something that was happening to him inside his skull: that his attention tended to wander whenever he attempted to concentrate on any one line of thought for more than a short length of time. And he was convinced that this was not caused by involuntary self-anger or anxiety or frustration on account of his unaccustomed helplessness. Such an unsettled state of mind he could have understood and come to terms with, since it would have been nothing new. But in the past, his attention had always been diverted from one subject to another. Today, the lapses in his concentration left his mind a blank. Or so it seemed. For certainly he could not recall what had pre-occupied him each time he was aware of having been lost to what was happening around him. Whether it be simply the changing mountainscape over which he was maintaining a careful watch, or if he had been listening to what Francisco Cortes or Conchita said to him.

Then, it seemed to him, the frequency of these aberrations increased the more concerned he became that the bullet had done more than mere physical damage to his head. But, he decided as they reached the village and Sosa called a halt, if he could reason that he was going out of his mind, did this not mean that he was entirely sane? Was he not, maybe, creating the limbo of total detachment as a defence against driving himself crazy because of the untenable sense of impotence he felt? And would continue to feel for as long as he remained powerless to help himself . . . himself and his daughter.

While he sat in Morton Reed's cantina and Conchita bathed his wound with refreshingly cool water, the half-breed resolved to abandon concern for such a tenuous factor as his sanity. He faced up to the fact that he was no longer responsible just for his own safety and wellbeing. This lovely young girl was his own flesh and blood.

In the wake of the killing of Ysidora Garcia and the way the corpse had been disposed of, none of the women riding the wagon had demanded silence in which to sleep. In fact, their brooding melancholy had seemed to be relieved when Conchita began to speak about her past life. And received more vocal encouragement to continue from Cortes than Edge.

She had not been born in the re-named town of Peaceville where her mother had worked as a waitress in Honey's restaurant. When the tall redheaded Gail found out she was pregnant soon after Edge left to take up his life as a drifter, she came south into Mexico. In search of the father of her unborn child, she was to tell Conchita when the girl was of an age to understand such things. But Gail gave up looking for him after her baby was born in a tiny village on the Chihuahua Al Pacifico Railroad south of Temosachic. Here she was given shelter by the local priest, Father Domingo Lopez. Gail kept house for the priest during the first ten years of Conchita's life, but then she caught a fever, and within five days of taking sick she was dead.

For a year or so after her mother's death, Conchita remained in the priest's house. He treated her, just as he had always treated her and Gail: as a close and much loved relative. And she took his family name as her own. But there was talk in the village. There had been talk before, about Father Lopez and Gail. Such a scandalous alliance, if it existed, was frowned upon by most of the priest's parishioners, but a blind eye could be turned toward it. For she was a full grown woman – and a *gringo*. But Conchita was a child. Albeit a child who was developing physically at a particularly early age. And although her mother had been a *gringo* – and by all accounts her father was more American than Mexican to look at – their daughter had inherited hardly any Anglo characteristics: unless you counted the way she spoke their language. And this made the villagers even more protective toward the moral welfare of the girl of such tender years who shared a small house with a priest whose celibacy had been in doubt for some time.

'There, that will have to do for now, daddy. It's the same filthy bandage, but at least the handkerchief that's over the wound is clean.'

'Obliged, girl,' Edge replied, and discovered it required no effort at all to direct a smile at her. And realised from the easy warmth of her smile of response that his own expression sat comfortably on his heavily bristled face. Which would not have been the case had he extended his recollections of what she had told him beyond this point. But he felt no compulsion nor even temptation to dwell upon the harsh turn her life had taken after she was forced to leave the household of Father Domingo Lopez. If he was to lose his mind, he was not yet crazy enough to voluntarily invite back again the anguish of guilt he had suffered when his daughter had spoken of that period of her adolescence. Encouraged to do so by the ugly little man who drove the wagon. Which was maybe when Edge had first become aware of withdrawing into an emotional wilderness? Because he instinctively knew his conscience could not withstand such an assault of torment without forcing him into some brand of reckless physical action that was doomed to failure – would maybe get both of them killed?

It was a compelling line of thought. And one that seemed to have a solid foundation. For it seemed that he had total recall, in a neatly chronological order, of all the events in her life about which she had spoken up until this point. But after that the sequence went a little haywire. Or was that a sign that his instincts were involuntarily at work again – making it impossible for him to think clearly about her most troubled times so he would not be tempted to power into foolhardy action. For no good reason beyond a passionate desire to begin to make it up to his daughter that he had not been there to protect her when she had most desperately needed him before.

Shit, at least she had survived all that had happened to her back then. When he had not been around to get mad as all hell and get her killed!

'It's looking *bueno, hombre,*' Cortes said with a grin of his own spreading across his misshapen features. 'There does not seem to be any *infeccion.*'

'You sound like a man who cares, Francisco!' Vincente Vallejo said with a sneer.

'We should all care!' the little man countered defensively. 'If this *gringo* is sick with the fever of a poisoned wound when we get to San Sarita he will be of no use in freeing José Sanchez!'

There was a chorus of agreement and disagreement from the bandits crowded into the small cantina. Some of them aligned at the bar counter and others seated at tables. All of them were in ill-humour because they had drunk the one tequila each that Esteban Sosa had ordered should be the limit while the horses and burros were rested. They could eat all they wanted, and the fact that none of them had taken advantage of this offer did nothing to improve the gloweringly sullen mood of Morton Reed. For the tall and skinny, bad-smelling man was still full with resentment at having to provide the liquor free of charge. Just once after Sosa and Vargus and Raoul had left the cantina, the unusually taciturn American behind the bar had started a snarling complaint. This when Conchita was given shrugging permission by Vallejo to step out into the kitchen to bring a bowl of water so she could bathe Edge's wound. But Reed's contention that the kitchen was private property had been curtailed when Vallejo swung his Colt away from the half-breed to aim it at the cantina owner.

Just the action was sufficient and after Reed became broodingly silent there was little sound elsewhere: just an occasional brief and low-voiced exchange of complaints among the men rationed to a single drink and the less obtrusive noises the girl made as she carried out her ministrations. While she did this, as Edge sat alone at the same corner table he had occupied when he was first in the place, only Vallejo and Cortes also paid more than passing attention to him. The man with the drooping moustache keeping him covered because Sosa had told him to do this, while the even shorter and far more ugly bandit seemed simply to have assumed something akin to a proprietary interest in the prisoner. Both men sat at the next table, only Vallejo armed, watching Conchita with as much glinting-eyed suspicion as he directed at the half-breed, and said not a word until the girl gave her opinion about the bullet wound and moved away with the bowl of dirty water toward the archway in the rear wall that gave access to the kitchen.

Now, after the mass expression of opinion concerned with the usefulness or otherwise of Edge in the attempt to free *El Malo* from the Federale post at San Sarita, the cantina became wretchedly quiet again.

Vallejo was briefly tense as Edge dug the makings from his shirt pocket. A man began to whistle off key but was stopped after a few tuneless notes by a barrage of glowers. The girl made some small sounds as she cleaned the bowl in the kitchen on the other side of the bead curtain. Four men, including Cortes, seemed to be tantalised by Edge's moves in rolling and lighting a cigarette: to such an extent that they felt the need to smoke – two cheroots, a pipe and a tailor-made cigarette. A pair of bluebottles buzzed in through the entrance doorway and for a few moments drew occasional rasped curses from men who swatted at them to no avail.

After them, only silence drifted in off the street on the barely moving currents of stifling mid-morning heat. And there began to build an atmosphere of nervous expectancy as the air grew heavy with the body odours of every man in the room. A stink so pungent it soon masked the aroma of freshly poured tequila and less fragrant stale chilli that filled every corner of the place for a while after the bandits crowded inside. Then, from Reed's general store next to the cantina, the chimes of a clock sounded. Eleven times. And with each note struck the temperature in the room seemed to get higher and the smell of unwashed bodies more obnoxious. Then the scar-faced bandit eased the massed apprehension when he growled in Mexican:

'José Sanchez would not have allowed us just a single tequila! He would have been happy to have us drink our fill!'

'And Manuel Vargas, Hernan,' the man who rode Edge's horse and carried his Winchester added. 'If he were still our leader while José cannot be.'

'I think that, too, Antonio.'

Vallejo looked accusingly at both men and warned: 'We must all remain clear in the head if we are to free our leader, my friends. And I think Esteban would not be pleased to learn you are criticising his orders?'

'And if he finds out,' the black-bearded Antonio countered with a sneer, 'then we will all know who has run to him with the tale?'

'That is correct,' Hernan agreed, and his sneer changed briefly into a cold grin of irony as he added: 'Though I do not know how it is possible for Esteban ever to hear what

Vincente tells him. The way, Vincente, you always have your head so far up Esteban's ass.'

There were a few hollow laughs while Vallejo spluttered with rage before he was able to snarl:

'Take care, Lugo! You, too, Diego! I have been given authority in the absence of Esteban and if I have to use it, I will. On anybody!'

The man with a moustache too large for his otherwise undistinguished face raked a dark-eyed gaze over everyone in the cantina. And it was apparent that none of his fellow bandits held him in any more respect than did the bearded Antonio Diego or the scar-faced Hernan Lugo. But all knew he possessed for the moment the command he claimed and so none was prepared to call his bluff. And so his imperious scrutiny drew nothing more mutinous than answering scowls, some defiant exhalations of tobacco smoke, and two or three spits at the floor.

Morton Reed refused even to meet the man's glowering gaze: and perhaps was unaware of what was happening in the room as he stared at the bead-curtained archway to the kitchen. From beyond this now there came the appetising aroma of frying meat, and the tall and skinny Texan looked even more perturbed than before that the private quarters of his establishment were being used without his permission. But this time he confined the expression of displeasure to a grimace firmly set on his gaunt, unshaven face.

This as Edge met Vallejo's commanding gaze with a combination of glinting eyes and compressed lips that seemed somehow to lower the temperature by several degrees. The Colt in the Mexican's fist wavered in its aim and the man felt it necessary to challenge:

'Twice you have been shot at by men who ride for *El Malo, gringo!* But from far off. If I mean to kill you, from such a distance I will not fail.'

'You talk a lot and say nothing of importance, Vincente!' the tall and handsome Ramon Cabello growled, probably stung by the implied criticism of his marksmanship in the valley below Punto de Honra yesterday.

'I make a point,' Vallejo said, composed now as he shifted the aim of his revolver so that it drew a bead on the half-breed's chest, left of centre. 'To tell the *gringo* to keep this in mind. He may look as hard as rock, but a bullet fired at his heart will not be deflected by the flesh of a man, which is all he is.'

Edge had already started to reshape his mouth into the line of a smile of anticipation as several men gave voice to short-lived sounds of pleasure. All of them, including Vallejo at length, shifted their attention to the bead-curtained archway. Where Conchita Lopez re-emerged from the kitchen. In place of the bowl of blood and dirt sullied water she had taken out of the room, she now carried a tin plate on which a thick beefsteak and two fried eggs continued to sizzle as she toted the mouth-watering meal toward the table where the half-breed sat.

'What the hell do you think you're doin', girl?' Reed demanded, his voice shrill with rage. 'That food was for me and the missus!'

'Shut up, *gringo!*' Vallejo bellowed. And powered to his feet so hard he knocked his chair over backwards. 'It is for me to ask such a question! Who told you to prepare food for the prisoner, *puta?*'

The girl set down the plate on the table, the knife and fork rattling against it for just a final second or so as a tell-tale sign of her nervousness. But then she was abruptly in the grip of the kind of rage that is exclusive to women with Latin blood in their veins. And she whirled around from the table, planted her splayed feet firmly on the floor, punched her fists against her hips and delivered a stream of obscenities in both Mexican and American at Vallejo. Screamed them at the top of her voice, until her voice broke with the strain of high emotion after she had been hurling abuse in two languages for perhaps as long as twenty seconds. Then the rigidity drained out of her slender form and the vehemence left her pretty features. She looked suddenly very young and alone and afraid as all the men before her looked at her with expressions that ran the emotional gamut from mild surprise to burning resentment.

'Proud of your daughter, *hombre?*' Francisco Cortes posed, the gravity of his tone matched by the expression on his ugly face. 'All that *obscenidad* and she hardly repeated herself.'

Suddenly, the girl who had become a woman too soon swung away from the roomful of men, to drop hard to her knees alongside the chair on which Edge sat. And enormous tears were visible on her cheeks before she covered her face with both hands and wailed: 'I'm so sorry, daddy! I've been with these brutes for so long! I'm getting to be like them! Please forgive me! Please understand! Once you've done what they want and you and me are on our own . . . I'll change . . . I'll get back to being how I was when mother and me lived . . .'

The sobs began to come so uncontrollably fast and from so deep inside her, she had to abandon the attempt to explain. And now she chose actions after the words had failed her: leaned to the side and hooked one arm around Edge's leg as she pressed a tear-run cheek to the side of his knee. Still down in a part-kneeling, part-sitting attitude on the floor as she wept and her body shuddered. Her free hand formed into a tight fist and she twisted this hard against each eye, like she thought she could force the tears back inside her head with this violent grinding action.

Edge was briefly disconcerted as he looked down at Conchita and saw her for the first time as a child rather than as a girl-woman: and felt certain he was totally incapable of offering this stranger who was his daughter the least word or slightest gesture of comfort that could be received as sincere. For he was caught up in a situation that was completely new to him. Nothing even remotely like it had ever involved him during the many years of his life. He was not equipped, emotionally, to deal with it. And the longer she stayed crouching at his feet, sobbing and shaking and gasping disjointed pleas for forgiveness and understanding, the more firmly entrenched became his initial instinct to thrust her away. Not because of what had happened to her, what she had done and what she was doing now. Instead, because of what he was – what he had become over all those years since he left the woman who was to be the mother of this child. A loner with no responsibility for anyone: a self-sufficient individual without obligation to feel protective toward anything but what he owned. And he could not even take care of that any more. For all he possessed now was the clothing he wore.

Stretched second piled upon stretched second. And as each tiny section of the future became the present and then was stored irrevocably in the past, Edge felt sure he was nearing a stage where he would hate Conchita Lopez. For there hovered in the black depths of his consciousness a suspicion that the fates were using this beautiful young girl to taunt him: that once again he was being put to the test. Like so often in the past. How often . . . ? In mere material possessions, countless times. But in terms of that most complex of human relationships, love . . . ? His brother Jamie and his wife Beth . . . other women . . . ? No, not even the mother of this girl. Just Conchita now. Outside of his own life, she was all he must care about. Perhaps the cruel fates that ruled his destiny had dictated that their paths should cross at such a low point in both their lives. But he could not blame the hapless young girl for that. To do that would be like falling down drunk and sleeping on a sidewalk, then giving hell to the blind man who tripped over you.

'It's all right, sweetheart,' he said and it sounded in his own ears like a voice he had never heard before. Then, by a conscious effort of will, he forced himself to shake off the last vestiges of unreality in which he had been shrouded. Not for so many stretched seconds, he saw. For if any man had done much more than blink since he last saw him clearly, it was not so very much more. 'No sweat. You were starting to repeat yourself. Cortes tells lies. You don't know so many dirty words. It's okay.'

His hand had been clawed, as if in preparation to take hold of her dark-haired head and shove her violently away from him. But it was easy enough to reshape his fingers and palm into a gentle curve with which to tenderly stroke her tresses.

'*Hijo de puta, hombre!*' Cortes rasped. '*Pensar* . . . It looked *de momento* that you were going to kill Conchita!'

Edge drew hard against the cigarette angled at the side of his mouth. And welcomed the intake of breath as much as the sensation of the tobacco smoke filling his lungs. It felt like the first chance he had to breathe after a dangerously long period of near suffocation. And now his voice sounded close to normal as he answered on a stream of expelled smoke: 'We all make mistakes, feller.' He glanced down at the upturned, tear-ravaged face of the girl as he completed: 'I figure this is one I don't want to rule out of my life.'

'Hey, I just figured somethin' out, Edge!' Morton Reed yelled, suddenly agitated.

But he became the centre of attention for just a moment, before Esteban Sosa appeared on the threshold of the cantina and announced:

'Me, too, *Señor* Reed!'

He spoke in much the same tone of voice as the Texan, but whereas Reed was excited by an abrupt realisation, the young Mexican was elated by the effects of liquor and women. His voice almost slurred and there was a foolish grin on his face. He looked more drunk than he sounded. But perhaps this was simply because of how he stood between two of the women who had ridden to Punto de Honra aboard the wagon. Stood as if he needed the support they gave him, for each had an arm curled around his waist and both his arms were draped over their shoulders. The women were fully dressed, but more dishevelled than when they climbed out of the wagon with Conchita and Margarita and the others. Sosa had on his pants and boots, but above his gunbelt-encircled waist wore just an undershirt.

The brittle silence that his cheerful opening had brought to the cantina was first cracked by some discontented mutterings in which the terms *licor, sexo, puta, emborracharse* and *bastardo* figured a great deal. But this was abruptly curtailed when the liquored-up man on the threshold suddenly gave vent to slurring anger.

'You hear what I tell you, *gringo hijo de puta?*' he raged, glowering at the suddenly gulping and afraid Morton Reed. And then the women who flanked him cried out in alarm as he fisted a bunch of their hair in each hand. Next pain sounded in the shrillness of their squeals as he thrust his arms to the sides: and released his holds on their hair when the women started to stagger away at either side of the cantina entrance. Sosa splayed his feet then, to steady himself. And was able to remain rigidly erect with his right hand draped over the Remington butt jutting out of his holster while his left thumb hooked in the belt at the opposite side of his waist.

'Esteban, there was no trouble until the girl brought food for the prisoner and the men – ' Vallejo began to explain, his voice as obsequious as his expression as he attempted to extricate himself from any chance of blame.

'Shut your mouth and listen while your leader is talking, you snivelling pig!' Sosa growled, the final heeltaps of the afterglow from sex and alcohol now gone. But gone, too, was the impulse to hot rage. He spoke more slowly, making a conscious effort not to slur, and the ice of controlled anger glistened in the dark eyes that peered out of a face that looked oddly elongated within the frame of the bandage wrapping. 'We must prepare to leave at once. We have just received word from San Sarita. José Sanchez will hang tonight if we do not set him free. The new captain who commands the Federale post has ordered a fiesta to celebrate his appointment. It is planned that the execution shall be a part of the entertainment.'

Manuel Vargas and Raoul appeared on the threshold behind Sosa. They were fully dressed and there were no women with them, but there was a certain glazed look in their eyes and a lopsidedness to their stance that signalled they had surely been at the same party as Sosa. But any resentment the men in the cantina might have felt about this was immediately neutralised by Sosa's revelation about the hanging of Sanchez. There was another short-lived period of tense silence, then a chorus of harsh-voiced invective against the Federales in general and Captain Miranda in particular.

'Cursing the bastards serves no purpose!' Sosa shouted. 'Get to your mounts and have them ready to ride at noon! Conchita Lopez, go to help the other women prepare the wagon for leaving! Cortes, see the women do this properly!'

Vincente Vallejo remained where he was beside his overturned chair, the revolver in his fist still aimed at Edge. The girl was as quick as the rest to begin complying with the orders, and paused only briefly as she unfolded up from the floor, to direct an entreating gaze at the half-breed and whisper:

'It will be best to do whatever he demands, when he orders it?'

He nodded his agreement with this, and watched her for just a moment as she joined the mass exodus from the cantina. Then he nipped out the fire from his cigarette and stowed it in his shirt pocket before he took up the knife and fork and prepared to eat the no-longer sizzlingly hot meal.

Vallejo said: '*Yo en su o tu lugar . . .*' Then he shrugged and reached down to set upright the overturned chair as he growled: '*Que demonios?*'

Esteban Sosa spoke in American for the first time since his opening remarks directed at the again surly Morton

Reed. Asked in an even-toned voice: 'And just what the hell are you doing here still, Vincente?'

The man with the oversize moustache was abruptly servile again. 'But, *jefe* . . . You tell me to guard the prisoner?'

Sosa, Vargas and Raoul had stepped in through the doorway before the other men and Conchita hurried out of the cantina. Now, as the three of them angled toward the bar counter, the short and thickset Manuel Vargas received a nod from the taller and leaner Sosa to deliver the put-down to the overly deferential Vallejo.

'That was before, Vincente. Before Esteban, Raoul and me were here. You think, maybe, the three of us can't keep the *gringo* in line?' He had been speaking evenly and smiling indulgently, in the manner of an adult who spoils a difficult child. But abruptly he scowled and his words were spat out like a series of pebbles designed to hit Vallejo in the face with stinging force. 'You think we should go out and saddle your lousy horse for you while you take your ease in the cantina?'

'No, no . . . como no –'

'So move your ass out of here and do as I ordered you,' Sosa commanded.

Vallejo moved away from the chair so fast it tipped over again. Then he was out through the doorway and on the street that was no longer peaceful: instead filled with the noises of the preparations for the column to pull out. The activity that caused the barrage of sounds also stirred up powdery dust, and some of this drifted into the cantina. But the air currents were too lethargic to carry even so tenuous a burden across to the table in the corner where Edge ate the now tepid but nonetheless welcome food.

While he ate, he was aware of Vargas and the rangy Raoul watching him – their backs to the bar counter and elbows resting on its top – while between them Sosa was bellied up to the bar, gazing at Morton Reed. The Texan was trying not to show how perturbed he was by the scrutiny as he gathered up the empty glasses from the top of the bar counter. But they rattled against each other more than was usual because of the way his bony hands were shaking with fear.

'You were about to say, *Señor* Reed?' Sosa invited, falsely amiable.

'How's that?' Reed responded huskily.

'When I came in just now. I interrupted you. I had my say first. Now it is your turn, *amigo*.'

'Shit, I forget what I was gonna say, anyhow. Couldn't've been so important, uh? Look, why don't you three guys have a drink? No charge, like always?'

Edge pushed a final piece of beefsteak into his mouth and rattled the fork on the empty tin plate.

Sosa drew his Remington slowly out of the holster, and rested the base of the butt on the top of the bar counter before he thumbed back the hammer.

Reed had a glass in each hand and he dropped both of them as a gasp of terror ripped from his throat and he pressed himself hard against the wall in back of the bar counter. Neither glass broke on the dirt floor.

'Look, what you doin' this for?' the lanky, sixty-plus Texan managed to force out from his constricted throat. And now his voice was squeaky rather than husky. 'Ain't I always been good to you? And the rest of them that ride with Sanchez? Okay, I beef about havin' to serve you free liquor and not gettin' no pay for the supplies you take outta the store, but that's only natural, ain't it? I ain't never done you no wrong and – '

'You said to *Señor* Edge that you had figured something out, as I recall it?' Sosa broke in.

Reed was able to tear his sunken-eyed gaze away from the bandaged face of the Mexican and peer past him at the half-breed. This as Edge struck a match on the underside of the table to relight the part-smoked cigarette. If the skinny Texan was desperately seeking help from the man at the corner table, he saw nothing in the impassive face and nonchalant attitude of Edge to inspire hope. But suddenly, as Reed's slack mouth started to tremble, he saw something that triggered an idea.

'Yeah, now I remember it!' he blurted, and his lips formed a smile line as he returned his eyes eagerly to Esteban Sosa. 'It was the chow!'

'*Que comida?*' Sosa asked and he sounded genuinely intrigued.

'I bawled the girl out for cookin' him the beef and eggs me and the missus was gonna have soon as I closed up after you guys left. But then I figured out it didn't make so much difference. Hell, there are some cold cuts and some . . .' He had started to respond with enthusiasm: worked at holding the smile in place as he blurted the explanation. But something he saw in Sosa's face – or perhaps simply the realisation of just how lame-brained he sounded – forced his expression into a grimace as mounting apprehension squeezed huskiness and then squeakiness into his voice. Now he squealed: 'Oh, Jeeze – '

Sosa squeezed the trigger of the Remington. Raoul fisted a hand around the butt of his Smith and Wesson and Vargas draped a hand over that of his Frontier Colt. But Edge did no more than tighten his mouthline and narrow his eyes in response to the gunshot, so neither man drew his revolver.

Reed took the bullet in the right shoulder and pleaded: 'No.'

Sosa thumbed back the hammer of the Remington and tracked the muzzle toward a new target. Blasted a second bullet into the left upper arm of the skinny old Texan, who moaned: 'Why you doin' this to me?'

Because the shots were blasted at so short a range into the sparsely-fleshed man, the bullets tunnelled through Reed. They made small entry wounds, and larger holes where they burst clear behind him. Little blood oozed out to stain his shirt at the front. But great welters splashed against the bullet pitted walls in back of him. The crimson stains seen after Reed began to slide down the wall, arms hanging limply at his sides while his head remained rigidly upright on his shoulders: thus was he able to direct a grimace of pained and terrified non-comprehension at the man who was torturing him. Then he was slumped down on the dirt floor, out of sight of everyone: except Sosa, who leaned across the top of the bar counter and pushed the Remington ahead of him as he thumbed back the hammer again.

'Why . . . ? For frig sake, just tell me why?' Although Reed's voice was shrill, it was also strong: powered by a depth of emotion that he perhaps had never plumbed in his life before.

'Because you are here, *gringo*,' Sosa answered and now seemed to be stone cold sober. 'And because you are a *gringo* . . . And I have no need of you.'

Reed vented a drawn-out scream of pure terror up at the face and the gun barrel that showed over the top of the bar counter. Which faltered when the Remington exploded a third shot. Then, as soon as the hammer was back and the cylinder had turned another live bullet into line, a fourth.

'You're killin' me, you greaser sonofabitch!' Reed shrieked. 'Two slugs in the guts are – '

'And one in the *cajones!*' Sosa bellowed: his voice forced to its loudest limit to make himself heard above the scream from Reed as the Texan saw the revolver move to aim at his crotch.

The fifth crack of a shell leaving the gun muzzle abruptly ended the scream. But Sosa did not consider the brutal business over before he had emptied the cylinder of the handgun of its final live bullet.

Then he turned around, blinking as the acrid black powder smoke of the six shots bit at his eyes. In the total silence that had come to the cantina and the village beyond it in the wake of the extended barrage of gunfire from a single revolver, the air felt hotter and heavier. Then Sosa began to turn the Remington's cylinder, and used the ejector rod to push the expended cartridge cases out of the chambers. On his elongated face there was an expression of satisfaction laced with the spite that had not been fully negated by the sadistic manner of Morton Reed's death. Until he suddenly vented a short, strident laugh and glanced at each of his companions before he fixed his grinning gaze on Edge and said:

'Hey, the body of a woman I know all about. But a man? I had to shoot that *gringo* six times before I found his heart. And unless a man is shot in the heart, you can never be sure he is quite dead? Is that not right?'

The gleeful voice of Esteban Sosa acted to trigger renewed activity and its accompanying noises outside the cantina.

'Tell you something, feller,' the half-breed said evenly, tobacco smoke trickling out of the corner of his mouth.

'It will not take long?' Sosa asked as he began to reload the chambers with fresh rounds.

'You should take anatomy lessons from Conchita.' He pinged the rim of the tin plate with the flick of a finger. Smiled with just his mouth at the puzzled looks on the faces of the three bandits aligned at the bar counter. 'She knows the way to a man's heart is through his stomach.'

Thirteen

ESTEBAN SOSA was not such a stickler for punctuality as Manuel Vargas. For although the column was reformed and ready to head out of Punto de Honra before the clock in the general store chimed noon, the order to start was not given until several minutes later.

During this wait in the high heat of midday, most of the men fretted tacitly: just the way they sat their mounts and the expressions on their sombrero-shaded faces revealing the extent of their resentment. Others – toward the rear of the column and thus far removed from Vargas, Vallejo and Raoul – occaionally engaged in terse, growled exchanges that disclosed it was not simply the unnecessary delay which stirred their sour disgruntlement.

'They are still angry that Esteban Sosa and his two *amigos de corazon* enjoy the wine and women while we have to wait in the cantina, *hombre*,' Francisco Cortes whispered softly to Edge as the two of them sat in their accustomed positions on the wagon seat. Which was the most comfortable place to be at this time of day with the rig facing north. Since the body of the former ambulance and the front projection of the roof provided them with ample shade. Inside it would be shadier still, of course, but the women had to endure the oppressiveness of stiflingly inert air fetid with their own sweat.

'Can see why that should be, feller,' Edge murmured and dropped over the side of the seat the butt of the cigarette he had lit after finishing the steak and eggs meal.

Their voices carried no further than any others: all of them sounding against the gently rising and falling but never obtrusively full-throated wailing of Morton Reed's widow.

'Now he is taking his leave of his mother,' the ugly little man went on. 'They are very close. She is the sister of José Sanchez, but I think you know this, *hombre?*'

'Yeah, feller. So I can see how nobody around here is going to try to stop Sosa doing whatever the hell he wants.'

Punto de Honra was a one-street village. And the double-file column of mounted men with a wagon and two-horse team at the rear stretched almost half the length of the street, stalled between the crudely-built and weather-ravaged adobe buildings that, with the exception of the cantina and one of the small houses, gave a false impression of being unoccupied. From out of the cantina emerged the wailing of the new widow. While, from time to time, there was the sound and occasionally the sight of somebody moving about beyond the open doorway of *Señora* Sosa's house. Most other doors, and even some shutters, along both sides of the narrow street of Punta de Honra were firmly closed. And nothing more tangible than a sense of fear, horror or hatred emanated from within these silent hovels where the peon families waited with even more impatient resentment than the bandits for Esteban Sosa to order a start northwards.

'*Si, hombre.* The people of this place gain nothing from having the sister of *El Malo* living among them. Perhaps, even, they are the losers because of it. Because the *sobrino* of José Sanchez comes here so often to visit with the mother he loves so much. But Esteban, he has no regard for any others here. The *Americano* who he has just killed so badly – that is the first really bad thing he has done here. He is like his *tio*. The *Americanos* he hates in the way it is natural for most men to hate those creatures that survive by eating the *excremento* of other creatures. But Esteban, he would perhaps have put to death the smallest *infanta* or *viejo* from any *casero* of Punta de Honra if that was what he wanted. And no one who lives here would protest.'

Although the dwarfish Francisco Cortes was speaking in low tones, directing what he said toward Edge out of the side of his mouth, there was a quality of compulsiveness about his manner. As if talk was a safety valve through which the volatile constituents of a bitter and powerful anger escaped and were neutralised: while his glittering dark eyes were never still in the depths of their sockets – like he was concerned that to look at anything or anyone for too long could result in the dangerous explosion of rage that talk kept in check. Just then, though, Esteban Sosa appeared on the threshold of his mother's house. His back was to the street for a few moments, as he spoke some final words of farewell. Which gave the men who were waiting for him enough time to wipe the expressions of sullen discontent off their bristled, sweat-run faces before Sosa swung around and strode purposefully toward the horse that Vincente Vallejo held for him.

Señora Sosa did not advance to the doorway or the single street-facing window to watch the departure of the column: the command to start yelled officiously by Vallejo acting on a peremptory inclination of his head by Sosa.

'And as for these *muchachos*, they will do nothing except talk about him behind his back,' Cortes went on, after the clatter of the column on the move had drowned out the wailing of the distraught new widow.

'As you are proving to be true!' Margarita said sourly in Mexican from inside the wagon.

The misshapen face of the little man briefly expressed anxiety that Edge was not his only listener. But he quickly recovered a degree of composure, and there was not even a hint of his earlier latent aggressiveness as he countered, in American: 'I do not deny what you say, *mujer*. For you know as well as I that Esteban Sosa would not hesitate to kill even a *compadre*, if he felt like it – in his present *estado?*'

The woman merely grunted, but there was a distinct tone of ill-humoured agreement in the sound. Cortes went on as the final buildings at the northern end of the village street were put behind the wagon:

'And as long as this thing did not endanger the plan to free José Sanchez, no-one here would do more than talk about him behind his back.'

There was another grunt from in the rear of the creaking, swaying, jolting wagon, even more distinctly in agreement with what the dwarfish Cortes had said. And other women gave vent to low-toned but powerfully expressed profanities to register that this was their sourly held opinion, too.

Through lips that hardly moved as the dust of the open trail billowed up from under the slow-moving hooves of travel- and heat-wearied animals, Edge asked: 'He always that unpredictable?'

'*Hombre?*'

'When he has a bellyful of liquor and gets his rocks off, feller? Or maybe it's just he doesn't figure a party's a party until he's emptied a gun into a griping old man?'

'I tell you this, daddy, Esteban Sosa could get to enjoy something like that, that's for sure!' Conchita snapped. And the vehemence of her hatred for the young man gave her American the coarsest tone Edge had yet heard in it. 'He is the meanest, most cruel – '

'He is a sonofabitch like no man I ever met,' one of the other women cut in, her Mexican words hard with an equal depth of ill feeling.

'But bad names are not going to harm him,' another growled. 'Nothing bad will ever happen to him for as long as José Sanchez is his uncle.'

'My Pa hurt him real bad!' Conchita argued with pride.

'Which has made him worse than he was before!' Margarita snarled. Then moderated her tone to warn: 'Which will mean the manner of your dying will be harder if your new-found father fails you, little girl.'

Conchita uttered a soft, terse groan – like the woman had done something to demonstrate the kind of pain that the future might hold for the girl. Edge felt his facial skin drawn taut to form an involuntary grimace and he forced himself to stare fixedly to the side: determined that Cortes should not see this visible sign of his reaction. But when he faced impassively to the front again a few moments later, he became aware of how his hands had bunched into fists where they rested on his thighs. Were clenched so tightly his knuckles ached and his fingernails felt on the point of piercing the flesh of the palms. He glanced at the ugly little driver, his mind churning with a turmoil of conflicting emotions while he made a conscious effort to unfold his fists without allowing his hands to tremble.

He felt compassion for the girl's suffering, hatred for the woman who hurt her, shame at his own helplessness, anger that he had let his coldly uncaring facade slip, relief that Francisco Cortes had not witnessed the lapse and . . . He gazed directly ahead again, over the backs of the two horses in the traces and the mostly sombrero-hatted heads of the double file column of bandits. His lips were compressed into a thin, hard line now and his eyes were glittering slivers of ice blue beneath their hooded lids. So that no one, even if they scrutinised him long and hard from close quarters, could know he felt a complete fool. Like the prize idiot of all time as he castigated himself for being afraid to show his feelings. For what did it matter if the little Mexican with the misshapen face saw he was affected by the pain of Conchita Lopez? It was only natural for a father to feel as he did in such a situation. He guessed . . . Yes, it had to be so, for it was the way he had instinctively reacted. But, of course, it seemed totally unnatural to a man who was a stranger to his daughter. Who had never been given the opportunity to experience the gradual strengthening of such a bond as a baby became a child and the child grew toward adulthood.

Shit, he told himself as he suddenly became aware just how familiar was the terrain over which the column was moving now. He was out of his depth emotionally, that was all. Unsure of what he should feel. What he did feel. Was he genuinely stirred by love for this lovely, slender young girl for whom he felt such a responsibility? Or was he so unfamiliar with such a powerful sentiment he could not recognise just what it was that he experienced each time he thought about or saw Conchita? Was he forcing himself to fabricate an illusion of himself as a father who cared deeply for his daughter? While his actual instinct was to reject her. To ignore her plight and be concerned only with his own survival. Which was a brutal view to take: but then life had progressively brutalised him in countless ways. And none of these were more effective than those few and far between occasions when he had known love for a fellow human being – only to harshly lose it.

So now, as he recognised that the column was snaking through the boulder-strewn *barranca* out of which the Federales had launched the attack that led to the capture of José Sanchez, Edge also pinned down the reason for the turmoil in his mind. And by doing this he was able to dispel the uncertainty that had begun to undermine his normally ice-cold selfconfidence. Conchita was his daughter. He had to believe that: and as such he felt duty bound to face up to a responsibility to protect her from harm to the best of his ability. Which entailed getting her out of the clutches of her murderous captors. Plain, simple and practical. Which was how he preferred things to be. And since there had been no time or opportunity for an emotional involvement to develop, it was senseless to try to conjure up such a complication. Maybe when this entire dangerous experience was over, there would be occasion to reflect on a brand of instinctive love he now felt guilty he was unable to feel.

If he survived . . .

And what if he survived and Conchita did not . . . ?

No! To attempt to project himself into the uncertain future with its many variables was as futile as trying to analyse his mental attitudes to the present. What he had to do was examine the reality of his perilous circumstances and figure out how he was going to survive – along with a dark-eyed and dark-haired lovely young girl who just happened to be his daughter.

'Esteban Sosa, he is not the most even tempered of men, *hombre*,' Cortes said in a sorrowful tone. 'His moods, they can change with the *pestaneo* of the eye.'

Edge directed a sidelong glance at the ugly little man driving the wagon. Saw on the grotesque features of the near-dwarf an expression of dispirited resignation. Which perhaps meant he had been delivering a monologue for some time and had abandoned hope of drawing a response: or maybe it suggested he had only now got around to replying to the query the half-breed had posed several minutes ago.

'At Punto de Honra, *por ejemplo*, I am certain it was his intention only to get more supplies from the store run by the *Americano*'s wife while the animals were rested and we refreshed ourselves. But the need for a *mujer* came upon him. And in his mind, the *voluptuoisidad* and the tequila go together.'

'The sonofabitch cannot serve a woman unless he is half drunk!' a voice sneered from the rear of the wagon.

The riders emerged from the mouth of the rock-strewn *barranca* without any call from Sosa to pause. For it was obvious that every member of the bandit group knew this was the scene of *El Malo*'s capture. For all had heard at least one version of what happened two nights ago. And the four almost fleshless skeletons of the scavanged corpses on three sides of the long-time-cold fire embers confirmed that this was the site of the camp where José Sanchez had been taken by the Federales. One sprawl of part-licked-clean and part-brown-stained white bones was unencumbered by any sort of clothing. This was the remains of the hapless Apache squaw. But what was left of the men – Ed Cody over at the base of the rock face and Miguel and Luis on the opposite side of the former fire – was mixed in with enough savagely-ripped remnants of fabric for the grim-faced, softly-muttering riders to know which of the bodies, picked over by coyote and buzzard, rodent and insect, had been those of their *compadres*.

Some of the riders spat, others made the sign of the cross at their chests, two looked abruptly away and one of these came close to choking as he fought down a dry retch.

'So this is the place where the mighty José Sanchez – the Evil One – allowed himself to be taken prisoner, uh?' Margarita murmured with heavy irony as she pushed her face close to the slit to peer out of the front of the wagon.

Cortes eyed the skeletons of Miguel and Luis with what appeared to be sincere sadness, before he turned his ugly head to direct an acrimonious glower at the woman as he rasped in acid-toned Mexican: 'I will listen to many bad things said of Esteban Sosa, and perhaps will agree with much I hear. I will not let pass any further insults you voice against José Sanchez.'

'Why you . . .' the woman began to snarl, but saw something in the misshapen face that warned her against completing the intended retort. And there was something close to a whine in her tone when she went on lamely: 'I don't know why a man like José Sanchez keeps a pathetic creature like you around, Cortes.'

The ugly little man continued to stare fixedly at her for a moment longer before he sighed and nodded and faced front to attend to the driving again. And reverted to American to mutter: 'Nor me, *mujercilla*. But he does, and that is why I will follow him into *tizonazos*, if that is what is required of me. Whether I am in *acuerdo* with his *ambicion* or I am not.'

He glanced to the side and met the coldly glinting gaze

of the half-breed without concern: tacitly reiterating what he said in the adobe hut at the *barranca* hide-out last night, and emphasising that he had not just now been talking for the sake of Margarita. He considered Sanchez an idealistic fool, but he would sacrifice his life rather than do anything to endanger the bandit chief. So, Edge could expect no help in an escape bid.

The half-breed drawled: 'Sanchez is locked up in a Federale prison and scheduled to be hanged before the day's out, feller. Bad mouthing him would be like kicking a man when he's down, seems to me?'

Cortes eyed the bigger, broader man for a few moments more: in a manner that suggested he was sure the American had misunderstood his unspoken message. Then he shrugged once more and resumed his front-facing attitude, steering the wagon up the slope toward the thick stand of timber from which Edge had witnessed the short, sharp skirmish two nights ago. A few minutes later, as the column made energy conserving progress through the heat of the afternoon along the rim of the *barranca* from where Edge had heard the piercing scream of Ed Cody's castration, Cortes again found the vocal silence too much of a strain.

'I was telling you of Esteban Sosa and his *de genio vivo* ways, *hombre.* Who knows why the *ansia por mujer* strikes us, uh? As men we feel the need, and if we are lucky we are able to fulfil it. But rage, that needs the *causa.* Unless a man is *loco*, and I do not believe this of Esteban Sosa.'

There was a scornful snort from in the back of the wagon. Any of the women inside could have been responsible for the sound. Nobody took issue with her, but there was a quality of petulant agreement with her sentiment in the silence.

'I know, *hombre*,' Cortes went on, 'just why he felt the need to relieve his feelings in another way – and made the unfortunate *Americano* at the cantina suffer for it. I think I know this, *de todas formas?*'

He paused after his tone had transformed the statement

into a query: and gave Edge the opportunity to prompt him as he took the time to light a cheroot. Then was content with the taste of the tobacco and unperturbed at the lack of encouragement by either word or gesture.

'While he and Manuel Vargas and Raoul Bandini were pleasuring themselves with the women and getting *bebido* with tequila, a peon who had been to visit a brother in San Sarita returned to the village. And brought news of the *fiesta* with which the Federales are to *celebrar* the hanging of José Sanchez. All of us who are loyal followers of *El Malo* are much *encolerizado* to hear such a thing. We are all enraged as we prepare to leave as Esteban has ordered. But Esteban, he has the rage and the guilt, too. That he is enjoying the women and the *licor*. Also, *hombre,* he has as a prisoner the *Americano* who cut him so badly. And I do not think Manuel Vargas was able to *convencer* Esteban, *totalmente* that it is a good idea to make use of you and your *hija* . . . your daughter.'

Edge was now aware of Francisco Cortes directing a series of quizzical glances at him, the ugly little man with the cheroot angled from his twisted mouth eager for a response. But the half-breed continued to gaze fixedly at the head of the column, where Sosa, Vargas, Bandini and Cabello had moved several yards out in front of the other riders. There they were engaged in earnest, secretive discussions. And, as Cortes felt drawn to look toward what had captured the American's attention, Ramon Cabello suddenly heeled his horse into a gallop that quickly carried him out of sight in such rugged mountain terrain. The other three men maintained the pace that kept them apart from the rest of the column: so they could continue with their confidential exchanges. And now, as before Cabello was ordered to ride on ahead, there were frequent backward glances that were either grim, sullen, bitter or angry.

'I think much of the talk is concerned with you, *hombre*,' Cortes said as he sensed, like Edge, that the wagon was the centre of ill-humoured interest each time one of the front riders looked back along the column.

'And I thought it was you bending my ear that was making both of them burn, feller,' Edge answered lightly.

'Please, daddy,' Conchita said anxiously. 'Think carefully about what he told you about that Sosa shi . . . You just never know where you are with him. I think Francisco Cortes has tried to warn you that what he did at the cantina to the American there . . . It could just as well have been you. And it was a warning to you. That if you do or you do not do what Sosa tells you, he is just as likely to get crazy mad and kill you. So do not trust him, daddy. And please do not even think of trying to trick him or – '

'I'm your father, girl,' Edge cut in on her flatly as her voice began to tremor with fervour.

'*Si* . . . Yes, I know this! And it is because of this I – '

'There were a whole lot of things I learned from your grandmother,' he interrupted her again.

'*Que?*'

'Don't tell me how to suck eggs.'

Fourteen

A SHARP whistle sounded and Esteban Sosa reined in his mount and thrust a hand high in the air to signal a halt to the northward progress of the column.

It was full night and the quarter moon with a misty ring around it was high in the almost starless sky. The evening air had been pleasantly warm in welcome contrast to the harsh heat of the long and dusty day on the trail. Then a gentle breeze had begun to stir across the Siérra Madre ridges, carrying with it a hint of dampness that could have promised rain. But the cloud cover never got to be that threatening. And by the time Ramon Cabello vented the whistle that brought the column to a stop, the refreshing breeze had dropped and the unmoving air was so humidly heavy that just the thought of blinking an eye was enough to break a man out in a sticky sweat.

'We are close to San Sarita, I think, *hombre*,' Francisco Cortes muttered, and sounded irritably close to exhaustion as he brought a long vocal silence to an end: as if the night with little sleep and the day of driving the wagon had finally caught up with him. And, perhaps, the bone-deep weariness of the ugly little man was made harder to bear because of the subdued sounds of the women as they continued to sleep peacefully in the back of the wagon.

Edge did not reply, although he could have confirmed that Cortes had made a right guess: for he had recognised several landmarks in the shape of eroded rock formations as the column wound up the steadily rising trail toward the jagged ridge that he knew overlooked the town of San Sarita. For it was only a couple of days ago that he had made the lone ride down from that ridge, passing those distinctive outcrops in the opposite direction.

There was a brief, tiny flare of yellow light up near the jagged crest of the rise, to the right of where the trail curved over it to begin the descent to San Sarita. Like Cabello had struck a match and shielded the flame on all but one side for the moment he allowed it to burn. Maybe three hundred yards up the slope from where Sosa, Vargas and Bandini now swung out of their saddles in response to this second pre-arranged signal. Then all three of them moved back along the column, Vargas rasping orders in a harsh whisper. All the men dismounted, their movements stiff from being in their saddles so long. Only Vincente Vallejo had been instructed to do more than get off his horse – and he moved forward to gather up the reins of the three animals that had been temporarily abandoned by the trio of men who halted alongside the wagon.

'Okay, *Señor* Edge,' Sosa said, and gave the courtesy title the tone of a curse as he scowled out of the frame of the dust- and sweat-stained bandage. 'I guess you know that our journey's end is beyond the hill here? Now you get down from the wagon and come up with us to join Ramon. Get the girl, Manuel. Raoul, bring the spyglass. *Darse prisa!* Ramon signals there is ample time. But the situation can change *pronto,* uh?'

He had drawn the Remington as he commanded Edge to climb down off the wagon. Now he thumbed back the hammer and aimed it at the half-breed, emphasising his demand for haste. His harsh voice had awakened the women and they had already started to climb out of the rear of the former ambulance before Vargas and Bandini got there. But the gaunt-faced, thicker set and shorter of the pair cursed Conchita for her tardiness, anyway. And then fastened a grip on her upper arm that was tight enough to spread a grimace of pain across her sleep-heavy face. Edge was down on the ground by then, and maybe it helped him to conceal his reaction to the girl's hurt that his head and every joint in his frame were complaining at how he was moving after so many hours of inactivity aboard the wagon.

'*Bueno, vamos!*' Sosa snapped, after he saw Margarita hand to Bandini a brass telescope. Then he gestured with the revolver and told Edge: 'A man like you misses little, uh? You heard the whistle and saw the match that was struck. You will lead the way!'

The half-breed moved away from the front wheel of the wagon and for a few moments after he had nothing to lean against he was conscious of the danger that he could stumble and fall. But, irrespective of the consequences, he felt it essential to his self-respect that he stayed on his feet. And he achieved this by a combination of sheer willpower and pushing the dipper deep down into his much diminished reserves of stamina. He doubted at first if it was going to succeed, but when he had taken twenty-three strides – carefully counted as a part of the mind-over-matter exercise – the ground remained stable beneath his booted feet and the jagged skyline of the ridge upon which he fixed his gaze ceased to tilt one way and then another, and came into sharp focus against the less dark and far more nebulous sky that was its backdrop.

If anyone – the men who stood or squatted on their haunches beside their horses or those who trailed him – said anything to him during those first twenty-three paces, he was deaf to their words. But no gun muzzle nor hand was shoved into his back to urge him to greater speed. And when he was clear-headed and in natural control of his muscles again, he realised there had been no need to goad him. For he was on the correct, shortest route between the end of the stalled column and the place where the light had shown, and he had made good progress up the slope. A slope that had got steeper the higher they climbed – away from the trail and then toward it again after it had completed a wide swing across the hill and back to reduce the grade for wagon traffic.

They passed close to where Ramon Cabello's gelding was hitched, relieved of the saddle, to a thicket of black greasewood. And a few seconds and steps later, the man with the neat black moustache and very white teeth who was the finest marksman in the bandit group greeted:

'*Buenas tardes, amigos.*' And his use of the Mexican language was taken up by all those who joined him. But Sosa established the tenor of the talk when he snarled:

'It is not such a good evening for my uncle at this moment, friend!'

'I am sorry, you are right, Esteban,' the chastened Cabello answered.

'How goes it?'

'Preparations are still being made. See for yourself.'

The man sent ahead to scout out the situation at San Sarita had chosen a good vantage point from which to keep surreptitious watch on the town. It was some fifty feet to the right of where the trail crested the rise, at a place where some ragged chollas and stunted sagebrush clung to pockets of soil among a scattering of weather-smoothed, small rock outcrops. The hatless head of one man, or those of half a dozen men, could have shown in dark silhouette among the rocks and vegetation on this section of skyline, and – provided there was no undue movement – it was unlikely any but the most eagle-eyed of sentries in the town beyond the ridge would spot the watchers.

Because the ground at this point took a sudden upward surge to form a hillock on which the cover of rocks and brush and cacti were spread, it was safe for everyone else to remain standing while Sosa, hatless and with the revolver holstered, went down on his belly and snaked his way up to where he could see beyond the ridge.

He had taken the telescope from Raoul Bandini, who drew his Smith and Wesson but held it low at his side, pointed at the ground. For by then Manuel Vargas had drawn a knife which he held with the blade a half inch from Conchita's throat as he continued to fist his other hand tightly around her upper arm. Although Vargas's sombrero brim cast a deep shadow over his face, Edge could sense the eyes of the thickset man glowering at him with heavy menace. Bandini, who had removed his hat so that it hung down his back, did not have the kind of face that was capable of projecting an intimidating threat: but he looked tense enough to lunge into violently reckless action at the merest hint of trouble. Perhaps he was sweating a little more than Cabello was seen to be – and Edge felt he was himself as the humidity of the night air seemed to get more oppressive by the moment. Certainly Bandini was breathing the heaviest of all of them from the exertion of the climb up to the ridge by the steepest route.

Conchita looked like a working waxen figure of a young girl as she stood perfectly still, unmoving except for her breathing, in the grip of Vargas and under the threat of the knife that glinted in the moonlight.

'Hey, Edge!' Sosa called down from the ridge in a rasping whisper. And although no more than a minute could have elapsed since the last word had been spoken, they were all startled by the unexpected end to the tense silence. 'Come on up here with me.'

'Do as he says,' Bandini felt the need to instruct. And some of the tautness in his expression and stance seemed to be drained off with the opportunity to speak.

'You will be with Esteban, American, but some of your thoughts will be with us, uh?' Vargas growled as the half-breed dropped down on to all fours.

Conchita winced and the merest suggestion of a cry of pain escaped her twisted lips.

'I don't think you'll ever be out of my thoughts, Vargas,' Edge told him before he started up the hillock. 'Until the day you die.'

A few seconds later, complying with gestured directions,

he was lying flat out to the left of Esteban Sosa, their bandaged heads at either side of a small block of granite and moon shadowed by sagebrush.

'Take a good look and do not think about anything except what you see,' the Mexican instructed in a strained tone that was taut with anxiety rather than threat. 'While my uncle's life is in danger, I am as expendable as Conchita Lopez.'

Edge had only glanced at Sosa as he began to speak the warning. Then he raked his narrow-eyed gaze over the familiar scene to the north of the ridge. Familiar from a different viewpoint, anyway: for he had spent two nights and a day in the town of San Sarita. Fitfully sleeping or broodingly awake as he began the gruelling process of coming to terms with a degree of failure he had never before experienced. But that was all in the past . . .

The ground immediately below the north side of the ridge fell away more sharply than to the south. And the trail took more than just the one sweeping curve to negotiate the steep slope. Then the terrain swept more gently down to meet a band of rugged high plains country that spread up toward the international border between Sonora and the Territory of New Mexico. The small town of San Sarita was sited on the rim of the mesa-featured plain, on the final area of flatland before the ground started to rise up to the high ridge. On the lower, gentle slope there was sufficient soil to support a number of small farmsteads: and tobacco, corn and cotton were the crops in most of the fields. Here and there was a small meadow on which, during the day, a few head of cattle grazed.

Having seen this pastoral vista in the sun-bright harshness of the Mexican daylight, Edge knew that the idyllically serene setting that it appeared to be in the misty moonlight was a totally false impression. The *labriegos* who worked the fields and ran the livestock were used-up shells of men, old before their time from the long days of backbreaking labour to provide for their families.

The townspeople were, for the most part, in better shape. Many of them maybe as grindingly poor as the farming families: but the work they were required to do in the making and supplying of what could not be grown or reared on the farmsteads was not so cruelly exhausting. The town in which they lived was no more than a single plaza with short streets leading off it from three sides. To the west, the street became the trail that curved across the farm land in a swing that headed it toward a meandering southward direction, up and over the ridge fifty feet to the left of where Edge and Esteban Sosa lay. Northward was the continuation of the trail that led up to and over the border. The street that left the plaza to the east led at its end to the town cemetery that was sited at the base of a towering cliff face that was a part of the same massive rock formation on which the two secret watchers were positioned.

'The message I received was true,' Sosa rasped, continuing to speak in his native tongue. 'Those Federale bastards intend that the execution of José Sanchez shall be the highlight of a fiesta.'

He spat a globule of saliva over the ridge. It hit the rocky ground no more than five feet away. The closest building of San Sarita in his line of fire – the Federale post that was spread across the entire southern side of the plaza – was more than a half mile distant. The brass telescope, which Edge saw from an inscription had a similar United States Army heritage as the ambulance, had the effect of reducing the range by a little over a third. But some definition was lost because the spyglass had been mistreated and its rear lens was badly scratched.

The half-breed first studied the close-up but blurred view of the plaza which had at its centre a group of contorted cottonwoods, struggling to survive, with four benches beneath the gnarled limbs of the trees. These were permanent features of San Sarita's central square. Tonight, much else was cluttering its rock-hard, rutted and potholed, dust-powdered surface. And predominant among the new features was the gallows that was in process of being constructed in front of the double-gated entrance of the Federale post. It was not being built from scratch. Instead, under the supervision of a non-com Edge thought he recognised as Sergeant Mendoza, uniformed figures were carrying it out section by section from somewhere in the post. And re-erecting it in a place where the doomed bandit chief could be publicly strung up without need for the audience to leave the immediate scene of their revels.

And revelry was certainly planned. For along the west side of the plaza, out front of a restaurant and a general and a hardware store, a run of trestle tables had been set up, and these were being laden with dishes and bowls of food and bottles of wine and liquor. Civilians were attending to these chores – women bringing the food out of the restaurant and men carrying the bottles across the plaza from the cantina on the opposite side. The men had to make a detour immediately outside the cantina, for here there had been set out an arc of chairs and music stands and, facing these, a conductor's podium. A fiddle, two guitars and a trumpet were already resting on four of the chairs.

At present, enough lamplight spilled out from the unshuttered windows and open doorways of every building that faced the plaza for everyone to see what he or she was doing. But a mixture of Federales and civilians were engaged in erecting ten-foot high poles with torches which would be ignited later at their tops.

'Hey, you notice something about all those bastards down there, Edge?' Sosa asked as the half-breed tracked the telescope away from the well-lit centre of activity to scrutinise the north trail and the one that left town westward but soon swung to the south.

Edge replied in American, in a pensive tone that suggested his mind was elsewhere. 'Yeah, feller. From up here it looks like everyone down there is really excited about the hoedown that's going to happen soon.'

'That is right!' the Mexican snapped bitterly in his own language. 'Those people my uncle plans to make proud and prosperous by winning back the land the *gringos* stole from us are happy at what is to take place! They laugh and sing and joke with the women even more than do the Federales, it seems to me.'

'It's nothing personal, I'd guess,' Edge countered evenly as he raked the telescope slowly back and forth across the fields that flanked the trail toward the foot of the slope. Now double checked with the naked eye and decided there were just the two sentries posted on each trail into San Sarita. Who, from their positions, were able to maintain an effective watch over broad areas of the country to the south, west and north, which were the only directions from which a mass attack could be launched.

'Nothing personal to laugh and joke before a great patriot is to be executed?' the young Mexican rasped, and snatched back the telescope that was offered to him.

'Figure parties are few and far between in that town,' Edge explained. 'Little enough to enjoy at any time. With the eating and drinking and music making, it's my guess those people would be just as happy if it was you, me or the new captain at the post who was going to get his neck stretched.'

Sosa scowled and gestured with his bandaged head for Edge to slide back down the hillock. 'That is beside the point, as far as José Sanchez is concerned,' he growled as he wriggled backwards out of the brush and rock in the wake of the half-breed.

'You have a plan, Esteban?' Cabello asked brightly when they were both standing to their full heights with the others again.

'I have not been up there admiring the view, idiot!' Sosa snarled at the eager-to-please man. Who clamped his lips tightly together to hide the very white teeth that had been displayed in a flashing smile. 'Of course I have a plan!

Your part in it is to return to your post and keep watch. And signal to me if you see anything down there you think I should know about!'

He had drawn the Remington again and now he levelled it at Edge as he handed the telescope to Cabello. The man with the neat little moustache was patently pleased to be left on his own while Sosa was in such an irascible mood. And he wasted no time in obeying the order – the spyglass in one hand and the Sharps breechloader with which he was such an expert in the other. This as Bandini holstered his revolver with a barely perceptible sigh. And Vargas returned the knife to the sheath on his belt, but maintained his painfully tight grip on Conchita's arm.

She vented several truncated groans during the walk back down the slope to the trail. She and Vargas led the way on the return, with Edge immediately behind them and the other two Mexicans bringing up the rear. Everyone sweated a great deal and all of them breathed raggedly as they approached the group of men and women gathered beside the wagon.

'Does it look good for us to rescue José, Esteban?' Vincente Vallejo called out anxiously.

Sosa spat forcefully at the ground and thrust the revolver back in his holster, apparently considering it unnecessary to keep the half-breed covered now he was again so heavily outnumbered. 'It would look much better,' he snapped, 'if many more of my uncle's band had rallied to join us!'

His dark eyes were alight with fury barely held in check as he raked his gaze back and forth over the group of men and women. Who, individually and as a whole, looked more dejectedly wretched with each moment that elapsed while Sosa scanned them.

'Esteban, none of us here is to blame for those who are missing,' Francisco Cortes argued from where he still sat up on the wagon seat.

Sosa jerked his head around, on the point of snarling a contemptuous retort at the ugly little man. But Bandini was the first to speak, and although his voice lacked power, the wisdom of what he said demanded attention.

'He's right, Esteban. We are here and ready to do whatever is asked of us to free José Sanchez. Who can say how many of us do not know of the danger he is in? How many learned of it too late? How many are at this moment making haste to join us here? But we cannot lose time waiting for men and women who might come. Or might not. Just as we should not use time with recriminations among ourselves while the Federales prepare to – '

'Right, here is what I have decided we should do!' Sosa broke in at length, as nods of agreement with Bandini became more numerous and more emphatic with each point he made. The fires were still in his eyes, but they burned less fiercely and he looked at nobody for longer than a part of a second as he began to pace up and down a ten-stride line as he spoke. 'I and five men will ride in the back of the wagon which will be driven into San Sarita by Edge. He is a gringo and so would not be suspected of plotting to free my uncle in any circumstances. But he is even less likely to arouse suspicion because he is known to the townspeople of San Sarita and many of the Federales.'

Most of the group listened with rapt attention and Edge was one of these – nothing in their expressions revealing at this stage what they thought of Sosa's plan. Raoul Bandini looked like he approved, or perhaps he was still relishing the satisfaction of having won personal approval from men who normally had scant respect for him. Manuel Vargas wore a quiet grin that showed not a hint of sadism as he continued to keep his fist clenched around Conchita's upper arm: and probably he was enjoying the fact that his decision at the start to keep Edge alive had been vindicated by the very man who had wanted him vengefully dead. While the girl . . .

She stood with her head bowed and her shoulders stooped in an attitude of misery and defeat. And each time that Edge saw her thus when he surveyed Sosa's silently attentive audience, he felt a mixture of futile anger that she was still enduring the pain and humiliation of captivity, and relief that her face was averted so that he was not able to see what was in her eyes.

'Once the advance party is in town, we will create a diversion,' Sosa went on, warming to his own strategy that he seemed to think improved with the telling. 'With an explosion or gunfire. It will be sufficient to bring all the Federales running to discover the cause. Then the rest of you will take advantage of this to sneak into town. We will all meet together at the rear of the cantina, and by this time the Federales will have forgotten the diversion and be enjoying the fiesta. Then we will enter the post and rescue José Sanchez. By stealth if it is possible. With an open assault if it is not. We will then make our escape with Federale horses, since our own mounts will remain here. As will Conchita Lopez, of course. In the care of Francisco Cortes.'

He curtailed his pacing and fastened his gaze on the face of the half-breed as he voiced the implied threat. Showed the thinnest of smiles in the brief silence before he asked: 'You realise, of course, that you are not essential to our efforts, gringo? Perhaps one of the women would serve equally well as driver of the wagon? Federale guards are as easily charmed by a pretty woman as other men? Or we could abandon the use of the wagon. Wait until the fiesta is under way and – '

'No one's indispensable, feller,' Edge broke in, speaking American.

Sosa expanded the thin smile to a broad grin and his mood infected most of the others. There were gasps, sighs, grunts and some shuffling of feet as the tension was abruptly dispelled in the oppressively humid air: just before, or so it seemed, it was about to impress its palpable presence in the night with a raucous crackling sound. Then Sosa said in the half-breed's language:

'So okay, we have the understanding, uh?'

'No, feller.'

There was a burst of angry and shocked talk. Ended when Sosa snarled:

'Que demonios?'

'Daddy . . . ?' Conchita cried. Then caught her breath when Vargas smoothly drew his knife and held it at her throat. Much closer this time, so that the blade actually touched the pulsing flesh.

'*Madre de Dios*, no jokes now, *hombre!*' the ugly, dwarfish man up on the wagon seat implored and there was something akin to plaintiveness in his voice. 'Always he makes the crazy jokes at the craziest of times, Esteban! I beg of you to hear him out before you do something you could regret! For José's sake?'

When Edge swung his cool-eyed gaze back at the other man with a bandaged head, he saw that Sosa's right hand was draped over the butt of the Remington. But the young Mexican did not draw the revolver – like he was afraid he could not control his own actions if he should bring the gun to the aim.

'No sweat, feller,' Edge told him evenly to end a short, highly charged silence. 'Nobody being indispensable doesn't have to mean anybody has to be dispensed with. For no good reason.'

'*Y eso?*' Sosa hissed the exclamation through clenched teeth.

'Your plan stinks.'

Esteban Sosa, who was facing Edge over a distance of some six or seven feet, closed his hand around the butt of the Remington. But confined the release of anger to a Mexican obscenity that came out so forcefully it burst his teeth and lips apart. It was Raoul Bandini, rigid with tension, who snatched his revolver out of the holster, snarling a cruder curse. His draw was also clumsily lacking in finesse. And Edge saw this telegraphed to him from some four feet to his left. So was prepared to respond to the instinctive reactions of a nervous man who he did not trust to think before he completed the dangerous move.

Edge pivoted on his left leg and swung his right up off the ground. Used his arms for balance as he whirled through a half turn. But, a part second after the top of his boot's toecap impacted with the crotch of Raoul Bandini, he started to push his arms above his head in the unmistakable gesture of surrender. He was still leaning sideways from the waist when he began this. But before the injured man's scream had risen to the limit of its shrillness and while the revolver he had hurled away was still sailing through the air, the half-breed was standing upright, both feet on the ground and hands as high as he could get them.

By now Sosa had his Remington out of the holster and aimed at Edge's chest, left of centre. A barrage of harshly whispered exclamations began to compete with the now less strident moans of Bandini as he dropped to his knees and toppled onto his side, both hands clawed at the source of the intense pain.

'*Silencio mundo!*' Sosa snarled, and held back until even Bandini had managed to stifle his whimpering before he told Edge: 'Except for you, *gringo.* You I allow to tell me why I should not kill you for this?'

'Daddy!' Conchita pleaded.

'*Esteban, cuidado!*' Vargas advised.

'I say only the *gringo!*' Sosa raged. And brandished the revolver.

'Not much to choose between the report of that Remington and his S and W, I'd guess,' Edge said evenly. 'And maybe the sound of a shot fired this side of the ridge will reach the men on guard on the trail on the other side?'

'Nothing disturbs the dead, which is what you will be . . . Now, why is my plan so bad it causes you to risk your life? And that of your daughter?'

'Because I've got a better one. That doesn't need any overstrung fellers like your buddy there to make it work. Or screw it up.'

The start of some more talk was instantly checked when

Sosa snapped: 'How better, *gringo?* And keep this in mind, *amigo!* You have refused to do what I want of you. And so if I fail to be impressed by your idea for getting my uncle out of the hands of the Federales, you are of no further use to me.'

'Nor is your so-beautiful young daughter!' Vargas growled.

'So impress me with your brilliance, uh?'

Edge explained what he had in mind and during the less than a minute and a half it took to accomplish this, everyone gazed fixedly at him. Most expressed mounting interest and many heads were bobbing with eager approval by the time he was through. Then there was a babble of talk that in the main urged the scowling Sosa to agree to the half-breed's suggestions. But, because the plan directly involved Francisco Cortes, the ugly little man on the wagon seat was vociferously against it. And Raoul Bandini, too, snarled through teeth gritted in pain that Edge's idea would not work: this as he struggled to his feet but was not yet able to stand fully upright as he continued to clutch his injured crotch.

'*Basta ya!*' Sosa ordered and the voices were instantly silenced. He gave the matter a few more moments of thought, then nodded once. 'A little better, perhaps,' he allowed. 'Yes, I like what you say, *gringo.*'

Cortes groaned, then arranged his misshapen features into an expression of resignation that he was again to be handed the short end of the stick.

Bandini began to object: 'Esteban, *creo que no* – '

'We have nothing to lose by agreeing,' Sosa broke in, the earlier scowl softening toward a thoughtful frown. 'It is the same as if my plan . . . But with less risk to us. The life of his daughter in exchange for the life of my uncle.'

'So we want much the same thing, feller,' Edge said. 'Relatively speaking.'

Cortes sent a stream of saliva between the rumps of the two horses in the wagon traces and growled caustically:

'You will probably die with a joke on your lips, *hombre.*'

'Prepare to do what is needed!' Sosa snapped. 'This is no laughing matter.'

'I am not laughing at him!' Bandini rasped sourly, staying where he was as the others began to move about him. He had managed to stand at his full height, but he still clutched at the base of his belly with both hands.

'Yeah, you're showing some real self-control now, feller,' Edge drawled. 'Since you took such a firm grip on yourself.'

Fifteen

HIS HEAD began to thud again as he drove the wagon down the twisting trail toward the town where the preparations for a fiesta were now almost complete. And he was sweating so heavily it felt as if every thread of his clothing was pasted to the clammy flesh it covered. He also experienced the burning taste of bile at the back of his throat at short, irregular intervals. He was sick and would get sick to his stomach if he did not consciously struggle to fight down the threat of nausea.

The two Federales watched the wagon roll toward them, their carbines held sloppily at port arms. And as he closed with the uniformed men he attempted to will himself to stop sweating and to control the need to vomit without gulping. But, as the time drew near when he would have to break the tight-lipped silence he had maintained since climbing back aboard the wagon, the image of the lovely young girl with a knife blade pressed against her skin became more clearly defined in his mind. While at the same time he was increasingly conscious of being watched through the telescope from up on the ridge.

'*Alto ahi!*' the Federale corporal ordered.

Edge reined in the team to roll the wagon to a halt so that the seat was level with the men at the side of the trail. And now he felt abruptly icily calm. His throat burned with the aftertaste of acid bile and his skull seemed to have shrunk so that it was squeezing his brain, but he was certain he could contend with this degree of discomfort without it affecting what he had to do. Then, just for a moment, he almost shuddered with the cold as the sweat ceased to ooze from his every pore.

'Something wrong?' he asked in American and his voice sounded more or less normal to his own ear. And the men who peered up at him, their faces illuminated by the misty moonlight, continued to express bored indifference. He did not recognise either of them, from the time he spent in San Sarita or from the group he had seen when Sanchez was captured.

'Only that we were assigned this duty and will miss the fiesta,' the enlisted man complained bitterly.

'Say, you're one of the Americans who was at *El Estelar Cantina* the night Captain Gomez was killed?' the non-com recalled.

'Right, *cabo*. Edge.'

The corporal stepped back and eyed the dilapidated wagon with disdain. 'Have you gone into the freight business, *señor?*' He gestured for the enlisted man to go to the rear of the rig while he moved to take a closer look at the horses. And was even less impressed by the sway-backed geldings than the wagon they were hauling.

'It beats walking, feller,' the half-breed answered, starting to feel better by the moment as he became self-confidently aware that he was in assured control of his own destiny again. So that the raising of a hand to touch fingertips to the bloodstained bandage around his head was a considered move not caused by the easily bearable ache beneath it. 'After I lost my horse the hard way, it had to be either this or walking.'

'*Algunos que otro cajas,* Alfonso,' the man at the rear reported after peering inside the wagon and seeing a number of wooden crates were stacked there.

The corporal nodded as he moved away from the horses. Asked: 'Have you seen anyone else on the road from Punto de Honra, *Señor* Edge?'

The half-breed shook his head and began to mistrust his new feeling of well-being. Maybe it was just another symptom of his sickness.

'*Buenas noches,*' the non-com said and made a sideways gesture of his head. 'I hope you will enjoy the fiesta.'

'Fiesta, cabo?'

'*Si.* It is to mark the appointment of Captain Miranda as the new *comandante* at San Sarita. And to celebrate the capture of the bandit known as *El Malo* who will be hanged later tonight, *señor.* This is why I ask if you have seen anyone on the road. It may be that some of those who have followed *El Malo* in the past will attempt to prevent the execution. I do not think this will happen, but I suppose it is wise to mount the guard.'

Edge flicked the reins and clucked to the horses. Had driven the wagon about halfway around the first curve through the farmsteaded area to the south west of town when Francisco Cortes rasped out of the aperture close to his right ear:

'Is that sonofabitch going to get a surprise, *hombre?* Him and the rest of them that don't think we care about José Sanchez being – '

'For as long as your buddies have my daughter, I care one hell of a lot about what happens to your top hand, feller. Easily enough to kill anyone who screws up my plan to save his lousy neck.'

The ugly little man who had emerged from the crate in which he had been hiding, and now peered out of the slit at the silent and darkened farmsteads on either side of the trail, failed to catch the implied threat that was latent in Edge's not quite even tone. And there was fervour in his own voice as he agreed:

'I can understand that, *hombre.* That Esteban Sosa will not hesitate to order your daughter killed if – '

'I said anybody, Cortes,' Edge broke in on him again. 'So best you get back to pretending there's nobody but me aboard this wagon.'

'*Hombre,* I do not think you are yet in a position to threaten – '

From the town there came the sound of a trumpet. For the first few notes the playing was tentative and the music seemed like the introduction to a mournful dirge that would have been wailingly appropriate to the misty night and the gallows. But a few moments later, as the pole-mounted torches were set brightly alight, the guitars, fiddles and a harmonica swelled the sound and the tune at once burst into a confidently lively beat.

'Get back into your box, little man!' the half-breed said, and the wagon was still far enough away from the suddenly noisy centre of San Sarita so that he did not have to raise his voice for the harshly spoken words to be heard by his passenger.

'You make me sound like the animal so many of my *compañero de armas* treat me – '

'All human beings are animals,' Edge countered the embittered accusation, and spoke more loudly now, as he heard the ugly little man moving to return to his hiding place.

'Some human beings are more human than others, *hombre.* And I had thought of you as one of these.'

'Some animals are more wild than others, feller,' Edge muttered, unconcerned that Cortes probably did not hear him.

The wagon was down off the slope now, and rolling around the final curve toward the start of the street that entered the plaza from the west side. There were some voices raised in raucous, undisciplined singing: in discord with the music. Other voices were shouting in good-natured ridicule of the singers' efforts and there was much laughter. On the level straightaway into town, Edge was able to keep control of the wagon with just one hand on the reins, and he dug out the makings and deftly rolled a cigarette. The paper was made a little moist by the sticky sweat of his fingertips, but his hand did not shake. And he let the match burn almost all the way down the stick after he had lit the tobacco: drew back his thin lips and narrowed his eyes to mere threads of glinting hardness to smile with ice-cold satisfaction at the way the flame was like something unflickeringly solid until he shook it out and tossed the dead and blackened twist of wood to the ground at the point where the trail became the street.

He sure as hell felt like a wild animal. One that had been hunted and injured. Endured pain and degradation while in captivity. Had been forced to become tame. No, that was wrong. An animal of the truly wild kind can never be tamed. It just sometimes appears that this has been achieved. Remove all the restraints and the wild streak is immediately the predominant driving force.

But he had not yet been unshackled from all restraints, of course. Would not be in such a situation until Conchita Lopez was as genuinely free as he appeared to be as he drove the wagon on to the crowded, noisy, brightly-lit plaza at the centre of the small town. He had both hands back on the reins again now, and was poised to grab for the brake lever should the horses in the traces be spooked by the noise and light and bustle. But whatever spirit had been in the sway-backed animals at the start of the trip had apparently been squeezed out of them during the day-long trek to town. And they seemed oblivious to all else but the reins as the music blared, the torches flared and smoked, and people jostled out of the path of the wagon – men, women and children of all ages and variously dressed in ragged work clothes or the best of what was in their meagre wardrobes: and uniforms, of course.

There were shouts and screams, most of it good natured, at the dishevelled man with the bandaged head who passingly interrupted the festivities as he drove the wagon carefully onto the plaza. Sometimes his name was called out, and here and there he recognised a face in the mostly happy throng.

There was one of the elderly merchants who had been

playing poker in the shade of the cottonwoods when he first rode into San Sarita just a few short days ago. And Manuel Martinez who ran the local cantina. Fernando Ruiz who was *patron* of the restaurant. A half dozen or so Federales from when he was last in town. Sergeant Mendoza and two or three other uniformed men from the ambush at the *barranca.*

Those who shouted and laughed the loudest had maybe started to drink before the music was struck up and the torches were lit to signal that the fiesta was officially under way. They were determined to kick over the traces, no matter what. But even the majority of the more sober and staid – civilians and Federales alike – showed not a sign of being disturbed by the scaffold with the noosed rope suspended from the gallows: which cast many shadows in different directions because of the light from the surrounding torches. Some of the older children were even playing games on the sinister looking structure – bounding up the steps, across the boards that rang hollowly to their footfalls, and then leaping off the other side. A few of the taller boys even sprang up to try to hook a crooked arm through the noose.

'*Hey, a su salud, Americano!*' a sergeant who was familiar to Edge yelled happily, and thrust a half-full bottle of wine up at him.

He accepted the gift and acknowledged the toast with a nod and a smile that the non-com did not see failed to inject warmth into the glittering slits of the hooded eyes. For the two men looked at each other for just a moment: before the sergeant returned his eager attention to the full-bodied woman who grasped his arm, and the half-breed resumed his careful survey of the milling crowd. He could not see any officers in the press of people, and marked his approval of this by taking a swig from the bottle to swill the dryness from his throat. This as he tugged on the reins to swing the rig into a tight turn around the gallows to head for the post entrance. And now he grinned with something akin to relief: for he was sure the occasional glower and scowl that had been directed at him from out of the throng of people were triggered by mere irritation with his intrusion upon the festivities. Nobody suspected him of coming to town to make trouble.

Both wrought-iron gates in the fifteen-foot-high wall that extended the full width of the plaza's southern side were wide open, and there was no sentry to guard the entrance to the Federale post. Which had once been a fine Spanish colonial style private house. But that had been long ago, and since the Federales had taken it over the house and grounds and the surrounding wall had been neglected by the men quartered there, and wantonly ravaged by anti-Government factions.

The gates were rusted and the wall at either side was bulging and crumbling and daubed with mostly old and faded slogans. Beyond the entrance, through which Edge drove the rig without hindrance, was a hard-packed dirt area with a flagpole at the centre. The flag had been hauled down at sunset. What had started out as a stone-encircled flowerbed at the base of the pole still boasted enough loosened dusty soil to support a few straggly but obviously tough weeds. He steered the wagon slowly around this tiny area of what might be termed cultivated ground and reined in the team out front of the two-storey house with its weathered but still elegant porticoed entrance.

Then he took another, longer drink of the wine that was red and warm and full-flavoured. For the sheer enjoyment of the taste this time, as he raked his gaze over the facade of the thirty-roomed mansion. None of the windows at the front spilled light, but some light did reach weakly to the open doorway from somewhere in the rear of the building. He had already seen that the stable block – dating back as far as the house – and the ugly, more recently built barrack blocks and other newer buildings to either side were in darkness.

Suddenly, he snatched the bottle away from his lips: and

an instant later there was not a trace of pleasure on his heavily bristled face. For he had just recalled the name of the sergeant who gave him the bottle. Ramon LOPEZ! As in Conchita Lopez! Why, there was a woman who worked in the town restaurant whose name was CONCHITA Romanos . . .

But it was not much of a coincidence. The given and the family names were not exactly uncommon in Mexico. It was just the fates twisting the knife again . . . Or was it? For surely it was a good thing for him to be reminded that he now had a beautiful young daughter who was in great danger. And only he could prevent her from being brutally killed. So there was no time and there should not even have been the inclination to indulge in the luxury of taking a drink! Unless to steady his nerves? But that was not his way. Not even when his body was run with sweat, he could taste bile in his throat again and his head throbbed in painful time to the music.

'*Que* . . . ' a man called from just inside the threshold of the house. Then stepped into sight and switched to American and lightened his tone as he recognised the half-breed in process of swinging down off the wagon seat. 'Hey, it's you, *Señor* Edge? What are you doing driving a – '

'How are things, feller?' Edge cut in evenly as he swung around and showed a grin to the skinny, good looking, twenty-five-year-old corporal whose name was also Lopez – the younger brother of the sergeant. 'I got something in the back here your new *comandante* ought to see.'

'*Capitan* Miranda? I do not know. *Señor* Edge . . . He does not wish to be disturbed. He is in his quarters, *entretenido* the other officers. With the good American whiskey. Before it is time to hang José Sanchez. I think he would not like it if – '

'Best go bring him, *cabo*,' Edge advised earnestly. 'What I've got in the back of this wagon will make his night for him.'

He set the bottle down on the footboard of the wagon and delved into his shirt pocket for the part-smoked cigarette he had stowed there while he sampled the wine.

'What shall I say to – '

The half-breed hung the unlit cigarette at the side of his mouth and moved toward the rear of the rig. And there was irritation in his tone as he broke in again on the disconcerted Corporal Lopez: 'That it's something he'll find highly interesting, *cabo*. And hurry it up, will you? Time's awasting and the way everyone's eating and drinking so fast out there on the plaza, could be there'll be nothing left for latecomers.'

The skinny young Federale hesitated for just a few more moments. While he gazed fixedly across the portico and down the steps at Edge who now stood at the rear of the one-time United States Army ambulance. Then, after a softly rasped: '*Que demonios!*' he swung out of sight again. And reappeared with a carbine to augment the revolver in his unfastened hip holster. But he carried it at port arms – a sloppy but at least completely-equipped sentry as he scuttled into the depths of the rich family's mansion become a headquarters of law and order.

'Okay, out of the box and shove the gun back here, feller,' Edge ordered, his voice low and taut. The attack of feverishness had been quelled while he spoke with the sentry. But he continued to experience a nagging worry that his customary ability to think coolly in the most danger-fraught situation was likely to desert him at any moment.

'*Loco bastardos,* that is what we are to be here like this, *hombre!*' Francisco Cortes muttered as he clambered out of the crate, flexing the muscles of his small frame to get rid of the cramped stiffness. Then he reached back into the crate, brought out a double barrel shotgun and held it possessively for perhaps two seconds before he pushed it reluctantly toward Edge. 'Stark, raving mad is what we are!'

Edge glanced at the house doorway, but decided he only thought he had heard voices and footfalls. For the noise from the plaza was too raucous. He accepted the shotgun by the barrels and turned it so the stock was toward him when he rested it on the floor. Then he eyed the ugly little man with the most fleeting of smiles as he drawled: 'And all along I didn't figure you were crazy about any of this.'

Sixteen

NOW FOOTFALLS thudded on the uncarpeted floor of the hallway, and a few moments later elongated shadows were cast out over the threshold. Three men halted in the doorway, two of them in front of the third. Corporal Lopez was at the rear of the small group, standing rigidly to attention. A lieutenant who was slightly older than the non-com was familiar to Edge by sight, but he had never known his name. The man to his right was the tall and slender, classically handsome Captain Miranda. Both officers were smartly turned out in their dress uniforms but were minus their caps. They perhaps looked especially neat because of the contrast with Lopez whose uniform was so ill-fitting. Both officers were smoking cigars, and both had the bright eyes and flushed complexions of men who had recently enjoyed some easy-going social drinking. But they were far from drunk, and there was a kind of studied amusement in their expressions as they peered out into the night at Edge.

'The sentry informs me you have something I should be desperate to see, Mr Edge?' Miranda opened, his tone of voice so cultured it approached natural arrogance.

The half-breed inclined his head and stepped a single pace back from the rear of the wagon. Made an ushering gesture with both hands as he answered: 'I said it would make your night for you, Captain.'

It was the lieutenant who responded with words as

Miranda stepped out of the doorway. He spoke American, too, but without any educated polish. 'The last time you had any business with the *comandante* of this post, *gringo,* it ended in killing.'

'Come, come, my good friend,' Miranda chided without rancour. 'As you told me yourself, that was hardly the fault of Mr Edge, who was simply seeking to recover property stolen from him. Gomez was a sadistic fool who . . .'

The captain had reached the rear of the wagon and his cultured voice faltered as he peered inside: was able to clearly see what was there in the light of the match that Edge struck as he moved up alongside the uniformed man.

'*Madre de Dios!*'

'*Cabo!*' the lieutenant gasped, instantly realising that something was badly wrong. He took a pace out of the doorway and the corporal was just a moment behind him. And as he hurled away his cigar and fumbled to unfasten his holster flap, Lopez clumsily struggled to bring his carbine down from his shoulder and level it in a double-handed grip.

'*Espera!*' Miranda snarled. His tone was shrill with fear but his face was hard set as he swung his head to glower at the men on the portico. They came to a sudden halt and his tone was more restrained as he ordered: '*Armas.*'

Lopez snapped to attention and ported his carbine again.

The lieutenant dropped his hand away from the still-buttoned holster, and asked apprehensively: '*Que pasa, comandante?*'

Everyone sweated heavily. And Edge had to consciously renounce a light-headed notion that the exuberant sounds from the plaza contributed to the humidity of the night air. But he acknowledged it was logical to assume that his head hurt worse because of the noise.

Miranda dropped his cigar to the ground and carefully turned his boot heel back and forth on it to mash into extinction every glowing ember of tobacco. As he did this, he returned his gaze to the interior of the wagon and replied in American: 'The matter, *teniente,* is that we are all in imminent danger of being blown to bits.'

Edge lit the part-smoked cigarette and flicked the match several feet away from the wagon. This as the Federale officer at his side stepped back a half pace: so that the two men on the portico could see the half-breed had a single handed grip around the frame of the shotgun – held it so its twin barrels rested at an upward angle against the rear of the wagon bed.

'There are explosives inside?' the lieutenant forced out in a strangled tone. And took a half pace backward himself.

'The new dynamite, it seems to me,' Miranda replied, his composure returning by the moment. 'Many sticks.'

From out of the wagon interior, Francisco Cortes informed mournfully: 'Thirty-two of them, *hombre.* I counted them as they were placed – '

'The *gringo* has a hostage?'

'Not a hostage, Lieutenant,' Edge corrected.

'A patriot who is willing to die for the cause he believes in!' Cortes augmented with a reasonable degree of fervour.

Edge glanced in the direction the shotgun was aimed. And Miranda's grimacing attention was also held there for a moment more. The both of them seeing in the meagre moonlight that filtered into the rear of the wagon the same ominous sight that had earlier been brightly – and dangerously – illuminated by the flaring match. The dwarfishly-built man with the misshapen face no longer wore his *serape* and he was also minus his usual straw sombrero. Thus there was nothing to obscure or throw a shadow over the sinister sticks of dynamite that were hung around his waist from his belt and lashed to his chest by two loops of rope.

'They are at the back as well as at the front,' the ugly little man assured miserably. And turned briefly sideways-on to display the truth of what he said.

'You have come for José Sanchez?' Miranda asked of the half-breed.

'Right, feller.'

'And unless I agree to hand him over to you, you will fire the gun at the human bomb?'

'You've got it.'

'*Comandante?*'

'*Silencio, idiota!*' Miranda flung at the junior officer, but did not shift his cool gaze from the gaunt face of the half-breed. 'If you are not bluffing, *señor,* you will die also.'

'I ain't bluffing.'

'You are a man of few words.'

'Actions speak louder, feller. In this case it'll be a whole lot louder.'

He and Edge locked gazes for a moment longer, before the Federale wrenched his head around and ordered: 'Bring the prisoner!'

'*No mas que* – ' the lieutenant began to argue.

'*No me ponga peros, tonto!*' Miranda cut in. And when he spoke his native language the extent of his fear was plainly evident. He suddenly seemed to realise this, and the conscious effort he made to bring himself back under control could be seen on his sweat-beaded face and in the way he took a deep breath.

'Lieutenant, do as I tell you,' he went on, and his tone was now that of a long-suffering parent trying to be patient with a recalcitrant child. 'Take Lopez with you. His help will be needed because of Sanchez's injury. You will tell the guard nothing of why the prisoner is being taken early from the cell. Do this now, my friend. And remember this. If you or anyone attempts to interfere with the plans of *Señor* Edge, you or they should pray I do not survive. For if I do so, the culprits will face court martial. Now, please do as you have been ordered.'

The lieutenant recognised this mood of his superior officer. He was on tenterhooks, waiting for Miranda to be through. Then he instantly swung around, rasped a command to the stone-faced non-com, and the both of them hurried into the building.

'*El Malo* is injured?' Cortes asked anxiously.

'It will take a few minutes,' Miranda said to Edge. 'The cells are in the basement.'

'I don't have a watch, feller. But something's ticking away in my guts. It'll tell me if your boys are taking too long.'

'How is *El Malo* injured?' Cortes insisted.

'A minor leg wound!' the captain snapped. 'The noose would have killed him before that did.' He had directed the most fleeting of sneering glances at the worried Cortes. Now eyed Edge again with what seemed to be genuine interest. 'They have a hold on you, I think?'

'My daughter, feller.'

Miranda nodded. '*Si*. You would rather die than live knowing you had not done everything in your power to protect her?'

'Everyone's prepared to die for something.'

'You are counting on the belief that I am not prepared to sacrifice myself for a mere bandit?'

'The only sure thing in life is death, Captain. All else is long odds or short, and sometimes it's necessary to figure them.'

Now the Federale officer merely gestured with his head toward the hapless little man inside the wagon: perhaps because he did not like to look at the deadly sticks of dynamite threatened by the twin muzzles of the shotgun. 'Why such a ploy as this? A man rather than a –'

'A man can go wherever I want him,' Edge broke in, constantly looking away from Miranda toward the open doorway of the former mansion. 'This feller can, anyway – decked out the way he is. And since I didn't know too much about what was happening here in San Sarita tonight, I had to play it by ear.'

'When you have Sanchez here, what then?' the captain

asked as he, too, began to cast agitated glances across the portico at the lighted doorway.

'We take a drive up to the ridge south of town, feller.'

'*Nosotros?*' Miranda exclaimed, swallowed hard and translated: 'We? You do not think I – '

'So you are willing to die on account of Sanchez? Let's get it over with – '

He had tossed away the cigarette and taken a two-handed grip on the shotgun before the aristocratic Federale officer was able to find his voice after gulping twice more.

'No! What will happen at the ridge, *Señor* Edge? Will you still be playing it by ear then?'

There was an abrupt end to the music. Applause thundered. As the noise diminished to shouting and laughter, Miranda stared toward the brightly-lit scene beyond the open gateway. He had to peer past Edge to do this and the half-breed could see at close quarters the frantic light in the man's dark eyes and the runnels of sweat that coursed down his recently shaven face. It was almost as if the man was willing the music and dancing to start up again – afraid that anything less than a frenetic level of sound would signal a squeezing of the shotgun's two triggers. And when the music burst forth again, his face lit with a broad smile of relief.

'Hey, these pigs do not lie to me!?' José Sanchez exclaimed. 'They didn't come to get me to string me up!'

Miranda snapped his head around and the smile died when he saw the tall, powerfully built figure of the bandit chief on the portico. Sanchez was standing between the grim-faced lieutenant and the nervous-looking corporal, able to remain on his feet with the help of a walking cane. His grin was almost as bright as Miranda's had been – until something warned him to mistrust the situation.

'What's in this for you, *gringo?*' he snarled.

'It is all right, *jefe!*' Cortes called excitedly and suspicion gave way to confusion on the fleshy face of Sanchez. 'It is me, Francisco! This *hombre* is with us! Esteban and

Manuel and many more of our *compadres* are waiting for us to – '

'You ain't going to be hung, feller,' Edge rasped. 'But if you don't do what I tell you real fast, you'll come to an even stickier end.'

Miranda took another half step backwards to ensure Sanchez could see the gun in the half-breed's grasp. And said icily: 'It is aimed at many sticks of dynamite, *amigo!*'

'*Treinta y dos, jefe!*' Cortes called tremulously.

'You got nothing to lose but your life, Sanchez,' Edge pointed out. 'And a couple of minutes ago that wasn't worth a bent *peso*.'

'Do it, *estupido hijo de puta!*' Miranda snarled. 'He means it. If you – '

'Okay, *gringo*,' Sanchez announced with an emphatic nod of the head. Then he spread another broad smile across his face. 'On this *ocasion*, the *notorio El Malo* will save the lives instead of taking them. *Gringo*, you tell me what you want of me, uh?'

The music that had re-started so energetically as if by Captain Miranda's willpower had gradually slowed in tempo and become almost soporific. For long periods, as Edge issued terse instructions that were quickly complied with, just a trumpet wailed. Then, every now and again, guitar strings were struck and immediately silenced. No voices could be heard until a woman began to sing a love song. By which time the wagon was ready to leave from in front of the portico of the once fine mansion. There was nobody on the portico then – the lieutenant and the non-com were inside the house behind the closed door. José Sanchez and the *comandante* of the San Sarita Federale post were up on the seat of the erstwhile ambulance: the bandit chief with the reins in his hands and Miranda disarmed of his revolver. Edge had climbed into the rear of the wagon and was peering out through the slit between the heads of the grim-faced driver and passenger. His features were impassive. The shotgun, uncocked now, he held in one hand down at his side. Francisco Cortes was seated on an upended crate near the rear, muttering in a manner that suggested he was probably offering up a prayer for deliverance. And certainly he crossed himself hurriedly when the half-breed commanded softly through the aperture:

'Okay, let's get this show on the road.' Then he thumbed back both hammers of the shotgun and in the wake of a low cry of alarm from Cortes, added: 'And hope we don't bomb.'

Seventeen

THE WOMAN who was singing of a love that was lost to her forever had a fine and perhaps beautiful voice.

Edge, who was no music lover, came to this instinctive conclusion as the wagon was steered around the stone-encircled base of the flagpole. Then he silently cursed himself for a fool as the sway-backed team hauled their burden wearily toward the open gateway in the wall. His brain beneath its bullet-furrowed skull had set his mind wandering off along an inconsequential track again. Even if it was the Swedish Nightingale herself on the plaza, and Jenny Lind was performing to the playing of some famous visiting European orchestra, what the hell difference did it make?

The wagon would be seen again as an unwelcome intrusion on the evening's entertainment. But it would not be allowed to roll across the plaza unhindered this time. For the first person to do a double take and recognise the two men up on the seat would not keep the discovery a secret . . .

His throat felt dry, but there was no acrid taste of bile in it. His stomach, that had begun to churn just before Sanchez was delivered out of the house, was now calm. His mind raced over the reduced options but his head no longer ached. He was aware of his bristled, sweat-beaded features resuming their customary impassive set after the scowl of self anger was banished. He was genuinely devoid of all emotion as the wagon rolled between the rusted, wrought-iron gates and angled to the left, to go around the scaffold with the gallows that threw shadows in so many directions. He was now fully committed to going through with this audacious plan to save the life of his daughter: or he would die in the attempt and take as many people as he had to with him. The vast majority of them innocent, maybe. But if that was how it had to be, then so be it. There was no other way after he had come this far. And no more time to doubt his own actions or to try to predict what others would do.

The crowd had divided into two groups. The larger section was gathered on the eastern side of the plaza, listening with rapt attention to the melancholy song. The rest were spread out at the long run of tables on the other side of the clump of cottonwoods: eating and drinking from the plentiful supplies with the kind of unseemly haste that suggested they feared a halt would be called before they had taken their fill. The most voracious eaters seemed to be the children who had earlier worked up an appetite with games on the scaffold. Most of the men in the area of the liquor table wore the drab grey uniforms of Federales.

'*Maldita sea,* half your pigs are drunk as skunks!' Sanchez rasped, fear in his tone.

'*Me importa un bledo, bandito!*' Miranda countered, coldly contemptuous of the man at his side. 'Watch and listen, *amigo!* And I will give the great *jefe* a lesson in how to handle men!'

'*Gringo?*' Sanchez rasped, still afraid of the situation. But also angered by the insulting attitude of Miranda.

'No sweat, feller,' the half-breed drawled. 'The captain knows what kind of an explosive situation we have here. Do like he says.'

Sanchez murmured bitterly: '*Cuando llegue la hora o el momento, comandante!*'

He spat between the rumps of the two horses. The woman, who did not have a beautiful face to match her voice, brought the song to an abrupt halt. This was how it was meant to end, for there was no surprised pause before the applause commenced. And then this came to a more faltering conclusion as shouts of alarm from across the plaza captured the attention of the appreciative audience.

'Stop the wagon!' Miranda told Sanchez in Mexican, his voice low but firm.

Edge used the same language to stress: 'Do it!'

Most voices that had been raised in alarmed query or angry exclamation were diminished as the wagon jerked to a halt midway across the corner of the plaza between the post entrance and the start of the street that led out to the south trail. And within moments just the voice of Sergeant Mendoza was clearly audible against a murmuring of many others. This as he strode purposefully through the throng: which was mostly unmoving until he barked:

'You men, come with me! All children go to your parents! All civilians withdraw to the – '

'Sergeant!' Miranda bellowed. 'It is I who will give the orders!'

Everyone on the brightly-lit plaza responded to the commanding tone of the man's voice. From Mendoza down to the youngest of the children. And there was a stunned silence, during which all seemed rooted to where they stood, sweating and tense. Until the officer went on:

'There is no need to panic, but you have to be told this wagon is laden with a large amount of high explosives!'

A chorus of voices were raised to express shock and fear. Many people began to back away, further isolating the stalled rig. A few women dashed forward, intent upon reaching children who were too afraid to move as they peered up wide-eyed at the two hard-faced men on the wagon seat.

'He said – ' Sanchez began to roar in anger.

'I said there is no need for panic!' Miranda cut in on the other man. There was just the threat of rage in back of his harsh tone. And most of the noise and movement was curtailed. Mendoza rapped out terse orders that brought to the plaza a silence that was kept from being absolute by the soft hissing and crackling sounds of the overhead torches. 'That is good,' the Federale captain said. 'The explosive will only be detonated if there is an attempt to prevent this wagon reaching the ridge to the south of San Sarita. I detail you, Sergeant, to maintain order here until my junior officers emerge from the post. All right, Sanchez, drive on.'

The non-com made as if to advance on the wagon, his mouth opening to form the first word of an objection. But something in Miranda's handsome face was sufficiently forceful to change the man's mind. And as the rig rolled into motion, Mendoza whirled, thrust his arms in the air and bellowed:

'Everybody remain silent! Nobody will move!'

A child wailed in fear. There was a discordant twang of strings as a hand brushed accidentally across a guitar. A dog barked from the northern fringe of town. The hooves of the two geldings clopped and the timbers of the dilapidated wagon creaked in counterpoint to the squeaking of two ungreased wheel hubs.

'You did well, pig,' Sanchez said flatly as he ran a bare arm over the sticky sweat on his forehead while the wagon rolled down the street. 'But you have the uniform with the gold braid that demands respect. I . . . I remain in command of my men because they know I am the best of them all.'

'That is the absolute truth!' Cortcs confirmed enthusiastically. He had been peering out of the rear of the wagon and as he turned around he grinned his relief that Miranda's edict was being obeyed – no one was following them. But his high spirits were immediately dashed when he saw the twin muzzles of the shotgun continued to draw a bead on him.

'It ain't over yet, feller,' Edge told him in American.

'And it won't be over even after we're past the pickets south of town.'

The ugly little man nodded emphatically, and then only the wagon and horses broke the silence until the two uniformed figures stepped out onto the trail where it started to climb steeply away from the area of farmsteads.

'What is wrong? Why has the music and dancing and . . . Oh, Captain Miranda! I did not . . . Attention!'

The corporal looked like there were a hundred more questions he wanted to ask as he ported his carbine and came rigidly erect. The enlisted man, who assumed the same rock-like stance, stared in utter amazement at José Sanchez.

'You are relieved of your duty here,' Miranda told them coldly. 'Report to Sergeant Mendoza in the town. At the double. Move!'

'Sir!'

Both men broke into a loping run to the same side of the wagon as Sanchez flicked the reins to start the horses. And it was the rescued bandit chief who spoke first, and chose the American language.

'Now I'm not going to say I'm ungrateful for what's happening here, uh? But is anybody ready to tell me how and why it's all happening the way it is?'

'I may be permitted, *hombre?*' Cortes asked eagerly, moving carefully forward as the wagon bed tilted on the steeper grade.

'You like to talk, feller,' Edge told him. 'And you've got yourself a willing listener.'

'Two,' Miranda corrected. 'I, also, am an interested party.'

Sanchez vented a harsh gaffaw, then growled: 'But it is no longer a necktie party with me as the most important guest, uh?'

Edge remained standing so that he was able to maintain his watch through the slit. And he only occasionally glanced down at the ugly little man who sat on the upended crate again. There was no need to break in on the account that Cortes gave. For it was accurate and concise, and probably the tension of the circumstances acted to dissuade him from wandering away from the point. When he was through, Sanchez said in amazement:

'My little Conchita is the daughter of this *gringo?*'

'*Si, jefe!*' the little man confirmed eagerly. Then swallowed hard after he glanced up and saw the hardness in Edge's features. And hurried to add: 'But you should not speak disrespectfully of her to this *hombre,* who – '

'Of course, *amigo,* I could not,' Sanchez assured. 'How could I say anything bad about such a fine . . . And you, Francisco? You were the *voluntario* for this most dangerous rescue of me?'

'*Si, jefe!*' Cortes exclaimed, and shot a surreptitious glance at the half-breed. Was caught in the act and spread across his misshapen features a look that pleaded for understanding and support of the lie.

'I picked him, feller,' Edge growled through the aperture. 'I figured I wouldn't get so many gripes from the others if he was the patsy. Only he did.'

'Because I was afraid, *jefe!*' Cortes blurted defensively.

'That I can understand, *mi amigo,*' Sanchez placated in a detached tone as he peered up at the ridge, anxious to see in the misty moonlight a first glimpse of his men on the skyline. 'But after you have shown such *bravura* tonight, Francisco, all will hold you in high respect.'

The man with thirty-two sticks of dynamite lashed to his dwarfish frame grinned with pride. He had failed to recognise from the tone of voice that the man he admired so much was talking for the mere sake of saying something. Perhaps as a prop to his composure as he scanned the skyline over varying perspectives as he steered the struggling team around the sharp turns of the steeply climbing trail.

'Hold it right here, feller,' Edge instructed when the wagon was about to start up the final stretch of the trail that angled some two hundred yards across the slope to its crest.

'*Ni pensarlo!*' Sanchez snarled. And made to crack the reins for a dash to the ridge.

'So let's all find out what hell is like!' Edge snapped.

He took a two-handed grip on the shotgun and whirled to press the twin muzzles against the dynamite lashed to the chest of Cortes.

'*José, lo dice en serio!*' the little man screamed, flinging himself back against the side of the wagon.

The rig came to a sudden halt as Sanchez snarled: '*So!*'

'*Cretino!*' Miranda gasped breathlessly. 'Is it not obvious to you that a man like this means business? You will get us all blown to pieces!'

'Enjoy your name-calling, pig!' the bandit chief taunted. 'Soon I will be *El Malo* again and one day you will – ' He was forced to break off and vent a strangled cry of pain.

'*Señor* Edge, what is to happen now?' Miranda asked evenly, and sounded fully in control of himself after the moments of panic.

'Just sit tight, feller,' the half-breed answered as he gestured with the shotgun for the trembling, sweat-drenched Cortes to rise from the crate and climb down from the wagon.

'I think the pig is having to sit very tight, *gringo,*' Sanchez rasped, obviously still in pain. 'To keep from filling his pants with the – '

'You want some more of this?' Miranda snapped.

'*Marrano!*' Sanchez said bitterly.

Then Edge, the shotgun pressed into the back of Cortes, was in a position alongside the wagon to see what had caused the bandit's new agony. For the Federale still held the walking cane in a way that threatened another rap on the bullet-shattered kneecap. The appearance of the two men below the seat of the rig drew the quizzical attention of the two up there. Until Esteban Sosa called from among the rocks and brush on the ridge:

'Hey, José! You are okay?'

'Tell him the truth, feller,' Edge encouraged after Sanchez had glanced eagerly upward, then anxiously back at the half-breed.

'Okay, *amigo!*' Then, after Miranda had thrust the walking cane across his thighs. 'A wound in the leg! *Poco cosa!* I can make it with a stick!'

'Edge, you are ready?' Sosa called.

'Sure.'

There was movement on the ridge to the left of the broken ground behind which Sosa was concealed. Then the slender form of Conchita Lopez appeared on the trail at the crest of the hill. She was leading a saddled horse by the reins.

'Help your boss down, feller,' Edge told Cortes.

Sanchez needed the assistance of the ugly little man, and even with it, he sweated and sometimes vented small cries of pain when his smashed kneecap protested the movement.

'You get down here too, Captain,' the half-breed instructed and spared the time to direct a glance back at San Sarita below. Where the plaza was empty of people. But in the light of the torches that spilled past the gallows on the scaffold and through the gateway into the Federale post, it could be seen that many uniformed figures were bustling to and fro. There were horses, too.

'I am to be handed over to the – ' Miranda began in a tone close to resignation as he climbed down from the seat.

'Feller up there named Ramon Cabello,' Edge cut in. 'Pretty good shot with a rifle by all accounts. Wouldn't want your men to get the idea I made you a sitting target.'

'*Comprender, lo siento mucho,*' the Federale apologised as he glanced anxiously at the ridge. And licked some beads of sweat from his top lip.

'I am here to be handed over to – ' Sanchez began harshly.

'Just hope that the girl starts down as soon as you start

up, feller,' Edge told him. 'For all our sakes. Move it.'

'*Si, gracias,*' the crippled bandit chief acknowledged. And began to hobble forward, not yet expert with the cane.

Conchita started down the trail, and gave a gentle tug on the reins so that the half-breed's chestnut gelding came with her.

Edge made an equally gentle motion with the shotgun against the sweat-sodden shirt of Francisco Cortes and murmured: 'Off you go, *amigo*. And remember, one wrong move – you and your boss won't just be dead. You'll be gone, too.'

'*Si, si!*' Cortes blurted. '*No lo quiera Dios. Adios, hombre.*'

He went in the wake of Sanchez, who attempted to hurry so that the gap did not close between himself and the ugly little man carrying so much dynamite. When he realised his injured leg would not allow this, he began to snarl obscenity-laced commands at Cortes. But Cortes refused to slow down, go back or veer to the side: sobbed as he struggled to convince Sanchez he was certain Edge would not hesitate to explode the awesome threat into lethal reality.

Miranda said in a rasping whisper: 'I think there is something you have overlooked, my friend.'

'There's still time, I guess,' Edge allowed as he shifted his attention briefly away from the trail on which Conchita and the horse came down at the same gruellingly slow pace as the hobbling man and the one laden with dynamite went up. Briefly directed his glinting-eyed gaze toward the town, where a double file column of mounted Federales were trotting through the post gateway and angling across the plaza.

'When the girl and those two pieces of excrement meet, all are in the same danger of being blown to bits. And surely it will be assumed by the bandit pigs that you will not cause – '

'Like I said earlier, Captain,' the half-breed reminded. 'The only sure thing in life is that it'll end in death. I've figured the odds the best that I can. And the way I saw it, they'll figure they've got the best of the deal and will let her come on down to me.' He shrugged. 'But that ain't certain. So we'll just have to wait and see.'

Miranda nodded. Then asked with a wry tone in his voice: 'I suppose, too, you have figured the odds, *señor,* on escaping the rope that still hangs from the gallows in the plaza? Assuming this is successful.'

He waved a hand toward the trail up to the ridge.

'Was going to mention that, Captain. I have a deal to offer you.'

'You do?' He seemed to welcome the even-tenored discussion as a kind of safety valve for the tension. But he continued to sweat as much as Edge, for a different reason.

'Let them take off and I'll show you where they've started to hole up since the last *comandante* of the San Sarita post flushed them out of their last hide-out.'

There was about a fifty yard distance between the girl and horse and the two men now. At the foot of the slope, the front riders of the column had come to a halt at the point where the trail swung from west to south. The Federales behind began to fan out to each side.

'Ah, now there is a point you have certainly overlooked!' Miranda countered with a brief smile of triumph that momentarily masked his anxiety – until he looked at Edge as he explained: 'Since they are aware you know where this place is?'

The hard-set profile of the half-breed forewarned the aristocratic Federale officer that this aspect of the offered deal had been considered.

'Not if they think I'm dead, Captain.'

'But why would they think that?'

'I'm going to be crazy happy when the girl gets close. You'll see that and come at me. Grab the gun. I'll be too crazy happy to notice. Start running up to meet her. You'll wait until I'm close enough to go at her with a flying tackle. And you'll fire the shotgun.'

'But I don't – '

'You can probably kill me and her, too,' Edge went on, speaking at a faster rate but in the same monotone. 'And take a chance on you and your men gunning down Sanchez and a handful of his group in a running battle. Or you can aim low and trap the whole bunch in a *barranca* they figure they can't be caught in.'

Miranda looked in the same direction as Edge and scowled his indecision when he saw the double line of mounted uniformed men at the foot of the hill. Then the two of them swung their heads to peer at where just ten paces separated the girl with the horse behind her and Sanchez who was trailed by Cortes.

'It is your life you are to place in my hands, *Señor* Edge. And that of the daughter for whom you have already risked so much. I must agree to your deal.'

'Much obliged, feller,' the half-breed acknowledged, and altered his stance so that the Federale officer would have easy access to the shotgun. Pain was pulsing in his head again and his voice sounded strange to his own ears. Beads of sweat hung on his eyelids and blurred his vision. There was a dryness in his throat that felt constricted and he needed to make a conscious effort to breathe.

José Sanchez and Conchita came to a halt, facing each other with only a matter of inches between them. Francisco Cortes did not stop. He swung into a clumsy about face as the reins slipped out of the girl's hand. Maybe there were tears of despair mixed in with the runnels of sweat that glistened in the misty moonlight on the misshapen face of the little man. Certainly the wail that was vented from his gaping mouth was of abject misery.

As he lunged into a headlong dash back down the trail.

As the girl stepped to the side and swung around: hooked an arm about the waist of Sanchez and began to help speed his hobbling progress up the hill.

As Sanchez bellowed: '*Romper fuego!*'

And the bandits on the ridge showed themselves as they obeyed the order – sprayed a barrage of gunfire down the slope.

'Goddamnit to hell!' Edge groaned, and shook his head violently as if he strove by this physical action to rid himself of the pain that pounded inside his skull.

The horse was spooked into a plunging bolt by the screaming of the suicidal Cortes. And kept galloping across the slope when the ugly little man made uglier by the dynamite he carried, curtailed his cry. And roared:

'You die, *hombre!* We will all die so that *El Malo* may live to have the great victory over the – '

He clutched at his right leg with both hands and pitched forward. Rolled over and over down the slope.

'Do it!' Edge snarled at Miranda as he continued to stare fixedly through the blur of salt moisture at the receding figures of Conchita and Sanchez. 'Take the Goddamn gun!'

The barrage of gunfire continued, but none of the shells were aimed at the wagon and the two men beside it.

'*Si!*' Miranda snapped, and reached to wrench the shotgun out of the half-breed's loosened grasp.

Edge powered forward.

Cortes scrambled to his feet.

Both barrels of the shotgun were discharged with a report that masked the fusillade of rifle fire for a moment.

Edge threw himself to the ground as he gave vent to an animalistic roar. That could have signalled his death agony or the depth of his despair.

The Federale officer hurled himself beneath the wagon.

Cortes took one staggering, lop-sided pace forward. Which maybe brought him to within fifty full paces of where the half-breed was sprawled. Then one or more bullets struck the dynamite. And the dwarfish man with the ugly face exploded into smithereens, the intense heat of the massive detonation acting to instantly dry every droplet of moisture from the tiny fragments of flesh and bone that were scattered in every direction. The impact of the blast seemed to have more palpable substance than the gritty remains of Francisco Cortes in the suddenly stinking night air.

The almost exhausted horses in the traces of the wagon pricked their ears and scraped at the ground, but did not have the spirit to bolt. The reeking smoke cleared and the air felt hotter and stickier than before the explosion.

Captain Miranda removed his arms from where they had been folded over his head and lifted his face away from the dusty ground. This as the buzzing in his ears from the detonation suddenly ended and he heard the half-breed rasp:

'Tell them I'm dead! You hear what I say, Miranda? Yell it to them! Goddamnit to hell, do it!'

The Federale peered at where Edge lay, face down across the trail: totally inert and not looking at him. Then he had to gulp a number of times to clear his throat before he was able to get sufficient volume into his voice. He used his native language to bellow:

'If it makes you feel even better, excrement, the American is dead! But I live, still! And I will not rest until you and the excrement which rides with you are all dead!'

Sanchez and the girl had been sent sprawling to the ground by the blast. By now had picked themselves up and made it almost to the ridge. A few moments later they were at the high point, and the men and women waiting there clustered in on either side of them.

'If we both live one million years, pig, you will never capture me again!' Sanchez challenged. 'But the American, there is the kind of man who might have been a match for me! I am sorry he is dead! I grieve for him almost as much as I grieve for my good and faithful friend, Francisco Cortes! For did they not both die so that I might live?'

He roared with harsh laughter. But cut short the sound and snarled for those about him to remain silent as Conchita raised her shrill voice to be heard:

'You will do something for me, Captain? You will place for me upon the grave of the man named Edge a wreath of beautiful flowers. And upon the wreath place a card on which is written: From Conchita, his beautiful daughter, who could never love him as she loves José Sanchez!' She vented a piercing laugh. Ended it to shout: 'You do this for me, Captain?'

The whole group on the ridge laughed. Until Sanchez snarled the order to leave. And within a moment they were all out of sight. Any sounds of their departure from the far side of the hill were masked by the thud of hooves as the Federales spurred their mounts up the north slope.

Miranda wriggled out from under the wagon, rose to his feet and dusted off his uniform with both hands as he approached where Edge lay. The half-breed was still sprawled out on his belly, unmoving and with his head turned so that his face was toward the now empty ridge.

'*Señor*, you are all right?' the Federale asked anxiously. 'I aimed low to – '

'I feel like death, maybe,' Edge answered in an embittered tone and still made no move to rise. 'But I plan on sticking around awhile longer.'

'Good,' Miranda acknowledged with a note of relief, as he delved into a pocket of his uniform jacket for a tin of cigars.

'It's said a family is supposed to enrich life, right?'

'I think so,' Miranda said as he struck a match and drew gratefully against the aromatically-burning tobacco.

'Whatever, feller,' Edge murmured and now began to rise. 'Until I can take mine with me, I ain't going to go.'

Eighteen

IT WAS just after a sun-bright dawn a day and two nights after the escape of José Sanchez when Edge rode his chestnut gelding over the crest of a rise to the south of Punto de Honra. And started on the downslope of the trail straightaway that cut across the foot of the long hill to the west, into which was cleaved the *barranca* which was the new bolt hole for *El Malo* and his bandit group.

Behind him were two wagons which were not at all like the one-time United States army ambulance in which he had travelled northward to his apparent death on the ridge above San Sarita. These were much newer, Mexican built rigs patterned on a tradesman's vehicle: painted in Federale livery and decked with the force crest on the side and rear panels. A Federale sergeant drove each wagon, and behind the vehicles rode a lieutenant, a corporal and eight enlisted men in a double-file column.

Edge knew that the sentries at the tree-screened mouth of the *barranca* were sure to be alert and would have seen him and the wagons and the column as soon as they came over the rise. But even if the guards were using the less than perfect telescope, he thought it unlikely they would be able to recognise him over such a range. Not least because he was wearing a wide-brimmed straw sombrero that threw deep shadow over his face and he was draped from shoulders to hips by a ragged *serape*. Also, he was supposed to be dead as far as the bandits were concerned.

And, anyway, it could well be the sentries up there in the trees at the top of the rocky and brush-featured slope did not even know what he looked like – were members of the group who had returned to it after Sanchez was freed from the San Sarita Federale post.

Not that it mattered, Edge acknowledged tacitly to himself as he tossed away the butt of the cigarette that had gone out as it hung from the side of his mouth. And he returned his hand to his face to rasp the back of it along the several day's growth of bristles on his jaw. All this consideration of inconsequentials was yet again a conscious exercise in blocking from his mind equally unimportant but far more painful thoughts.

About his bitch of a daughter and how she had made a sucker out of him!

He spat to the side and now needed to make an effort to force the scowl from his gaunt face. And achieved this to the extent of replacing the soured expression with a tight grin of satisfaction as he tugged gently on the right rein to head up the broken slope, on the same line Cortes had driven the wagon down it on an equally bright morning the day before yesterday. He did not take the trouble to look back and check that the wagons and riders were following him. He could tell from the clop of hooves on hard-packed ground and the creak of wagon timbers that all was well in this respect. And he had no desire to see on the grim-set faces of the uniformed men the expressions of the fear he could sense emanating from them.

Nor did he have the inclination to tell the men that he had a strong feeling they were no longer under surveillance from among that timber at the *barranca* mouth. For he could be wrong. The way so many of his instincts had gone haywire since the bullet gouged his skull, a lot of time would have to pass before he entirely trusted them again. And, anyway, it was good for men to carry a burden of fear into a dangerous situation. For when the shooting started they would be keyed up and ready to react: so that what had seemed a shameful streak of cowardice at one instant became a reflex sharpening benefit the next.

Edge felt fear as an ice-cold ball concentrated at the pit of his stomach. Even while he smiled with drawn-back lips and eyes that glinted without mirth. But the smile was not one of bravado. It was not in the nature of the man called Edge to harbour such a futile emotion. However, it was in his nature to experience quiet pleasure from the knowledge that he was again in possession of certain belongings which had seemed to be gone forever.

For at least the double-crossing sonsofbitches had unintentionally kept part of the deal when the girl let go of the reins and the gelding bolted. Recapturing the spooked horse was easy enough. He was winded but not hurt from the explosion: and the half-breed's sense of satisfaction was intensified when he found all his gear was intact on the saddle and in his bedroll. The Winchester he had taken off a dead man named Marshall Troy was in the boot. And in a saddlebag was his razor in the pouch on the necklet of beads and his gunbelt with the ancient Navy Colt – confiscated from a dead man named Calvin Terry – in the holster.

This morning, as he neared the naturally-screened mouth of the *barranca* on the Sierra Madre hilltop, he did not have the Navy Colt in the holster tied down to his right thigh. Instead, his own more modern Frontier Colt. Which Delmar Pyle stole from him and lost in a card game to an enlisted man at the San Sarita post. The man's name was Jaime Carrillo and he was young and an inveterate gambler: but he was not experienced enough at two-handed draw poker to recognise when he was being suckered by a cheat. So he had not been too concerned about losing the revolver to the legitimate owner – and he was even smiling as he left the table in *El Estelar Cantina.* For the half-breed had felt guilty enough about the cheating to work the cards so that the youngster won back the money he had lost before he was persuaded to bet the Colt.

This left Edge still totally out the money that Delmar Pyle had stolen from him and gambled away along the trail out of New Mexico and into Sonora. But he could live with the loss. It went against the grain to cheat an honest man, even for what he considered a valid motive.

Then, as he reined in his mount some twenty feet short of the thicket of brush and timber at the top of the slope, it required no conscious effort to void his mind of all thoughts about what was past. For there was no longer any danger that it would fill with futile notions of what he might wishfully desire for the future. It was time to put theory to the practical test and as he heeled the gelding forward again, and signalled with a hand gesture for the mounted Federales to ride by the stalled wagons and close up on him, he allowed himself to be certain of just one factor. Whatever was about to happen, he intended to exact vengeance for all that had been done to him since he took the shot to the head – so he certainly was not going to allow his mind to dwell on anything unconnected with achieving this aim.

The lieutenant, who was flabby-faced, pot-bellied and too old for his rank, rasped a low-voiced warning to the corporal: who was probably not yet twenty. Ordered him in Mexican to stay behind Edge. Which did not bother the half-breed. The non-com was young and eager. And although there was nervousness audible in the officer's tone, he spoke for the right reason. Miranda's agreement to go along with this approach to rounding up *El Malo* and his bandit group – as opposed to a full-scale frontal attack – was dependent upon Edge being the first man to risk getting blasted out of the saddle.

Beyond the timber, the chestnut gelding was reined in again. And because of the caution of the overweight lieutenant, all ten Federales were still in the cover of the trees and brush. Not yet visible targets for anyone in the *barranca* with its sloping floor and splayed sides that dead-ended six hundred feet away at the sixty-foot-high, hundred-and-fifty-foot-broad cliff face.

By the same token – they were also concealed in cover – there was not a living creature to be seen in what, north of the border, would be called a blind canyon. But they were down there, Edge was sure of that. And he was not indulging in wishful thinking. He had sensed watching eyes since he rode within sight of the *barranca* mouth, and he had known when the sentries, and those summoned to see what they had seen, withdrew. Now the hair stood up on the nape of his neck, and his pores were oozing much more sweat than was merited by the pleasant warmth of the newly risen sun.

Close by, his narrow-eyed gaze saw a confusion of sign in the dust. Hoof and foot prints, and even a trace here and there to show where the wagon abandoned at San Sarita had passed back and forth. A couple of matches and a dried-up cigar stub. Such sign could be followed on down the slope, beyond the adobe shack against the north wall where Edge had been a patient and a prisoner. All the way down to where the three tunnels started into the cliff face at the very bottom: this area still out of reach of the new day's sunlight. Doubtless there was plenty of sign, too, in the areas outside of the two tunnels that could be seen in the south cliff, and the one that old-time prospectors had dug into the north side.

All of the tracks and prints were useless to Edge and he saw them only as facets of the whole deserted, silent vista spread out before and below him. This as he saw again the *barranca* which he had last seen bustling with activity before the start of the trek to save Sanchez from the gallows. Now, as then, he realised there could be other mine tunnels hidden behind brush or boulders piled up from long-ago rockfalls. And also now, as then, he had no way of knowing which, if any, of the old mine workings provided an escape route out of the *barranca*.

'*Señor,* do you see anything?' the lieutenant whispered.

'Just what I figured I'd see, feller,' Edge muttered. Then did a double-take at something that he had seen to move on the periphery of his vision. Drew back his lips to show the most fleeting of smiles when he saw at this second glance that the fire out front of the small shack had not been entirely doused – an ember still gave up an occasional wisp of grey smoke. 'Everyone ready back there?'

'*Listo, señor,*' one of the enlisted men confirmed.

The lieutenant felt it necessary to elaborate: '*Dispuesto para el combate.*'

And Edge, impassive-faced again, touched his heels to the flanks of his horse to set off down the slope. Satisfied the still-wisping smoke confirmed the *barranca* was not so eerily empty as it appeared. At the same time, he accepted his limitations as a normal human being: with time-honed instincts but without any supernatural powers. In this instance, he surely had known from the outset there were hostile eyes watching him: but without some kind of physical evidence seen by his own eyes or heard with his own ears, he could not possibly know their position.

The Federales had swung out of their saddles. They emerged into the open behind him and, once clear of the trees and brush, spread out to either side of the mounted half-breed to form a single line of advance. Their fear as they offered themselves as targets to the guns of an unseen enemy had an almost palpable presence in the early morning air.

Each of the uniformed men carried his cabine at an angle across the front of his body. When the slow-moving line was complete, Edge slid his Winchester from the boot, and rode with the base of the stock resting on his right thigh so that the barrel pointed straight up at the cloudless sky.

Everyone breathed heavily.

Four hooves and ten pairs of booted feet stirred up powdery dust.

Dark eyes flicked back and forth across sockets.

Tongues darted out to lick salty lips.

Sweat-greased hands fisted with greater force than necessary around the frames and barrels of carbines.

Grey uniform tunics began to spread with deeper, damp patches at the armpits.

One man spat.

A second, at the far end of the line to the right, began to mutter in the low, reverent tones of a prayer.

The man who was advancing beside him rasped obscenely that it was too late for a sinner like him to try to talk his way into a heaven that didn't exist anyway.

Edge said: 'Far enough.'

He reined in his mount and cautiously took off his sombrero. Then placed it on the muzzle of the Winchester, which he thrust high in the air and began to move with a circular motion. In the surrounding silence, tense with the fear of death, the hat made a whooshing noise through the air. The low sun from behind sent long shadows. Edge was aware of the perplexed faces turned briefly toward him. The word *loco* was muttered scornfully several times.

'It ain't the hat that's going to throw lead at you!' Edge rasped. Then moved the rifle faster. Jerked it forward. To scale the spinning sombrero further down into the *barranca* than its shadow had been cast. A split second after the hat was sailing through the air, the stock of the rifle was against his shoulder and right cheek and his left hand was fisted in a rock-steady grip around the barrel. He cracked the first shot at the shack, pumped the repeater action and exploded a second toward the tunnel entrance nearby. Tracked the Winchester across the *barranca* as he worked the lever and blasted a third shot at one of the adits cut into the north wall.

Tension stretched time. It seemed to have been many seconds since the third bullet blasted out of the muzzle of the Winchester as the whirling sombrero closed with the rocky ground. And the Federales to either side of Edge remained in their rock-like attitudes of inaction. Seemingly unable to move the muscles of even their eyes, which stared fixedly at whatever they looked at when the first gunshot cracked out.

Then the hat hit the ground and the half-breed grimaced at the theatrical self-indulgence he had allowed himself with the arrogant gesture. He snarled:

'Get to it, Goddamnit!'

It wasn't their fault. The agreed signal was the first firing of the Winchester.

'*Pronto, pronto!*' the lieutenant yelled. And lunged forward, swinging his carbine down and turning it to aim in the direction he was lumbering.

But maybe the crazy game with the hat had served a useful purpose. Had proved to be more than a mere challenge . . . Held the bandits transfixed in their confusion for longer than the perplexed Federales.

The men were just part of a second later in plunging after the officer. Thrusting their weapons toward unseen targets as they overhauled the flabby lieutenant to reform the line of advance at the double.

Edge was giving them covering fire by then. His impassive face beneath the filthy bandage giving no clue to the sudden, gut-wrenching doubt that had gripped him. What if there was nobody down there in the shack and the old mine workings? That was no sweat. It would just leave him with egg on his face. But what if there were hundreds of men? Loyal followers of *El Malo,* fired with patriotic fervour? Men who were prepared to go through hell to have the chance to join the rebel army of José Sanchez as it marched to war against the United States? Such men would not be panicked into a reckless move against a handful of Government . . .

A single gunshot answered the one-man barrage laid down by Edge. Exploded out of one of the tunnel entrances at the lower end of the *barranca.*

The lieutenant bellowed an order and he and his men

broke from the line. Whirled and raced back up the slope without firing a shot. On past Edge and into the cover of the trees. As the half-breed continued to sit his gelding and blast shot after shot through the drifting black powder smoke of those which had gone before.

And now there was a similar pall of smoke building in the previously clear air of the *barranca's* far end. For that first shot had signalled a whole fusillade of others. Bullets cracked around the half-breed and now he was showing a killer's grin on his gaunt, heavily bristled face. The business with the sombrero had been as *loco* as several of the Federales had growled it to be. And he had been *loco* to give his imagination free rein. José Sanchez was a no account bandit with a dream he could never fulfil. Who had gathered about himself a bunch of other no-hopers. All of them the kind of men who would not be able to contain themselves if they saw they had the enemy on the run . . .

The hammer of the Winchester sprang forward behind an empty breech while the final expended shellcase was still twisting toward the ground. Men shouted at him from the trees. Others were shouting from a lot further away, in front of him. He glimpsed many men who had spilled out of the tunnel entrances. And he saw, too, that the door of the shack was now wide open. With gunsmoke and muzzle flashes exploding out of it. More men than had been on the trek to San Sarita were advancing up the slope. A large force, but not hundreds.

There was no time to look for familiar figures. No point. No inclination. He had been on borrowed time since he showed himself at the top of the hill. And this had started to run out a whole lot faster from the moment his shots had drawn a reply.

He thrust the empty Winchester into the boot, took up the reins with both hands and jerked at them to wheel the gelding as he thudded his heels to the flanks of the horse. Into his mind as he hunched low in the saddle and pressed himself against his mount's neck there came a vivid image of Ramon Cabello – the most expert marksman of the bunch – as he drew a bead on him with his sniper's rifle.

The cover of the trees seemed to be an impossible distance away. But they were close enough for him to see bark and twigs and leaves flying through the air as bullets smashed into them. He could not see any uniformed men and they no longer shrieked encouragement at him. Nor did they provide him with any covering fire. But they were not supposed to: for that was all part of the battle plan to flush out the bandits.

Then Edge was in the trees. Brought the gelding to a rearing, flailing, snorting halt as soon as he was out of sight of the men down in the *barranca.* Some of them kept up the barrage, firing blindly into the trees for several seconds. But then the gunshots faded away and the triumphant shouts of men tasting victory filled the air.

The half-breed was down off his horse by then. He hitched the reins to some brush and drew the Colt from his holster. Only then took the time to glance about himself. At the more than forty uniformed men who were hunkered down in the cover of the timber, cocked carbines at the ready.

Here there was an opportunity to recognise some men. Sergeant Mendoza and the Lopez brothers. Jaime Carrillo. The two lieutenants. And Captain Miranda. There was no talking as the men convinced they had their enemy in full retreat came far enough up the hill for the thud of their pumping feet to be heard amid their strident shouts. But expressions of excitement, fear, determination and cold impassivity revealed more emphatically than words could have done just what the men were thinking as they waited for the order.

Edge looked back at the aristocratic *comandante* after he had surveyed the entire body of men. And smiled coldly and nodded that he was impressed. Miranda's smile was warmer as he inclined his head in a mannered gesture of appreciation. Then he was rigid-framed and grim-faced as he drew the revolver from the already unfastened holster on his hip. Aimed it skywards and squeezed the trigger.

Every man responded as if the bullet that blasted from Miranda's Colt had cracked perilously close to him. He jerked up from his haunches and powered forward. Many – perhaps all – gave full-throated vent to their feelings as they burst clear of the timber. And suddenly the cacophony of gunfire again drowned out all other sounds.

Edge and the Federale captain lunged for the fringe of the trees in the wake of the bellowing men with the blazing guns. But it was not their intention to move as fast. So when they were in a position to gaze down into the *barranca* the running battle had already been carried some distance down the slope.

And the first casualties were slumped totally motionless in death or were writhing in fear and agony on the blood-stained ground. Bandits and Federales both had gone down in the opening exchange of fire as the surprise counter-attack was launched. And now, as the half-breed and the captain came to a halt, each holding a cocked but silent revolver, the brief battle became a brutal rout. When the bandits who had felt assured of victory just moments before were suddenly forced into terrified retreat. Their terror sparked and then fanned into enormity by the realisation that there could be no surrender. Only death. Because the Federales had been ordered to take no prisoners.

Thus, men either stood their ground and fired at the wave of uniformed figures plunging toward them – fired wildly behind them as they fled: or hurled away their weapons and ran in utter desperation. For they had already seen that anyone who came to a halt and thrust his empty hands in the air was savagely shot. Or clubbed to the ground with a rifle stock by one Federale so that another coming down the hill from behind was able to blast a revolver shot into the sprawled form.

'It shocks you, *amigo?*' Miranda yelled, grinning with

sadistic excitement as he looked at Edge after raking his gaze over the battleground.

'How's that, feller?' the half-breed answered evenly as he continued to peer down the slope.

'You look upon this victory in the making without pleasure.'

Edge sent a globule of saliva to the ground and shifted his glinting-eyed gaze from one bullet-shattered, blood-spattered corpse to another as he replied: 'I'm happy Manuel Vargas is in hell, feller. And that Antonio Diego has a bloody hole where his left eye used to be. That Ramon Cabello doesn't look so much of a ladykiller while he's choking on his own blood. Cabello I'd have preferred to kill myself, since he's the feller that shot me in the head. Diego ought to have been mine, too. On account of he was riding my horse and carrying my guns for awhile. But I'm happy enough they're dead.'

'Soon, all of the men who rode with José Sanchez will be dead!' Miranda predicted, rasping the threat menacingly through teeth exposed in the smile that became more filled with sadistic pleasure as each one of the defeated bandits became a crumpled corpse.

Edge nodded and eased the hammer of his revolver gently forward before he pushed the gun back into the tied-down holster. Then he hoisted the *serape* over his bandaged head, and used part of it to rub the sweat off his face before he dropped it to the ground. The attack was almost over now. The Federales were within a few yards of the apparently blind end of the *barranca*. Some still yelled in triumph or hatred but there were no more gunshots. If any of the bandits had survived the rout, they had gone from sight into the old mine workings. Some uniformed men moved into the tunnels. But they advanced cautiously now. Nervously aware that any of the enemy who had made the tunnels – or never emerged in the first place – knew that no prisoners were being taken. So had nothing to lose by putting up a fight. Other Federales started back up the slope, carrying out assignments ordered by the overweight lieutenant. Some checked on their own dead and wounded, of which there were something close to a dozen. The remainder made tentative approaches to the sprawled figures not in uniform – fired a flesh-twitching shot to make sure of any they were doubtful about. Now and then finished off at close range a bandit who had survived but was unconscious. Or played dead.

'So let's go see how many you missed by,' Edge drawled, and made to turn away from the corpse-littered scene that was now brightly lit by the sun which had risen above the tops of the trees.

'*Comandante!*' a man called.

And Miranda halted in the process of lighting a cigar to peer, with the half-breed, down at the adobe shack. Where Corporal Lopez who had called to the captain, and Jaime Carillo, were shepherding out of the building a half-dozen women who were variously cowed and afraid or sneeringly defiant. Conchita was not among them.

'Is that all of them?' Edge yelled when it was apparent there were no more to emerge from the shack. 'Dead or alive?'

'The one you seek, *señor,* she is not in the building!' Carillo supplied.

'*Comandante?*' the corporal posed again, and in the single word both a question and the preferred answer were implied.

And other Federales, spread far and wide over the floor of the *barranca*, peered between the women and the officer with looks in their eyes that matched the young non-com's tone of voice.

'To the victors go the spoils!' Miranda allowed with a magnanimous wave of a hand that held the freshly lit cigar. 'Do as you wish with them!'

A cheer was raised and all the women were prodded with rifle muzzles until they had their backs against the wall of the shack. While men who had completed the chores detailed to them hurried across to start a line.

A handgun was fired twice in quick succession. The sounds came from somewhere on the slope below the mouth of the *barranca*, and when the first shot cracked everyone froze for the instant until the second report. When the signal was recognised and all activity resumed again.

'It would seem likely you were right, *Señor* Edge,' Miranda said evenly as he watched the half-breed unhitch his horse from the tree branch.

'Sometimes it happens,' Edge drawled as he started to lead the gelding by the reins and the Federale officer fell in beside him.

They emerged into the direct glare of the early morning sun beyond the tree-filled mouth of the *barranca*. And went between the two wagons, the rear doors of which still hung open after the secret back-up force of Federales had climbed out. Not all the men who rode here in the wagons had joined the attack in the *barranca*. Ten had climbed into the saddles of the horses that were left in the timber. And had waited and watched the broken ground of the slope. Ready to gallop at high speed toward the first sign of a break-out from the escape tunnel Edge was convinced existed.

And it did exist. Exited in a rock-strewn hollow a hundred yards down the hill to the north of where the half-breed and the Federale captain moved away from the stalled wagons. Each of them eager for his own reasons to reach the tunnel exit: but neither with any reason to hurry. For José Sanchez, Esteban Sosa and Conchita were already secure captives. Encircled by the ring of carbine-aiming mounted Federales. The mouth of the escape tunnel, that emerged between two low outcrops of rock in the steepest side of the hollow, was blocked by Sergeant Mendoza and the lieutenant who had followed the two bandits and the girl.

Sanchez was seated on the ground, wincing with pain as

he clutched with both hands at his shattered right knee. Sosa was trying to appear defiantly unafraid as he stood to one side of the older man, glaring at Edge and Miranda. Conchita was on her knees at the other side of Sanchez, weeping and murmuring comforting words to him. But her attempt to appear something she was not could be seen to be as much of a pretence as Sosa's desperate charade. But it was equally obvious that Sanchez was suffering excrutiating agony from his leg wound. And out of this was triggered genuine rage as he lashed out at the girl and sent her sprawling on her side away from him.

Mendoza stepped forward and deftly withdrew the Remington from Sosa's holster.

The lieutenant needed to stoop to confiscate the revolver Sanchez packed.

Edge gazed fixedly at the whimpering, shuddering young girl. And felt physically and mentally numb. Which was something that had never happened to him before.

The lieutenant struck a match on a boulder to light a celebratory cigar and proclaimed brightly: 'It is as you wanted, is it not, Captain? All of them dead, except for *El Malo!*' There was depthless contempt in his use of the appellation. 'And even better, perhaps? This *heces* is his nephew, is he not? To hang him, too – '

He broke off suddenly and both he and Mendoza stepped hurriedly back. The way his voice had trailed off was pointed enough to draw the attention of Sanchez away from his injured leg and also penetrated through the girl's misery. But it was only after Miranda had drawn his revolver and cocked the hammer as he raked it to the aim that Esteban Sosa realised what was to happen.

'On the gallows as elsewhere, *mi amigo*,' the captain said coldly as Sosa gulped with terror and his face in the frame of bandages was contorted into ugliness, 'two is company and three makes a crowd.'

He squeezed the trigger. The bullet took the slim young man in the chest, left of centre. He remained standing for a stretched second, trying to bring up his hands to where the bloodstain blossomed on his shirt. Then he was dead on his feet and his staring eyes remained unseeingly open as he corkscrewed to the ground.

Sanchez needed to lean painfully forward to keep from being struck by the crumpling corpse.

Miranda had removed the cigar from between his lips to deliver the even-toned reason for the summary execution on this sunlit hillside. He took another elegant pull against the burning tobacco as he slid the still smoking Colt back into the holster. But removed the cigar from his mouth again as he turned to tell the half-breed:

'I intend to hang both of them, *Señor* Edge.'

Conchita caught her breath.

José Sanchez spat.

Edge was still feeling oddly numb and detached from the here and now of this grim situation. He had never experienced such a sense of impotence before. But for several days he had been feeling not the man he thought he had become. Now his voice sounded distant to his own ears when he replied to Miranda without shifting his narrow-eyed gaze from the tearstained, fear-twisted face of the girl:

'That so?'

'That is so. You have been of much assistance to me in bringing the criminals to justice. And I will honour the word I gave and not execute you for aiding the escape of this excrement. But she must hang.' His tone was cold and the gaze that Edge failed to meet was challenging. Then, just for a moment, Miranda was disconcerted at the lack of reaction from the half-breed, before he said: 'I have been given to understand that you object to having guns pointed at you?'

'Right, feller.'

'So I will not provoke you to retaliation by ordering any of my men to cover you with their weapons. But I tell you this, *mi amigo:* if you attempt to interfere with my plans to do as I intend with Sanchez and your daughter who is his mistress and *confidente* – '

'Daughter, ah!' Sanchez blurted contemptuously, the power of his emotions able to transcend the pain that so viciously gripped him. His dark eyes blazed hatred at Edge as he taunted: 'You think you played the fine trick on *El Malo,* uh? When you play dead. Then you bring the Federale pigs to where you know we make our camp. Where my men gather for the march against the United – '

'Get to the point, feller,' Edge cut in coldly, and his voice sounded more like it should to his own ears. And the sense of near paralysis began to desert him. He could think more clearly, too – enough to know to check the movement of his right hand toward the butt of his Colt when the ring of mounted men made to swing their carbines away from the prisoners toward him. 'What about my daughter?'

'That was the master trick, *gringo!* I cannot claim the credit. But I can claim that only the best of men ride with *El Malo! Hombres* with the *inteligencia,* uh? Not just the *valiente* fighters! And our women, too, uh?' He extended an arm and Conchita Lopez slithered with grateful eagerness into his embrace. And from the physical contact with his powerfully-built body she seemed also to draw on his emotions. For her lovely face was suddenly lit with a smile that was as filled with pride as his. 'It was all the lie, *Americano!* The lie built on the *pocos* things you spoke of when you were *delirante!* When you talk in the sleep. Did she not give the fine performance, by all accounts? To fool such a man as you, uh Edge?'

'*Si,* it is true!' the girl confirmed. And she was as scornful as Sanchez in her tone of voice and in her eyes that mocked the stone-faced half-breed. 'You are the *tonto,* that is sure! I surely twisted you around my little finger, didn't I? Like all daughters are supposed to be able to twist their daddies . . .'

Edge was no longer listening to her ranting voice as he

stared fixedly at her sneering face and saw, too, she had extended a finger from one tight fist. But not the little one of which she spoke. The middle one, thrust forcefully upwards in a crude gesture to match her expression and the tone of her voice. And as he looked at her in this hellcat attitude, he tried to come to terms with the revelation that she was not his flesh and blood. Which should have made it easier to swing away from her and begin to live with the fact this little whore had made a complete fool of him.

But that would take time. For now, the ring of mounted men with carbines at the ready were what guided his actions.

'*Señor* Edge,' Miranda said, and his insistent tone cut cleanly through into the private world where the half-breed had almost totally withdrawn.

'Yeah, Captain?' Edge replied as there came into his mind a vivid image of Morton Reed as the man was gunned down in his cantina. Before the garrulous Texan could stupidly blurt out that Conchita Lopez could not be what was claimed for her.

'I repeat, these are my prisoners and will be under my protection until it is time for them to be executed on the gallows at San Sarita. If you wish to take issue with this . . .'

'No, Captain,' Edge drawled, and swung sharply around and up into the saddle. Then his slitted eyes under their hooded lids glittered like threads of blue ice as he gazed at Conchita and murmured: 'It appears this is an unrelated issue.'

Nineteen

EDGE AND the parish priest of Pueblo Rojo – Father Claudio Rodrigues – were ready to leave El Mision de Vallecito at first light, after a night the half-breed had not intended to spend at the derelict church in the valley.

But weariness bordering on exhaustion had overtaken him the previous evening: and he had drifted lethargically into what might have been a shallow sleep as he half listened and indifferently watched the elderly priest prepare to make attonement as a part of his annual pilgrimage. But his punished body and ravaged mind was in need of more than a cat nap. Maybe the weak wine he had helped Rodrigues to drink had contributed to the depth of his sleep, too. And even the mere presence of the white-haired, clear-eyed, tall and slender priest could have encouraged the degree of relaxation he allowed himself to feel just before he sank without a struggle into a deep, long, untroubled sleep.

Or it had seemed untroubled to him. Until the priest asked:

'You will permit me to come with you to the town of San Sarita, *Señor* Edge?'

They were outside the arched doorway of the unimpressive church with the crumbled belltower. The sun was not yet risen and the post-dawn air was just beginning to lose the chill of night. The cassock-garbed priest had already saddled his sway-backed burro and now stood beside the doleful animal, holding his biretta in both hands as he watched Edge straighten up from checking the cinch buckle beneath the gelding.

'How'd you figure I'm heading for there, preacherman?' the half-breed answered with a query of his own. And although his tone was even, there was a glinting light in his slitted eyes that made an insistent demand for an honest response.

'Your sleep, it was *turbado*,' Father Rodrigues explained hurriedly and apologetically. 'It cannot be helped that I hear some of what you speak of . . . *Lo siento*.'

'Shit,' Edge rasped.

'May I go there, too?'

Edge was impassive again. And the shaking of his hands as he made a cigarette was barely perceptible. He said: 'This far out in the boondocks, preacherman, you live in a free country. You can go wherever you like, I guess.'

'I have the good *razon* for wishing to go there.'

'Something I yelled in my sleep?' Edge asked as he struck a match on the butt of his holster Colt and lit the cigarette. Then swung up into his saddle.

'*Señor?*'

'Your reason for wanting to go to San Sarita?'

Claudio Rodrigues shrugged his narrow shoulders. 'I have made my *expiacion* for past *pecado* . . . For those sins I committed since I last came here to El Mision de Vallecito. I have no wish to offend *el santa* . . . So soon, you understand?'

'No, preacherman, I don't.'

'I am a poor *parraco*. I seldom have the opportunity to travel far from Pueblo Rojo. San Sarita I have visited. Not often and always for the matters *eclesiastico*. For the good *razon*. To see my good friend Father Filipe Chevez, perhaps? To visit there without this . . . I would feel *malo*. Guilty, you know? When I should be with my *congregacion*. But if I visit with you, so much troubled in the spirits.

Because of your daughter? Who is not a good girl? And lives in San Sarita?'

'That all I raved about in my sleep?' Edge asked, scowling darkly.

'You did not rave, *señor*,' the priest corrected earnestly. 'You only talk. I do not understand much of what you say. Not because of the language . . . It is all not clear. The Federales . . . A *hombre* named Sanchez . . . ?'

The half-breed nodded and his face became impassive again as he said: 'Figure I've just got to go back to San Sarita, preacherman.' He touched fingertips to the blood-stained bandage on his hatless head as the first ray of morning sunlight shafted down on the mission church in the valley. 'Night's rest eased most of what ails my body. But I think I'll have to go on a kind of pilgrimage of my own to get rid of what's bothering me in the head.'

'I may ride with you? I make the *promesa* that I will not offer the guidance *espiritual* unless you ask for this?'

'I won't.'

The priest put on his biretta and climbed astride the burro. 'But I will feel good to know I may be of some help if it is necessary, *mi amigo?*'

'Not to me, preacherman,' Edge said as he heeled his horse forward and the priest started his mount. 'But there'll be a service someone like you or Filipe Chevez can perform for somebody at San Sarita.'

'*Como?*'

'A dead one. A funeral service.'

Twenty

THE HALF-BREED had relented on the long ride from El Mision de Vallecito, and had satisfied the priest's curiosity by telling him the basic facts of what had happened since he took the shot to the head. Thus was Father Claudio Rodrigues prepared for the scene in the distance below when they rode over the ridge of the high hill to the south of San Sarita. But he crossed himself, anyway, as Edge drawled:

'Looks like there's not going to be a party this time, preacherman.'

It was night and the pole-mounted torches were lit to augment the again misty glow of the crescent moon. In the bright light of the flames, the audience was gathering for the double hanging on the plaza. But it was a far more subdued throng than before, comprised of townspeople and those Federales from the post not assigned to play a direct part in the execution of Jose Sanchez and Conchita Lopez. For there was no music nor food and drink to encourage high-spirited enthusiasm for what was shortly to be witnessed.

'Both at once?' the priest murmured, grim-faced.

'That's a new twist, too,' Edge replied.

The scaffold was in the same place as before – sited between the open gateway of the post and the clump of stunted cottonwoods at the centre of the plaza. But it had been adapted, so that now there were two gallows to cast their shadows in many directions from the flaring torches. Also, tonight, there were no sentries watching the trail from the south. Or, if there were, the men remained hidden off the trail and made no attempt to halt the pair of riders approaching town.

All the farmsteads were in darkness and the only unobtrusive noises to come from them were made by livestock. The adobe buildings flanking the short street that gave on to the west side of the plaza were just as devoid of lamp or candlelight, and were even quieter.

The murmuring of much low-keyed talk faltered and then was silenced entirely, leaving a tense atmosphere of hushed anticipation as Edge and the priest were seen to ride their mounts into the brightly lit area. Many questions, or perhaps just the one, could be seen tacitly expressed in many pairs of eyes as the half-breed reined in his gelding but stayed astride the saddle. His companion climbed stiffly but gratefully down from the burro.

The talk started up again, and from the surreptitious glances and gestures in the direction of the newcomers, it seemed most people were asking each other the questions they had earlier shown only in their eyes.

Edge ignored those who were so avidly interested in him, and peered unblinkingly toward the gap in the weathered and vandalised wall behind the scaffold surmounted by two gallows. But had his attention diverted when a woman softly called:

'*Claudio, por que –*'

'*Señora,*' the priest interrupted with enforced severity before the fine-looking middle-aged woman could start to put into words the eagerness that shone in her eyes. Then he looked sheepish when the cold gaze of Edge intercepted the confidential wink he directed toward his real reason for wanting an excuse to come to San Sarita.

Rodrigues seemed to be about to offer an explanation, but a new silence abruptly blanketed the crowded plaza. Punctured by muted sounds from within the Federale post, toward the ungated entrance of which everyone was irresistibly drawn to look.

A door closed. The sound of a voice carried out of the post without the spoken words being discernible. Then footfalls. At least four people. Out of step. Some members of the waiting crowd shuffled their feet. Some began to whisper, but were hushed into silence.

Captain Miranda, immaculately attired in what looked to be a brand-new uniform, was the first to saunter aristocratically out of the gateway, a freshly lit cigar angled from a side of his mouth. Behind him came two enlisted men carrying a litter on which José Sanchez lay on his back, his arms forced beneath him in such a way that they were obviously tied there. The girl came behind the rear litter carrier. Her arms were also bound at her back and an enlisted man escorted her at either side, tensed to reach for her upper arms and hold her upright at the first sign that she might be about to collapse. The four men responsible for getting the condemned prisoners to the double gallows probably looked more sloppily turned out than they were because of the contrast with their *comandante's* smartness. Sanchez and Conchita were still attired in the same peon outfits they wore when they were captured below the mouth of the *barranca.* Except that their hats were gone. So that sacks, black in colour and with eyeholes cut raggedly in them, could be pulled down over their heads and be loosely tied at the throat.

'*Madre de Dios,* I do not like this,' the priest murmured. And his whispered words were masked to all except Edge by the hollow rapping of Miranda's booted feet on the steps up to the scaffold.

'The Mother of God has to care, preacherman,' Edge rasped through gritted teeth as he shifted his right hand down the length of his thigh to where the Winchester stock jutted from the forward-hung boot close to his knee.

'Lo siento mucho.'

'No sweat.'

The rest of the exchange was covered by other footfalls on the steps and across the scaffold.

Edge eased his hand forward, fisted it around the frame of the Winchester and slid the rifle clear. He did this slowly, and just as slowly swung the weapon so that the top of the barrel rested gently to his shoulder. No one in the crowd realised what was happening until the move was completed, for at the same time that the half-breed was adopting this attitude with the Winchester, all attention was transfixed upon final preparations for the hangings. Then, when José Sanchez and the girl were standing with the nooses pulled firmly around their necks – the two litter carriers needing to hold the crippled man upright, while Conchita's escorts remained close but not touching her – Miranda revealed for the first time that he was aware of Edge sitting the horse some fifty yards away. And when the officer looked at the half-breed, so did everyone else. Perhaps the doomed couple, too, although they did not turn their hooded heads.

In Captain Miranda's dark eyes as he gazed at Edge and the chorus of murmuring began to diminish, there was a degree of arrogant self-possession that seemed to buffet the rifle-toting mounted man with a palpable force.

Edge made an almost imperceptible movement of his bandaged head – inclining it in acknowledgement.

The captain went to stand at the rear of the scaffold, where there was just the one lever to operate both traps. He placed the cigar back between his teeth exposed in a sadistic smile, so that he was able to use his two hands on the lever.

No words were spoken on the scaffold.

Father Claudio Rodrigues was murmuring what was surely a prayer for the souls of the man and girl about to die.

In the silent audience, hands moved through the sign of the cross. Some heads were bowed. Some people looked away.

The loudest sounds were made by the flaming torches. Until Miranda hissed through his grinning teeth:

'*Pronto!*'

José Sanchez snarled: '*Me impota un bledo!*'

Conchita shrieked: '*Madre!*'

The four enlisted men leapt to the sides, like they feared they might tumble down through the traps.

The Federale *comandante* wrenched back the lever. The doors opened. The doomed couple dropped. Edge already had the Winchester stock to his shoulder, the hammer back and his eye aligned behind the sights. He squeezed the trigger. The report cut across and instantly curtailed the massed venting of pent-up breath. And all eyes were fastened upon the front of the girl's shirt where it contoured her unprominent left breast. Saw the blood spurting from the bullet hole as the heart pumped a final time and the slender form jerked and twitched with the dying of the nervous system. It did not matter that it would never be known for sure if Conchita Lopez died from the rope or the bullet. Not to the man called Edge, who showed a mirthless grin on his heavily bristled face as he pushed the Winchester back in the boot.

'Somebody can only die once, *Señor* Edge!' Miranda called across the rising volume of eager chatter as the two victims at last became limply inert on the ends of the ropes.

'I let you have her neck, Captain,' Edge responded. 'But I figured her heart belonged to daddy.'

'But you said you were not her *padre?*' the parish priest of Pueblo Rojo exclaimed in confusion.

'I know that for sure now, preacherman. But she sure as hell kidded me . . .' He vented a short laugh of genuine humour.

'*Señor?*'

'I just figured something out,' the half-breed said. 'This is more like a wedding than a hanging, far as I'm concerned.'

'*Que?*'

Edge tugged on his reins to head the gelding toward the

street across the plaza that led to the trail north. Laughed again before he explained: 'She kidded me. I didn't so much just lose a daughter as gain a pun.'